LETHBRIDGE STEWART

BLOODLINES
THE SHADOWMAN

Sharon Bidwell

CANDY JAR BOOKS · CARDIFF
2019

The Shadowman © Sharon Bidwell 2019
The Nexus © Andy Frankham-Allen 2019

The character Eileen Le Croissette © Shaun Russell
Bill Bishop © Andy Frankham-Allen 2014, 2019
Characters from The Web of Fear
© *Hannah Haisman & Henry Lincoln 1968, 2019*
Lethbridge-Stewart: The Series
© *Andy Frankham-Allen & Shaun Russell 2014, 2019*

Doctor Who is © British Broadcasting Corporation, 1963, 2019

Range Editor: Andy Frankham-Allen
Editor: Shaun Russell
Editorial: Keren Williams
Licensed by Hannah Haisman
Cover by Paul Cowan & Will Brooks

ISBN: 978-1-912535-56-9

Printed and bound in the UK by
Severn, Bristol Road, Gloucester, GL2 5EU

Published by
Candy Jar Books
Mackintosh House
136 Newport Road, Cardiff, CF24 1DJ
www.candyjarbooks.co.uk

THE GUARDIAN watched as Eileen Younghusband was erased from the essential timeline, just like Brigadier Lethbridge-Stewart before her. Her own time period was no more; the work of the fracture point as it strained under the weight of the temporal collapse.

Still, the Guardian needed agents. Traverses and Lethbridge-Stewarts from the strongest divergent timelines, those that were closest to the essential timeline. They could fix things, acting on his behalf.

The Guardian of the Quantum Realm turned to face the young woman who had been brought to the nexus through her contact with the temporal beacon. It had not been the Guardian's intention to bring forth her. Standing before him should have been Edward Travers. Still...

He smiled with his manufactured mouth, a movement of the muscles that seemed to put corporeal beings at ease.

She would have to do.

'Eileen Le Croissette, your realm needs you...'

The Guardian explained, and Eileen, quite gobsmacked by the outpouring of information, could do little but listen.

Time was cracking. Falling apart. Two bloodlines were being disrupted, no longer entwined the way they ought to be. A fracture point in Earth's history, a key moment upon which hinged a multitude of future events, was splitting apart. New, unstable realities were being created. And as a result of all these things the essential timeline, the one from which all alternatives branched and intersected, was being destroyed.

This is what the Guardian of the Quantum Realm told

Eileen.

And she barely understood a word. Just like she barely understood the strange being before her. He looked like a man, after a fashion. Or rather three identical men, who constantly moved, the three bodies intersecting with each other, passing through one another as if they all wished to exist in the same space. Even the voices overlapped – all the same, yet three distinct voices.

'Do you understand the mission?'

That was the one thing Eileen did understand. The Guardian needed agents to act in the 'corporeal' world, the real world. It had sent that old woman, who he claimed was her from the future, to retrieve Professor Edward Travers. She could accept that. Already she had met aliens and people from the future. So why not herself from the future? Good to see she lived to an old age, that she survived the war. But the old Eileen had remembered wrong, and it wasn't Travers who had emerged from the secret bunker beneath London. It was, in fact, the young Eileen. And it was she who had been pulled 'out of time' to this nexus place.

Agents from the Travers and Lethbridge-Stewart bloodlines were needed. At least one from each. But time was being shredded quicker, and so he didn't have time to try again in 1943. Instead, Eileen would be sent to a newly created parallel timeline, a result of time trying to repair the damage done by the change to the essential timeline. In this alternative time, she was to retrieve another member of the Travers timeline.

'I think I understand it. At least the basics,' Eileen said.

'Good. It may take many attempts to actualise you; the timelines are weak, corrupted. Keep the temporal beacon on you. It will assist in the actualisation.'

Eileen looked down at the coin-like object she'd got from her old self. She placed it in her pocket for safe keeping.

'Okay. And I am to pass this one…' She held another coin. 'To Anne Travers?'

'And then I can bring you both back to the nexus.'

That seemed simple enough.

'Okay. When do I leave? Do I need any…?'

Eileen blinked out of existence.

2

PROLOGUE

WHO LURKED? Gaze narrowed, Christophe peered into the dark. Nothing. The blackness deepened, the night a solid thing, but no one stepped out. Still, someone watched. Couldn't be one of Lara's parents. They wouldn't hide, circling someone who dared lay a hand on their daughter.

A surprising sense of shame crept over him. An awareness of the way his mother would react if she knew how he behaved.

Lara.

Jerking his head to the left, he swore. The girl was halfway across the lawn. He'd no idea she could run so fast. No chance to choose wrong or right now. He couldn't finish what he'd started, or ask for forgiveness.

Not important. Not while something stalked him. Not while he felt unhappy, disgruntled, ashamed, frustrated, and many other emotions.

Scared. That too, because he was no longer alone. The closest form of safety was the house, not that Lara would open the door to him. How ironic. Served him right, but maybe whatever was out here wouldn't follow.

He should chase the girl, and pound on the door, wake someone. The need to explain was better than fighting off an attack.

The night drew in. The darkness thickened. Christophe stepped back, moving sideways. He needed to leave. Find his way back. If he didn't make his way through the forest soon, it might be so dark he'd lose his way to the road. His back to the darkness, he sprinted as fast as the uneven ground allowed. He didn't get far.

Someone grabbed his arm, and slowed him, made him

gasp. He tried to push but his hand slipped through nothing, through whatever held him let go. Christophe plunged ahead.

If the unseen thing grabbed him again, his heart might explode. The need to fight off the unwelcome touch became an unwanted glimpse into how Lara must have felt. A quick glance back revealed nothing there but the dark.

An exposed root tripped him. Without hesitation Christophe rolled, rose, tested his ankle – painful but good enough, thank God. He ran. Slammed into a tree, and pushed off, forced to slow down. Nothing behind him. In front…

Confounded, Christophe stopped. A silhouette of a man stood in a pool of moonlight.

No. A trick of the light. Nothing more. If a man blocked the path, he'd see him. It had to be an illusion. He grew more certain as the man dispersed, drifted apart, becoming once more a part of the night, of the shadows amid the trees.

He had no time for this nonsense, hurried on, glancing back, moaning as the darkness kept pace, the strange shape reappearing, gone, reforming, flying, and floating. Herding him. Christophe spotted Lara's house through the trees. God, whatever this thing was it had him turned around, heading back from where he'd come from.

A wild laugh rang out, Christophe's own, the sound disintegrating into a whimper, tears thickening, bitter in his mouth.

The wind sang his name. Shadows grabbed him again. Took him down into the mud. Flipped him over so he came up coughing. Spitting out gritty water and rotting leaves.

If he didn't get to his feet he was going to die. He'd never been more certain of anything. Lara's house. He must get to Lara's house. Beg her on his knees. Only he didn't know which way to go, unable to see. He opened his mouth, desperate for air, to shout for help, to plead, but before he could breathe, the shadow inched its way down his throat.

Invaded him.

Days earlier, in Paris, Bill Bishop gazed at the closed door, swallowing so hard pain tore through his throat. A bead of sweat trickled from his hairline to his nape. A second drop caressed his temple. Two of his fingers dipped into one of his pockets to remove a handkerchief, which he used to wipe away the evidence of his uncertainty. His career, a major in the United Nations Intelligence Taskforce, led him to face many assignments with less of an irregular heartbeat, but this next task tested his measure.

'Come on, fella. Get a grip of yourself.'

A seasoned officer shouldn't let his nerves best him. It was ridiculous. The missions he undertook with more fortitude were countless, but none struck him as so frightening a prospect as an upset wife did.

More precisely, an upset Anne.

Still delaying, Bill glanced at the small box in his hands, not brave enough to surprise his wife in all things. This holiday they took for their seventh wedding anniversary, an event discussed and agreed on weeks before. At dinner, Bill intended to spring a gift on her. A little something extra despite an agreement not to go to the trouble and expense of presents on this occasion. He might have stuck to the arrangement, if not for having thought of something unique. Something she should love, but there were no guarantees.

Enough dawdling. With the box in his pocket, he entered their hotel room.

The woman he cared for most sat brushing her hair in front of a gilt mirror. A few seconds passed during which Bill did nothing but stare. A sense of warm affection washed over him. He adored Anne for her intelligence and bravery, and loved her as much for the simple things: her smile, her kindness, her good heart, the sight of her doing something as mundane as preparing for an evening out, or for bed. Although why women made so much fuss with their hair before they went to bed – equal to a night out in his opinion – remained beyond Bill's understanding. The only thing he understood was the pleasure of watching her.

No doubt in his mind: he was a lucky man to have married Anne, unsure he would ever dare say so to her face, fearing she'd call him sentimental. These feelings surprised him more than they might do her, but were only the truth.

Catching her gaze via her reflection, and before more sweat dewed his brow, Bill stepped forward, kissed Anne's cheek and posed the question, 'Are you ready?'

'We won't be late, will we?'

'No, not as long as we leave within the next ten minutes.'

'I'm good to go.' Her gaze flickered over his face. A small frown creased her forehead. 'What are you up to?'

Bill took a pace back and blinked in fake astonishment. The woman read him too well. 'Whatever do you mean?'

'You're behaving twitchy.' Anne set her brush on the dressing table.

'Twitchy?' For his continued effort to feign ignorance, Bill deserved an Oscar.

'You're up to something. I can tell.'

'My only intention this evening is to make the night run to plan. To present my wife with the ideal celebration and proper representation of my feelings.'

Laughter rang out, merriment unparalleled, as Anne slipped a lipstick into her handbag. After adding a smaller brush than the one she used at the dressing table, Anne rose from the stool. As she faced him, Bill received a better view of the dress she had chosen for the evening. Bill let out a whistle, unable to contain his appreciation.

'New dress?'

'You noticed.' Anne's amusement came through. Her gaze danced. Her lips curved in the right direction.

'You look wonderful.'

'And you are handsome.' Anne took his hand. 'But you're still up to something. Don't worry.'

She paused by the side of the bed where her coat adorned the brocade bedspread. She handed Bill the garment, his help making it easier for her not to snag the few and subtle sequins on the dress. To add to his amazement, Anne took his arm and guided him to the door of their room.

'I won't pry. You may keep your revelation for the right moment,' she added as they moved into the corridor.

The only possible response was to flash one of his biggest smiles.

6

CHAPTER ONE
Treachery on the Home Front

BILL EXCUSED himself, leaving Anne with her thoughts, for a welcome interval. Everywhere she looked, light twinkled or sparked off a reflective surface drowning her in glitter. The only relief came from closing her eyes, though pain flickered in her heart the moment she did so. Several seconds slithered away during which she learned a lesson in how it was possible to be happy and sad in equal measure.

She should be happy. They'd been to the Palais Garnier opera house earlier that evening, moving on to enjoy an after-show meal. People would think her mad to know her heart weighed heavy.

Anne opened her eyes, blinking to clear her vision, one name bright in her mind: Samantha. Although glad to be alone with Bill, she missed her girl. Sam stayed, not for the first time, in London with her grandmother. A thing she did far too often because of her and Bill's work.

This time, Sam's visit allowed Anne and Bill to take pleasure in a romantic break, well-deserved and sorely needed. Their child, their relationship, their work: sometimes these things proved difficult to prioritise, but… seven years. Although positive neither she nor Bill suffered any itch, she did not intend to take their partnership for granted.

While she awaited Bill's return, and a dessert she might not find the room for, but was too weak to resist, the candlelight mesmerised, and recollections wandered to when Bill first suggested this trip. He'd made her laugh, speaking in a formal tone laced with humour.

'If you disagree, Annie, forget I mentioned it, but I hope you'll appreciate my intentions are for the best.'

With more fortitude than she felt, she'd taken the folder he presented to her, expecting a document inside to declare his need to work, a new assignment at the behest of Old Spence. Poor Bill begging forgiveness, detained elsewhere. Little more than a large envelope, the folder contained papers through which she flicked, eyes widening with every passing second. The next words to slip from Bill's mouth were to ask whether he should apologise.

Had she appeared thoughtful or, worse, pensive? Being nothing but pleased, guilt must have been the cause for her hesitation. For when Bill proposed Paris, to include a brief tour of other parts of France, her first notions were not of romance. She thought of a friend not seen for many years.

More light caught her gaze, reflected in the highly polished silver. Anne toyed with her dessert spoon, annoyed with her emotions. She was a traitor. Not taking a family for granted included not forgetting the romance. She had to do better.

She looked up and blinked. Standing before her was a woman. Dark hair, and dressed in the uniform of a WAAF officer, from over thirty years ago! Anne went to say something, but before she could the woman simply vanished. Anne glanced around; nobody else seemed to have noticed.

She rubbed her eyes. Perhaps she was more tired than she realised.

Bill returned as their desserts reached the table, along with the coffees ordered to go with them. A sigh of relief passed over Anne's lips as she straightened the napkin on her lap.

'Excellent timing.' The maître d' spoke to Bill in English, his accent French, and gave Bill a nod and a smile.

'I hope I have room for this.' Anne intended the comment for her husband, but captured the waiter's attention as he moved to leave.

'Take your time. Enjoy.'

The maître d' stepped back but stopped as Anne replied, '*Merci, pour cette excellente soirée.*'

The maître d' hesitated and blinked, before he inclined his head in her direction as though to say she was welcome.

'Shaming me, are you?' Bill teased once the man moved far enough away.

'Nothing of the sort. Being polite in case I don't finish the meal. I shouldn't eat all this.'

'Since when do you ever indulge?' Bill reached across the table and took her hand. 'You heard the man. Enjoy.'

As he pulled one of his hands away, with the other he placed a small box on the crisp white tablecloth. Ah… So, he broke his vow of no gifts. Anne tutted.

'Open it.' Bill's tone brooked no argument.

Suppressing a small sigh, for she had nothing for him, Anne flipped open the lid. Inside she spied a small white card with a name, a telephone number, an address, and a date. She read the name twice to make sure this wasn't pure imagination. Still, she required another minute before she found her voice.

'How in the world…?' Anne peered into Bill's eyes. 'You arranged this?'

'Yes. She expects us to stay for a few days. Time to explore the district ourselves, spend the evenings with your friend. I'll even make myself scarce for a bit, so you can be alone together. You'll note the date of our arrival.'

'I don't know what to say.' This was… marvellous, and Bill… A lump formed in Anne's throat. To think he did this for her. They had planned be in a different part of France for the next portion of their trip, but he made alternative arrangements without her knowledge. Anne fingered the card, still not quite believing the change in their schedule.

'You think I can't investigate when necessary? The moment I mentioned this break, I noticed something troubled you. I remembered you travelled before we met, and recalled you spoke of your time in France. At once, I checked your contacts to make sure I recalled correctly. Wasn't difficult to work out you wanted to take a slight detour, but you didn't like to ask.'

Bill often said she read his mind. Now it appeared they had been married long enough for him to do the same in reverse. The proof of his initiative – Treachery? – lay before her. No point in her trying to deny how this made her feel.

'Do you think it terrible of me?'

'Not terrible. Just very Anne. The woman I fell in love with.'

Despite the compliment, Anne struggled to accept. 'I feel

horribly ungrateful.'

'Anne, you've not seen Madeleine Bonnaire for longer than we've been together, though I know you've kept in touch with her. I should have realised suggesting France brought her to your mind.'

'Occasional letters.' Despite trying to sound dismissive, his expression said she fooled no one.

'Life is often too short. We know this better than anybody. This may be the one chance to catch up with her. I'm telling you to take it.'

Bill sounded decided even if Anne was not, the dear sweet man.

'I must admit, I would love to.' The admission felt daring and more than insensitive. This was their anniversary, but once she spoke the thought aloud, her words ran on. 'Madeleine now works at a private institute overseen by her father. I would love to meet with her again, talk over what she's doing. A great deal of her involvement sounds fascinating. I'm sure there's much she's not able to put on paper.'

Bill caught her meaning. 'Much she may discuss in person?'

'Quite, and it never hurts to know where one might find expert advice when it's required.'

'It never does.'

'So… You don't mind?' Although she kept her voice light, she failed to sound entirely innocent. The battle to keep her lips from curving was real and unsuccessful. If eyes could twinkle as brightly as the chandeliers, hers must have been. Bill's present was… perfect. She couldn't be more impressed.

'As if I could refuse you such a simple thing. What kind of man or husband would that make me, if I didn't appreciate that your scientific curiosity is one of the many reasons I love you?'

'I love you, too.'

'So, you're going to accept my proposal?' Bill's eyebrows lifted in question.

'The same way I accepted the one which led to this celebration.' With love in her heart and gratitude. 'I'll call Madeleine at first light.'

'She'll be up that early?'

'Up and working.'

'Of course, what other kind of friend would you have?' Bill took up his dessert fork. 'What have I let myself in for?'

Although he made fun, Anne struggled to restrain her excitement. He attacked his food as though a man starving. Or a man walking away from the gallows, causing Anne to fight a real battle not to break into wild laughter. Time to reassure him he was not in trouble.

'It's a perfect gift. Thank you.' She couldn't wait to meet with her friend again, and, if feasible, she would love to inspect the facility where Madeleine worked.

What were they in for, indeed?

'Good morning… *Monsieur* Larousse.' Madeleine almost called him Paul, but reconsidered. The man poked his head around the mahogany door of her office. At the mention of his name, he blushed. Madeleine battled the twitch of her lips, afraid of smirking, or giving in to outright laughter.

'Sorry, *Mademoiselle* Bonnaire. I intended to drop these off to you. The monthly reports?'

'I think you'll find you should drop them off with my secretary.' A moment of irritation on her part perished. Paul Larousse was new, and his mistake a mere slip of protocol. 'And it is customary to knock.'

'Oh.' He straightened, coming further into the room. 'My apologies. There's no one in the outer office and when the professor said to hand these to you, I didn't realise he meant your secretary. I'll remember… and… If there's any reason for me to… c-call on you, I'll announce myself.'

The young man swallowed but recovered most of his composure fast, which she liked. The stumbling utterances she put down to his attraction to her, her knowledge of which he appeared to remain unaware.

Madeleine glanced at the telephone on her desk, then at her watch. No wonder her secretary had left. Time ran away from her; too often the case. She needed to return a call but… One glance at Paul as he spun around, moving to leave the room, and she decided to spare a minute or two.

'I'll take the files this time.' Madeleine tapped her desk, amused to witness Paul's uncertainty.

He walked back as though he feared tripping, and, as she expected, hovered near after laying down the documents. Madeleine lounged back in her chair, regarding him.

'How are you finding the work here, Paul?' To hell with propriety, she was more entertained than ever when, at the sound of his Christian name, the man flinched as though she threatened him. 'Are you settling in?'

'Yes, it's… interesting. The facilities excellent and my accommodation more than I hoped for or expected at this stage in my career.'

Though Paul spoke too carefully, Madeleine nodded, showing him that she understood. Not unheard of for a scientist of thirty-two to make a breakthrough, but Paul arrived in the science field by a roundabout route. Struck by a solution during a lecture, and speaking up, brought his name to her father's attention. Victor Bonnaire often sought and hired people others might pass over. Said appreciation often made people work harder than a considerable salary, though he provided that too… if he saw results. Several might claim Paul had no business gaining such a prestigious position in a private facility owing to his age and his credentials. Be it as an assistant to one of their resident professors. Madeleine wasn't one of his critics, but, if she let Paul ramble, he'd start expressing his indebtedness to her and her father any second.

To avoid all that, and because she ran the risk of staring too long into his bright eyes, she spoke first. 'My father wouldn't allow you here if you weren't qualified or deserving.'

His flush this time spoke of embarrassment but also pleasure.

'And… What is it like to work with Cooper?' Madeleine hesitated though her reasons for asking were many.

The institution housed scientists from around the world, Cooper was not the only professor from England but… she disliked the man. She met Paul's gaze, he was ensnared by the question.

'He's… more qualified than I ever hope to be. It's a privilege to work alongside such a man with so… many… qualities and—'

A caught fish never floundered so hard. Best to cut in. 'Yes, but what is he like?'

If her interruption upset or surprised him, he didn't let it show. No. Paul's unease was with Cooper. No blame on Paul. Cooper was difficult, and she sincerely wanted to learn how things faired between the two men. Clearly, Paul didn't like to belittle his immediate supervisor. In a self-conscious gesture, he pushed his mop of a fringe back, making Madeleine take pity on him.

'Many consider my father eccentric in his way. Yet the work we do here, the work he instigates, produces amazing results. Our effort saves countless lives. Sometimes genius manifests in unexpected ways. I... hope that is the case with Cooper.'

Paul nodded but still said nothing. What more did she want the poor man to tell her, having put him in an ugly, awkward position?

'Thank you for these.' She placed a hand over the folders. 'I look forward to seeing you around.' Madeleine gave what she wished him to take as an inviting smile.

Paul flushed again before spinning toward the door and leaving. As he left, he only tripped over his own feet once.

Wiping the smirk from her lips, though not the warmth from her heart, Madeleine picked up the telephone. More work awaited her, but if she didn't return the call soon, life and her routine would interfere.

The connection went through, Madeleine tapping her nails on her desk blotter while she waited. At last, the voice she longed to hear on the other end of the line snapped out, 'Hello?'

Madeleine at once switched from French to English without effort. 'Hello, Anne! What? No. I mean yes! Of course I was up and working. Been out of the office. I'm so pleased to receive your call. Itched to ring back all day. This is my first chance.'

She listened, rotating her chair, and glancing out of the window without enjoying the view, thoughts as misty as the woods and fields growing hazy as dusk approached.

'You've no idea how difficult. I'm not wonderful with secrets. Not when friends are involved. I've been dying to call ever since Bill contacted me, but I didn't want to spoil his surprise. Wonderful. No. Nonsense. You must both stay with me. I'll see you soon. Trust me; I practically got the room ready the day Bill rang me. Not a good idea? Why ever not? Are you suggesting it's inappropriate?' Madeleine laughed. 'I am French, my dear. I can do what I like. Father? No. Don't worry about him. He's mellowed.'

She didn't say her father would accept Anne more now someone had married her. A woman without a man in her life was all too peculiar for him to withstand.

At the thought heat blossomed in Madeleine's face. Although her father would love to see her wed, she couldn't believe Victor Bonnaire would ever welcome Paul Larousse as marital material.

CHAPTER TWO
Anxious Meetings

THE CAR whisked them through the countryside, giving Anne a sense of displacement more comforting than disturbing. In as much as she adored her work with UNIT, her home in Buckinghamshire, her husband, her daughter, there was something to say for getting out of the office. When did she last stop to smell any flowers, let alone roses? A pity so few bloomed this time of the year, her sentiment more figurative than literal.

Bill switched on the heater. Warmth flooded the interior and the rhythm of the car passing over the tarmac lulled Anne into contentment. The trip became nostalgic as much as romantic.

Madeleine Bonnaire. Would she see many changes in the woman's face? In her attitude? The two women shared a sense of adventure once. Madeleine, perhaps more so, always talking of travelling, exploring the world. Yet Anne became the true peregrinator in mind and body. More things existed in the universe than Madeleine perceived. If Anne regretted anything, it was the inability to share all her experiences with her friend.

'Will we take much longer?'

'An hour.' They planned to stop for room and board overnight to break up the journey. Bill glanced over. 'Close your eyes. Sleep if you wish.'

'And miss the scenery?'

A gentle chuckle caressed her. 'You were almost asleep, anyway.'

'Not so.' Despite her protest, he was right. Her eyelids grew heavy and... Anne shifted in her seat, lifting a hand on which to rest her head. Perhaps she should nod off for a few moments…

Darkness enclosed her. Comforting. Warm. Rocking. Her sense of the car, of speeding through the afternoon in the confines of a box on wheels, fell away. Thoughts of Bill, of her friend, left her. Anne drifted, the car expanding into somewhere larger, perhaps a room, or a corridor. She lifted her head and peered upward, vision filling with jagged black spears against a grey delineation. The shapes swayed and creaked, reminiscent of tree branches.

Did she stand in a forest? If so, how did her footsteps echo as though someone confined her to a much smaller area? The way forward appeared oval, ceiling arched, walls painted black. Anne moved along, a train on a track, direction pre-determined.

As she progressed, a shape moved closer, or did she move nearer? Either way, the form took on the outline of a man, Anne shrinking under a malevolent gaze she sensed more than glimpsed. The contour expanded until it towered over her. Menace loomed. Much like a sleeper aware a threat crawled up the bed, Anne pressed into her seat, trying to back away. The air thickened, forcing her to breathe in a rich stew of acrid fog. She pushed against the unseen malignancy, hands tearing into nothing. Still the threat advanced, drawing in, forming, and falling towards her until there was nothing left but darkness.

Gleaming eyes pierced the gloom.

'Anne?'

A voice broke through, but fear shoved back. She tried to respond; failed. She glided, propelled by an unseen force. 'No.' She fought to shatter an invisible grip. The need to stop became paramount, the awareness of what lay ahead too clear.

The way through approached, and she tried to pass unnoticed, but whatever waited detected her presence. Knew her.

No astonishment, therefore, when a black cloud billowed out, engulfing her. Acid ate away her skin, Anne dissolving…

'Anne!'

A touch on Anne's arm jolted her back into the waking world, shivering, trying to throw off her confusion. Where was she? The answer came on the instant. In a car, a man at the wheel… He was taking her… somewhere.

Bill. Her Bill. She was safe. Thank goodness. Anne drew in a ragged breath, shaking her head when Bill gave her a concerned glance.

'Should I pull over?'

'No. No need. I… was dreaming.'

'You were mumbling. If a dream, I wouldn't call it a pleasant one.' Bill stared ahead, ideas shifting through his gaze. 'Are you sure you want to meet with your friend?'

Where did that notion come from? Puzzling over Bill making the peculiar connection, Anne asked, 'Why?'

'I'm uncertain. Strange for you to experience a bad dream when we're heading there, that's all.'

'Not strange at all. Memories crash in on us sometimes. Anxieties. No. None of them of Madeleine,' she added when concern etched lines into his features. 'I'm fine. Serves me right for falling asleep and leaving the driving to you.'

He may not have believed her, but Bill put his foot to the accelerator and continued. The road sped under the wheels.

They made progress. Good enough. Anne settled back into her seat, though now she wouldn't sleep. A sense of foreboding made her heart beat too fast, but long steady breaths slowed her pulse. She never ran from anything, wouldn't start. The universe moved by mysterious means. Their destination, and Bill's organising this excursion, might be more in tune with destiny than she cared to explain, making it impossible to shake a sense of something not right in the world. The sense of Madeleine needing her, and Anne and Bill rushing through the day to arrive where their presence would not only be welcome but was essential.

'Madeleine!'

'Father.' He hugged her as he did every time she stopped by. As if he missed her for more than a year, when no more than a week slipped away.

Gaze drifting over the interior of the old gatekeeper's house, she tried to spot whether her father completed any of the 'little jobs' he claimed he would get around to. Often he'd not touched a thing, though occasionally he amazed her. This was not to be one of those days.

He caught her gaping at a few tools laid out in a neat but untouched row since the previous week.

'I'll um... have the um... a new backdoor catch on by the time you visit me next. Yes, I will. The lock changed, the um... hinges oiled, the edges sanded. The door won't stick next time you call.'

Madeleine smiled, letting him interpret the gesture as he willed. He might well do as he said, but she didn't want to guilt him into completing any of the work. Despite the loving touches the cottage could well do with, her father had no reason to undertake these chores, but he chose to. Same as he chose to live in the cottage. He hadn't taken up residence at the head of the drive to the estate to keep an eye on who came and went. For Victor Bonnaire, renovating the place became more his hobby, a way to keep busy and de-stress.

After his last cardiac stutter, doctors said to ease back on his hours. Father seldom visited the main building except for meetings these days. The man filled his time with careful and researched refurbishment, claiming he enjoyed the work but just didn't know how to proceed with speed. Who would think hammering in nails and a little painting and decorating would calm her father? The thought at once delighted, confounded, and relieved her.

'I'll whip this place into shape. Perfect for a family.'

Madeleine said nothing, the implication that one day the entire estate including the institute would be hers. She would have the choice whether to live in the cottage or to stay in town; easy to grasp for which outcome her father longed. The reasons she didn't wish to debate the possibility were many, because he spoke of a time when he would no longer be around. The moment also touched on her living in an apartment too small for a family on the outskirts of the local town, a situation that suited her.

No doubt sensing she refused to be drawn into discussing the subject, her father said, 'Thought you'd forgotten about me this um...   week.'

Days sometimes went by before they saw each other at work, so she always made sure she frequently dropped in to see him at home.

'Never.'

A mere hour late because of the time spent arranging things with Anne, her father made too much fuss. An unnecessary delay, but Anne had needed a few reassurances she and her husband were not intruding.

'I may not always arrive when you expect, but I will never forget.'

Seldom did Madeleine step over her father's doorstep late, but it happened before and would again. Neither of them mentioned his comment, which amounted to a question. So like her father to enquire over a thing without asking. Although his was a superior intellect, in matters pertaining to human interaction he could be far more irresolute. Wanting people to like him, for people to see him as flexible and endearing, he went about things like a horse on a carousel. Much as that habit annoyed her, she loved him for it.

Madeleine gave him a smile warmer than the one she'd given Paul Larousse, a little disturbed the man remained in her thoughts during her drive from the institute. More so than her conversation with Anne. She thrust Paul from her mind now, afraid of what she might reveal in her expression.

She needn't have worried. Her father's eyes took on a twinkle so familiar, always present when he set eyes on her, causing a mixture of love and pain to spear her chest. No one needed to tell her she looked like her mother, more so each day as she aged. Enough photos provided the evidence, and, her parents once told her, owing to complications, she was a baby blessed to them late in their lives. Madeleine, now thirty-eight, might be destined to give birth the same way, if she ever did.

Turning her back on the room and her father, Madeleine took a moment to pull herself together.

Speaking of carousels, this day proved to be a merry-go-round of emotions. It was a consequence of knowing Anne was coming; an old bitterness surfacing that Anne was able to enjoy a lifetime of memories with her own mother. Most times, Madeleine thought of her mother, and their resemblance, without more than a twinge of sorrow for what couldn't be. This late in the day, afternoon fading into evening, reminded her of how she'd hated the dark during interminable nights after her mother's death, and how her father still did. Her father had lived on his own, a widower, for the last eighteen years.

Life might part them one day, but she stayed not only to further her career but also to remain near to her last surviving parent. Loyalty was one reason she gave up on her ambition of travelling – the dream she had once devised with Anne. She also lived with the fear if she took time off, she might lose her standing in the scientific community. She was an only child, and not allowed to forget it. Although her father frowned upon women becoming more involved in a man's world, his bigotry came from puzzlement, not malevolence. Sad to think his opinion of women in science was no isolated case.

Equally odd to think she and Anne Travers made friends during a time of women's liberation, a concept with which her father still struggled. Anne had been supported by her father, a scientist himself, before his death nine years ago. But Madeleine, being an only child, gave her own father the task of speaking with her. First over school, and then boys, and lastly her career, discussing the day when she would take over after he died. If married when she did so, her father might be happier. If she had a brother, her father would leave the foundation to him, but somehow she never complained about her father's unfair nature.

Aware she in part pandered to her father's whims, still an image of Paul Larousse rose in her mind. Her smile widened, causing her father to kiss her cheek, a smidgeon of guilt dimming her grin at his error. Her father believed her delight all for him.

The man pulled back, but held on to one of her hands, patting. 'You're not here to entertain an old man. Tell me about this um… visitor of yours you're expecting.'

'Anne, Father. Anne Travers.'

'Anne?' His grasp tightened to an extent where he made her winch. 'Oh, I'm sorry, my dear. I um… apologise.' He let go at once and stepped back but without an explanation as to his reaction, leaving Madeleine to flex her fingers.

'Yes, Anne. I'm sure you remember her. We met in 1965, thirteen years ago. We kept in touch, but this is our first opportunity to see each other again in years.'

Madeleine tried to escape the ghost of his grip. What was

that all about? Though her father had never taken to Anne, he couldn't begrudge their friendship after all this time.

'Yes, yes. Anne Travers.' A frown spread across her father's forehead and he became more preoccupied, providing Madeleine with the perfect opportunity to test whether he might relent.

'I hoped you'd allow me to give her a tour of the institute. Nothing too complex but I would love to show her where I work. To discuss a few of our lesser projects with her.'

'Discuss… Yes, well. That is… May um… be a potential problem.'

His manner turned to one of disgruntlement. What was so wrong with Anne visiting? Surely, he wouldn't deny his own daughter's request.

'I will give you any assurances you need and I'm sure Anne will be happy to sign a non-disclosure.'

'That's as well be but um…' His gaze wandered as though searching for something on which to latch.

As if he didn't want to meet her gaze.

'Father, forgive me, but I don't understand the problem. Anne isn't unknown to us. You've given more public tours yourself.'

'In the interest of external funding. On um… certain things.'

'Yes, but relaxed tours, and it's not as if I'll take Anne into any of the restricted areas.'

'No. No, you um… wouldn't. No, *you* wouldn't do anything wrong.'

He made it sound like Anne would escape Madeleine's clutches and fight her way into areas where she didn't belong. He stood, hands folding one over the other, as though he washed his hands without the aid of soap or water. A nervous habit she'd not seen in a long time.

'Let us… Yes, let us um… Yes, put the kettle on and you can um… tell me all about Anne Travers and what she's doing these days.'

His perspective perplexed her, made Madeleine speechless, though she opened her mouth to defend Anne, uncertain what to say. Perhaps the best thing was not to push.

'Well, for one thing she's married now. Seven years ago,

in fact.'

That stopped him on his way to the kitchen. What did her father think? That feminism translated to a dislike of men and marriage? Could well be. Many made the same mistake, women included.

'She's bringing her husband?'

'Yes. Bill. Bill Bishop.'

'Well, well, well,' her father chanted. 'To think, Anne Travers hitched. And she's bringing her husband... here?'

Madeleine half expected him to pose the question, 'Anne Travers wedded before you?' To her relief he didn't. He ambled off into the kitchen, muttering. 'I guess um... that means she no longer goes by the name.'

As much as she wanted to, Madeleine strove to correct him, but in the end she didn't bother.

'Yes, put it there, right there. Careful now!' The box slid off one corner of the trolley, but both of the deliverymen grabbed hold and transferred it to the floor. Clumsy oafs. Ted Cooper struggled not to dance around the box eager to be rid of them.

At last. A consignment from which he wanted to extract a single item. Despite his excitement, a yawn took over his jaw. God, but he felt worn from the drive to fetch the last of his remaining sample – a secret he refused to share with anyone – from a safe secure place some miles away. He recovered quickly.

The tube, nestled in a case in his pocket, and the crystal he wanted to remove from the institute's latest acquisitions, put a bounce in his stride, in his whole being. He was exhausted though, having to take a leave of absence for a handful of days and dash back at the last possible moment to intercept this delivery.

'Sign here, *Monsieur* Cooper.'

Ted Cooper gritted his teeth at the omitted title of professor. Ignorant louts. He entertained an image of security escorting them not only from the premises but shooting them in the heads for the insult to someone of Cooper's standing.

Ted closed the door on the men and spent precious minutes growling in frustration. To think he was reduced to thievery. No alternative.

'No. No time.'

Not a second more would he squander through no fault of his own, years of research done when and where able with inadequate provisions. Then the added months spent waiting to bring his real project into the laboratory... No, the time lost didn't withstand consideration.

A moment of nostalgia tinged with pain stilled Ted's hands, bringing a halt to the unpacking. If allowed access to everything he wanted in his earlier jobs, his work might have advanced more by now.

Stupid, melancholic dreaming. Ted tore a portion of the packing material apart with such savagery he might have been tearing open a throat.

Stop this. He must stop wallowing. No point wishing to retrieve misspent days. He'd suffered, the passing seasons taking their toll on his nerves and the aspect of his reflection. The lines on his face and watery eyes staring back at him each morning spoke of the sentence inflicted on his genius by men who believed caution wiser than a gamble.

Patience. Not his virtue, but hell if he hadn't needed to bide his time. Now he was here and, assured an outstanding laboratory, he could get to the most important aspects of his work.

Attractive old building, too. Many rooms. Several lived in the halls of residence, using the superb facilities, but his little corner of a ground floor was deadly silent even this early in the evening, as he liked it.

His footsteps echoed though old stone walls, which helped to deaden sound from the outside world. An old university, if he was not mistaken, set up as a records library. Members of the public had no clue what they examined and catalogued here. The experiments that took place. Good thing too.

Ted dragged off his jacket and threw the garment at the coat rack where it missed and hit the floor. He paid no attention. Time to prepare the lab.

He moved across the floor, pulled up short by a sharp knock on the door.

'Teddy?'

Blasted nickname. How often must he tell Paul not to use it? The man never paid attention. Ted was one of many hired to perform tests and to decide which level of threat to attribute to several artefacts. Boring stuff, and the reason he praised the day Bonnaire said he'd assign him an assistant, little knowing the helper would be Paul Larousse. He only put up with the man's annoyances because he had no choice. Still, the man had his uses. Ted fielded work Paul's way to distract him, keep him busy, and to make Bonnaire believe Ted cared. Paul provided Ted with a handy way to distance himself from Bonnaire – so clean-cut personality-wise actual dirt didn't dare touch him. Still, Paul couldn't carry out a greater travesty than interrupting at such a late hour. If Paul noticed him blow in, the man wouldn't stop pestering until Ted opened the door. Worse, the man would sulk. Then again, if Paul were unsure…

A glance revealed the hopelessness of that idea, the gap under the door wide enough to reveal the light shining within.

With no alternative, Ted unlocked the door and cracked it open, leaning into the aperture, frowning when Paul tried to peep into the room beyond. Up on his toes, head bobbing back and forth. Rude of the man. Upstanding character but untidy chap who didn't appreciate the invention of the iron. The man always needed a haircut. At least he did as Ted told him, quick to react to orders, and his English was superb, unlike Ted's French. Could be worse.

'Got a minute?' Paul asked, no doubt in response to Ted's silence.

'No. Sorry, Paul. Just got in.'

'I can see. Thought you'd fall into bed.'

'I may do, soon as I store a few items.'

'How'd your time off go? I finished the work you left. Are there any other interesting assignments for us yet?'

'Sorry, Paul. Not had the time to look. I'll sort you something out tomorrow. There's a consignment to catalogue.'

'Nothing you brought along yourself?' Once more Paul strained to peer over Ted's shoulder. Ted wedged the slot tighter.

'You know I can't tell you too much. You'll be assisting me where possible, but there'll be things I'll be working on I won't be able to mention.'

While in part true, reinforcing the statement helped

protect Ted's secret. He could tinker on his own project without Paul learning too much. If the man grew curious, Ted fell back on the need for silence. Their being one of many experts – though he used the term loosely in Paul's case – on site, supported this. So far, he maintained the ruse Paul could know only as much as necessary to help with any developments.

'Excellent.'

Ted's reply was little more than a rebuttal, but Paul still sounded upbeat, a fact to irritate Ted the more.

'Say, are you all right?'

'Hmm? What?' Surprise replaced irritation. Ted stared at Paul, taking in the way the man glowered at him, brow furrowed, a question in his eyes. God, what did Paul see? Ted tried to alter his expression, fearing he stared too hard. 'I'm all right. I told you, tired.'

'You're sure that's all it is?'

'What else can it be?'

'I don't know.' Paul took a pace back but kept one hand on the doorframe. If Ted slammed the door, he might fracture the man's fingers. The temptation to do so alarmed him. Alas, not as much as it should. 'You may be a little under the weather or been working too hard.'

Ted snorted, shocking himself and the younger man whose eyes widened. Paul didn't understand hard work, but Ted wouldn't say so. 'Tell it to Bonnaire. Let it get around in a place like this and the other scientists will call us both wusses.'

'I… guess.' Paul didn't appear sure. 'You're certain it's nothing else?'

'Last time I examined your credentials, you don't qualify as a physician.'

'No, but… well, you appear to be sweating.'

Ted started. 'Am I?' Well, if so, it was through eagerness and excitement while this fool got in his way. 'It's warm in here. Long journey. I need a shower. Can't wait to turn in.' Hell, he babbled.

'Pity.'

'Why?' What was the idiot on about?

Paul produced a bottle from behind his back. 'Thought we could have a celebratory shot.'

'Celebration?'

'More of a welcome back. I twiddled my thumbs the last couple of days.'

Last couple of...? The work should have taken Paul longer. Hmm. He needed to bear in mind the pace Paul maintained and give him chores more time-consuming. Well, what he lined up next should take Paul best part of a week or longer. As for the drink... The whisky... One look at the label revealed the brand to be an outstanding one and a different temptation made Ted Cooper itch.

No. Although he had more to celebrate than pleasing a rich bigwig like Bonnaire, he shouldn't waste any more time. Besides, Paul's gaze struck him as feverish. Paul still itching to enter the laboratory tonight and longing to catch sight of the delivery. Crafty bugger. He would be no happier when he found out and Ted set him to work in the morning, but let the idiot believe otherwise.

'Another night.' Ted rejected the offer.

Paul's face slipped from eager happiness to outright disappointment. Perhaps... something more vindictive? Possible, though Ted might have been judging the young man by his own standards.

'I guess it's goodnight, then.'

'Goodnight.' Ted lost no time closing the door and throwing the lock.

He stepped away, staring at the base of the door, beneath which Paul's shadow cast dark blotches. Paul took ten seconds, twenty, more, before he walked away.

At once, Ted hurried over to the box, which contained the crystals, and removed them searching for the one he wanted. He filled the next half an hour by transferring items to the floor around the box, almost dropping one in haste – possibly disastrous, as some were delicate. A few he set upon the workbench. He should log each one, but he would not do such measly work this evening. Any evening. That was for Paul to do. Ted intended to put most of the samples back in the case, leaving them as one of many menial tasks to assign to Paul. A more important venture awaited Ted, and moving a few of the specimens now might help to cover up the fact one was missing.

CHAPTER THREE
Generation Gaps

'I'M SORRY the apartment's so small.'

Surprise stopped Anne midway across the living room. Granted the room wasn't huge, but a pair of two-seater sofas, separate miss-matched chairs, a coffee table, sideboard and bookcase, left plenty of room to walk between the furniture. A sense of Madeleine's apology extending far beyond the limits of her home unsettled Anne, though she struggled to understand why. Before she could enquire, Madeleine pushed them into a whirlwind tour, cutting their greeting short.

The flat composed of two bedrooms, and one bathroom which Anne and Bill would have to share, something Madeleine felt the need to again apologise for, though they knew this beforehand. A small kitchen left an impression of a sizeable dining room – as though the intention was to make guests bring their own nourishment.

Back in the living room, Madeleine paced. What was wrong with her? Ever since their arrival, she gave off a nervous energy, perhaps best explained as friends meeting after a long absence.

'Your flat's lovely,' Anne said. 'Everything about it is delightful. Not to mention the amazing view.'

The bedroom, made up for her and Bill's stay, contained only a wardrobe, a bed, and side tables, but doors in place of a window opened out onto a Juliette balcony. The vista overlooking a busy thoroughfare, more than compensated for any ascetics the room lacked. Not the time of the year to keep the doors open, but Anne had peered out and taken in a deep lungful of crisp chill air with a sense of enchantment. Her reassurances appeared to do nothing to calm her friend. One glance exchanged with Bill told her he noticed.

'If you ladies will excuse me, I think I'll take a walk. We can unpack later.'

Ever the strategist, Bill left Anne with the opportunity to reacquaint with Madeleine. No sooner did she hear the door close, than Anne concentrated on her friend. The atmosphere grew heavy.

'I hope our dropping in is not an inconvenience.'

'No. No. Not at all.' Fingers skittered up and down Madeleine's arms as though she wanted to claw her skin. 'I'm being terribly inhospitable.' Madeleine stilled her wandering hands, by clasping one of her forearms. 'Forgive me, Anne, and please sit. I'll fetch us a tray of tea.'

How English. No point in voicing the thought. Anne made no offer to help as she thought Madeleine might relax better if allowed to carry out a simple task.

Not until Madeleine set the tray on the table, poured the beverage, sweetened hers, and the tinkle of teaspoons done stirring fell silent, did either woman speak again. Both rushed to talk, overlapping, falling quiet before laughing.

'Oh dear. We were never this inept.' A grin at least revealed Madeleine still to be the woman Anne remembered.

'It's been more than a while. Longer than I prefer. I have missed you.'

'Missed the things we got up to, more like.'

Anne chuckled aware Madeleine didn't mean the usual high jinks such as stealing or cadging smokes and alcohol, or dating. Women's liberation carried a different meaning for the two women. Anne and Madeleine always poked their noses in where their so-called superiors believed they had no business prying. Either because they were women or because they believed them to be less than intellectual equals.

'Do you recall when you corrected Professor Hébert?' Madeleine chose the shared memory that most delighted them.

'Something we will never forget. Such a boring lecture, and I told him he was wrong, he protested, you supported me and then—'

'We both walked up to the board and debunked his miscalculations.'

'I swear if he grew any redder I expected him to keel over.'

Anne drained her cup. 'How is work these days?'

A mischievous twinkle chased a dark shadow in Madeleine's eyes. 'Just visiting an old friend, eh?'

Anne pretended innocence, though Madeleine would not be deceived. 'Can I help it if it's a friend with whom I share much in common?'

'Shop talk.' Madeleine's smile blossomed, at last transforming her face. 'I can't tell you how wonderful it is to have you here, Annie. You couldn't choose better timing. Oh, nothing solemn.' She waved a hand in a dismissive gesture, no doubt spotting a question in Anne's expression. 'You know what work in the sciences can be like, for women.'

The situation had improved, but despite major historical breakthroughs from the likes of Marie Curie and Émilie du Châtelet – a favourite figure for Madeleine – and many others who helped to change the world, women still struggled. Alas, Madeleine's father was not the easiest of men or patriarch.

'I swear a few at the institute believe I receive a free ride because of my father's patronage, but I often work longer hours than many there do.'

Now Madeleine mentioned it, she seemed overburdened, not that any but the most observant might notice. The woman was ever stylish and always elegant, her hairstyle impeccable and her make-up almost flawless. Yet the skin around her eyes appeared a little dark, hollow in a way not even her foundation disguised. A few lines worked their way around Madeleine's lips, as if she often presented a pinched expression to the world. Their stares locked for an instant as Anne's gaze flicked over her friend's face. No way did Madeleine fail to note Anne's inspection.

'Still fine for my age.' Madeleine gave her a wink. 'Or so one assistant at the institute would say.'

Anne put on a show of mock horror. Something might trouble Madeleine, but Anne didn't mean to prise the information out of her. Patience would make Anne a better friend and Madeleine a more open talker. As for Madeleine's revelation…

'Are you talking of an irritation or temptation?'

'I'm French. I know all about temptation. No. Paul is… ' Madeleine's gaze took on a dreamy expression, though not one of a love-struck person. 'Paul is Paul. More intelligent than others give him credit for, which, God knows, I understand too well. I perceive an underlying determination and bravery, but his own self-doubt makes him a candidate for those who would take advantage. Doesn't help that my father has placed him with one of our vilest scientists.'

'In what way vile?'

Madeleine performed an actual shudder. 'Not a topic I wish to discuss on your first evening. Upon your tour of the institute if your paths cross it will be explanation enough. Though it's doubtful the man will crawl out of the hole he calls a laboratory. If I didn't know better, I'd believe he camped out in there.' A frown creased her brow.

'What's wrong?'

Madeleine gave a dismissive shake of her head. 'Nothing. Realised the man might be the only one to work longer than I do. Not saying he isn't brilliant, mind. My father wouldn't hire him if he was otherwise, but I'm glad to have little contact, though my emotions may colour my feelings for Paul.'

'Feelings for Paul?' Anne projected innocence.

'Oh, you,' Madeleine scolded. 'I mean, I don't envy Paul for having to grin and bear the cretin's company, despite what he might learn from him.'

Anne made a wild guess. '*If* Paul is given the opportunity.'

'Yes, that is a concern. Strikes me this scientist isn't much one for sharing, but it's too early in this year's programme to reach such a conclusion.'

'And your interest complicates things?'

Madeleine met Anne's gaze, poised, perhaps, to argue. 'Fine, I like Paul.'

'Are you crossing a line?'

A moment of consideration flickered across Madeleine's expression. 'My father outlines no precise rules about colleagues dating. Still, I'm uncertain whether to do so is wise, and not because of the reasons you're thinking. Paul is... well, younger than I by several years.'

Madeleine was a mere two years younger than Anne. 'Age is largely just a number, darling, and besides, you're not old.'

'But I'm not young, and I'm not married.'

Anne digested this comment and Madeleine's strangely

bitter tone. Perchance, approaching forty – an age many viewed as a milestone – her friend grew conscious of time passing and now regretted not having settled down. Might be Madeleine didn't have a choice. Not everyone met someone with whom they wanted to spend their life. Certainly, Anne hadn't been looking when she first met Bill, just after she and Spencer Pemberton had convinced the powers-that-be of the need for a United Nations Intelligence Taskforce. She would have been quite content without romance in her life, but now she had it… Anne felt sure Madeleine was of the same mind. Which suggested to her that…

'Is this your father speaking, or your own words?'

Victor Bonnaire had often encouraged their friendship, but Anne had nevertheless quickly realised that he hoped for a result different to what the women shared. The two based their relationship on intellect and an open and mutual admiration of each other's abilities. Back in the early days of their friendship, Bonnaire often viewed Anne as a method to remind Madeleine what it meant to be a woman. They'd spent many a night giggling over the idea he likely believed them out choosing perspective husbands. In reality, they poured over books, discussing the latest scientific discoveries.

Madeleine gave Anne a long and considering stare. 'We are products of our parents no matter how much we try not to be. He influences my thinking, no doubt.'

Anne thought of her father, how he had influenced her so much when she was younger. Yet having her mother around had tempered that development somewhat; reminded Anne that there was more to being a woman in the world than constantly fighting against male privilege.

'I wonder why now,' she said to Madeleine. 'You never talked about marriage when I was here last.'

The French woman twisted her cup in its saucer, staring at the patterned china. 'When younger, I thought meeting someone happened or didn't. I also witnessed how it tore my father apart to lose my mother and I wondered whether love was worth heartache. You have lost a parent, Anne, you have seen how much one grieves when they lose what they consider to be their life-partner.' She appeared surprised by the confession. 'Forgive me. I did not mean to sound so melodramatic.' She flushed a little. 'Don't let me alarm you. I didn't and don't spend long nights brooding. I left things to fate, I guess. If such a thing exists. Then... time passes in a blink and we realise opportunities may never present themselves again, if they ever did at all. I watch you with Bill... Anne, I can tell how much he loves you. How much you love him. I noticed the moment you arrived.'

The cup rattled again as Madeleine set it down. 'I'm sorry. I do not mean to put all this on you, and you not here an hour. It's not as if I saw you only a week ago. Time has made us different people to who we were, and I should not—'

'I am amazed to say so, but I do not feel the time we've spent apart.' Anne interrupted Madeleine, forgiving her own rudeness. Without a map to tell her where Madeleine tried to direct her sentences, Anne stopped her short of babbling. 'The years fell away the moment I stepped into your lovely home. The days and differences perhaps give us both unique perspectives. What is troubling you?'

For a second it appeared Madeleine would shake her head and laugh off her feelings.

'Your girl. Your Samantha. I see you and Bill and think of your daughter and you still working and... It's as though you are blessed with everything.' Madeleine's laughter this time sounded rueful. 'I may be a little envious.'

'That's one monster with which I can deal.' Good thing Madeleine wouldn't pick up on Anne's humour, but Anne launched straight into the next sentence regardless. 'You're not too old to have a child.'

'No, but it does rather mean I need to find a husband sooner than later and, well...' Madeleine's cheeks took on a rosy hue, her gaze furtive. 'When I think of Paul, sometimes I imagine what handsome children we would produce.'

She grinned like a naughty schoolchild, the smile blossoming into one of a much-older seductress, making Anne chuckle.

'The poor man doesn't stand a chance,' Anne said lightly.

'Such talk would scare him.'

'Paul may view it as premature, but he need not know. You don't have to frighten him off. We're speaking of a date, not wedding bells. Not yet, anyway.' Anne winked at her. 'But something tells me there's more to this.'

Madeleine huffed. 'Paul is not... I am uncertain my father would think of him as worthy.'

Unlike your Bill. Though Madeleine didn't say, she didn't need to. Bonnaire would view Bill's position as a thing to make him a worthwhile match for marriage.

'And there is the age gap.'

'A difference of...?'

'Paul is thirty-one.'

Madeline was thirty-eight. Seven years. A series of twitches ran over Anne's face, pulling her brow and lips in various directions and causing her to blink. A thing Madeleine spotted.

'Mads.' The old nickname slipped out, though Anne had forgotten it until now. 'Mads, I am forty, and Bill is thirty-three.'

The other woman's eyes widened. She drew her lower lip into her mouth, pressing her mouth shut, hard, before breaking into a laugh. She laid her hands over her face and peered between her fingers.

'Oh my goodness, Anne, I am so sorry. I didn't think. I assumed... Well, he seems a little younger than you, but...' She laughed again. 'Can you imagine? If we both become involved with men seven years our junior, whatever will my father say?'

'It will provide us with the perfect opportunity to point out seven years is no time at all. No one would say a word if the age difference were reversed.'

'That much is true. Do you suppose the day will come when women will no longer fight these prejudices?'

Anne took a moment to consider the question, pained to speak the truth. She'd seen the future, once or twice. 'Not in our lifetime, though things will continue to improve. So, I solved your problem. Is the age gap now not an issue?'

'Perhaps not, but there are other reasons I hesitate. My father doesn't object to a relationship at work, but it can be difficult, and there is Paul himself. He is... a timid man in some respects. He's interested, but he's never done a thing about it. Part of me wishes he would ask me out and he never gets around to it.'

'A woman can ask a man. Should, if we want to change the world.' Anne teased but not entirely. 'It may not surprise you, but I tired of waiting for Bill to ask me on our first date, so I asked him. Although, to even things out, he did propose first.'

'You're right and I may do so given time. Part of me wonders if he'll run away crying in fright.'

More laughter ensued. The moment their merriment petered off, Madeleine asked, 'More tea?'

'Lovely.'

'And when I sit back down the spotlight will shine on you. Tell me all about Bill. By the time the pot cools, he should return. After we eat the superb dinner I cooked for us,' – wonderful smells emanated from the kitchen – 'I want to know all there is to know about him. By the time I take you tomorrow evening to the delightful Bistro I told you about, I want us to put all this awkwardness behind us. I want us to remember what it's like to be the best of friends.'

Despite her wish to be cautious, Anne dove in. 'And must I wait that long before you'll tell me what else is troubling you?'

With widening eyes and a sharp intake of breath, her friend relented. 'What else but my father?'

Self-directed horror brought heat to Ted's face. Stupid. If he dropped the cylinder, it might have been the end of him. Would definitely spell doom for his hoped-for experiments. Mortifying!

The small cylindrical tube he'd fetched to the institute contained a potentially deadly organism and this, the last of the supply, made his hands shake.

The tricks and the tests he performed to date were about keeping the sample fresh and useable. Initially, he'd tried the general fixation method most often used in medical testing. The function to inhibit decay including autolysis – essentially, the destruction of cells by their own enzymes. This involved several considerations, namely the temperature in which to maintain the detail without the specimen deteriorating. So far, the best fixation temperature proved to be forty-five degrees centigrade.

The second concern was of size. Too thick and the fixative

measure took too long to penetrate the inner portion of the test material. Other issues were relative to volume ratio and time. With experimentation, approximately five percent of the solution lost, by accident and frustration more than intent, Ted worked out he need not worry. A low temperature, not so cold as to form ice crystals kept the sample in a suspended state. Though even this was unnecessary while using the liquid, they were mere precautions so as not to risk the sample degrading over time.

To collect a drop was riskier, but no science advanced without peril. Not that he feared the compound, not in its present condition.

The contents of the cylinder appeared to be solid black paint. Inert.

Though he didn't fear the sample, he was about to be stupid. Ted crossed the room and put the tube into an isolation unit, a glass box with gloves sealed on the side. With the lid clicked into place, he made sure the rubber ring around the top remained intact, creating a seal. A section at the side allowed him to introduce new elements. The outer door closed up tight, and, using the gloves, by unfastening the inner door of the compartment he gathered up whatever he placed there. By the same method, he could extract items from within the box. A glass dish lay in the base. Now he slipped his hands into the gloves, picked up the tube, and unscrewed the cap.

He took hold of an eyedropper, filled it, and then set it aside. He screwed the stopper back on to the container and sited the tube in a corner inside the outer compartment of the casket. Next, he again took up the dropper and squeezed the rubber end.

At once, the black substance poured out as a liquid. Fluid as water, the sample sat like an inky pool in the plastic base tray put in place for this purpose. Ted released the dropper and pulled his hands back to the side of the box, though not out of the unit.

He waited.

Not knowing what he expected, still a sense of disappointment came over him when nothing happened.

'Ridiculous.'

He was being ridiculous. He'd done this many times with

the same outcome, but always he waited. The fluid being inactive meant he achieved the longed-for result: a substance with which to work.

To judge by eye, and the level in the tray, as well as what remained in the capsule, he guessed he retained 300ml of liquid. He needed to use the drops sparingly and be on the lookout for any activity from within the pool. Already he set up a list of experiments. The next few days would prove interesting.

Hours moved on ticking into the night, long past the time he should leave the main building. Long past when he should make his way to his room in the halls of residence.

Nothing more occurred except his wasting another twenty-eight drops of the liquid. No reaction came from any of the chemicals added.

The substance didn't appear to be chemically lacking in any respect he perceived, but possibly the fluid decomposed on a level science to date couldn't detect. If he'd done anything wrong, based his dreams on mere stories, his existence was pointless, his life a failure. If nothing brought about the hoped-for change, then maybe he was the mad professor many believed him to be.

CHAPTER FOUR
Mad Scientists and Crazed Professors

'SHALL WE visit the museum or the art gallery?' Bill folded the map over, glancing around, trying not to act too much like a tourist. They sought something to do indoors, at least for part of the day, because the sky shone a slate grey. According to Madeleine, things would brighten up in the afternoon.

When he received no answer, Bill guessed Anne didn't hear as she was preoccupied with kicking a stone with some persistence against a pillar supporting the gate of an elegant house. A glance at the windows revealed no one peeking from behind the curtains. The thought of Anne scolded for yobbish behaviour proved more amusing than it should have been.

'Anne, are you listening? What do you want to do next?'

'Hmm?' She lifted her head and gazed around, seemingly shocked by her behaviour, turning her back on the house, and kicking the stone to the kerb. 'Oh… Can we amble?'

'Amble?'

'Yes. Take a walk.' She threaded her arm through his. 'Although not part of our original plans, the area is pleasant enough. Will be nice to see what's changed. Perhaps I can show you a few haunts of mine.'

'Where you and Madeleine first met?'

'I could.'

'Where you upset the lecturer, Hébert?'

'Maybe.'

'Where you used to both go for coffee?'

Anne paused. 'We frequented a delightful little café near to here. I would like to see if it's still there, though it'll be sad if it's not.'

'The library where you once stole a book?'

Anne gasped. 'I did not steal it. I forgot to take it back.'

'Where you kissed a boy?'

This time she slapped his arm. 'I did no such thing.'

'Not here.'

A light flush turned Anne's cheeks rosy. 'No, not here. I filled my stay here with Madeleine, study, and learning. With finding a woman with a keen intellect who didn't laugh at my hopes and ambitions.'

'So, no boys?'

'No.'

'I wouldn't mind.'

'Mind?'

'I mean, it no longer matters how many boys you kissed.'

'I'm telling you I didn't.'

'Good, but I wouldn't care is the point.'

In a few steps, they reached the end of the street where they would need to choose a direction, though Bill knew he would follow Anne anywhere.

'Why not?'

'Because you're mine.'

Bill always strove to conceal a hint of pride. That which made Anne dip her head, not from embarrassment, but something else Bill struggled to name. If not for the fact he often heard the same mutual admiration in her voice, she might tell him off for putting her on a pedestal. Not the case and, drawing to a halt, taking her hands in his, and starring into her eyes, he saw she understood him.

'What's preoccupied you all morning?'

'A sense of unease. I gather Bonnaire is not as eager for me to tour the institute as his daughter is, and I don't like putting her in such a position.'

'I can understand. Definitely understand, but from what you said, he's more than a little antiquated in his outlook. Nothing more. I'm certain you and Madeleine can handle him.'

'I can't help wondering whether there would be anything to handle if Madeleine was Bonnaire's son, and I, a male friend.' Anne took Bill's arm again and gestured around the corner. 'Three blocks from here we should find the café, if it still exists. I could do with a drink.'

Bill matched her step. 'Do you think Bonnaire is that

prejudiced? I mean, Madeleine will inherit the institute one day.'

'Only because there's no other heir, though I like to think otherwise.'

'You don't think he's changed at all?'

'Not from the conversation I shared with Madeleine last night. Oh, I don't know. Something's troubling me but I'm uncertain what. Possibly I'm searching for something which doesn't exist.'

Bill knew better than to put Anne's instincts down to feminine intuition.

'I'm glad to be here, I am, but I should tell Madeleine not to worry about speaking to her father. We can discuss her work without me having to set foot inside the institute.' Despite her words, Anne didn't sound at all certain.

She came to a halt, making Bill stop.

'Do you see her?' Anne asked.

'See who?'

Anne pointed. There was nobody there. He told her so.

Anne frowned. 'You're sure? A woman in a WAAF uniform.'

'Nope, nothing.' Bill turned her to face him. 'Are you okay? Anxiety over Bonnaire getting to you?'

Anne sighed, the expression familiar to Bill. She was becoming introspective. She shook her head. 'Must be that.' She smiled softly.

They continued walking, Anne silent, Bill concerned, when a sudden smile bloomed on her face. He followed her gaze across the road to the windows of a café.

'It's still here.' She tugged on his arm. 'Come on. I'm hoping to find the same tables and chairs. The same red chequered tablecloths.'

Seeing the expectant delight on her face, Bill hoped so too – though not the exact same tablecloths. Red chequered, but new would be preferable, lacking over a decade of germs.

Bill set off across the road with Anne. With luck, the café would look as she remembered, but if only he could remake the world into something where society didn't try to make her feel inferior to men. Where nothing ever wiped a smile from her face.

Love.

Perhaps love made fools of men, but he'd be a happy fool for Anne.

The telephone rang, making Anne jump. Should she answer it? Bill had yet to emerge from their bedroom, and Madeleine was in the shower, having insisted she go last, never taking more than five minutes to do her makeup. If Anne didn't know Madeleine better, she might consider the offer uncomplimentary, but experience taught her how little effort Madeleine made to appear so flawless. Still, that left no one around but Anne to deal with the persistent ringing.

Despite her hesitation, on the fifth ring, as if her hand possessed a separate intelligence, Anne lifted the receiver. A tinny compelling voice sounded through the speaker. A stunned silence greeted her initial, 'Hello?'

'Who is this?' The voice that eventually answered came through a little gruff.

'I'm sorry. You've reached Madeleine Bonnaire's residence. She's unable to come to the phone right now. May I take a message?'

'Well, as I um… This isn't a wrong number, you can um… answer my original question and…' The man broke off. 'Madeleine's friend. Forgive me; my mind's been on other things. I quite forgot. Preoccupied with um… Well, with work. It's Victor. I understand congratulations are in order, my dear. Anne Bishop these days, isn't it? I presume it's who I'm speaking to.'

Anne relaxed, though to talk to Victor Bonnaire felt more than a little peculiar. Did people ever relax around the parents of friends? Though she'd not seen Madeleine for years, the time that passed since she spoke with Madeleine's father stretched into eternity. The realisation had come to her early on that she wanted little to do with him, so she steered clear all those years ago. 'Thank you, only I often still go by the name of Travers.'

A lengthy pause ensued, during which she imagined the old man blinking into the distance. Perhaps unwise of her to speak so frankly, but it was long past time to drag Madeleine's father into present day reality.

'Oh... yes, quite.' A husky cough followed. 'I... Tell Madeleine... Tell her I'll catch her at the... um... at work.'

Why not refer to the institute by its rather odd name of the Repositorium? A hint of amusement softened the last of Anne's reserve. 'I will, and I hope to see you before we leave.'

She ought to say something more, but stopped short of asking him for a tour of the facility, even though Madeleine had tried to make those arrangements. 'It's so wonderful to spend time with Madeleine again, and to catch up with you both.'

'And I understand you'll... um...   You want to be poking around our little organisation.'

Bonnaire took her by surprise; she'd expected him to avoid the subject. 'With your permission.' Instinct made Anne err on the side of caution.

'You're... Well, I suppose.'

'If it's a problem...?'

'No, no. You're more than welcome. More than welcome.' His tone made her not welcome at all. 'Day after tomorrow?' A question, one he answered before she did. 'Yes, day after um... tomorrow. Under a watchful guidance. Can't give away all our little secrets.' The old man chuckled. 'I always admired your father and can do no less than to extend the same courtesy to his daughter. In his absence.'

The man did well for a moment, but spoiled the attempt to sound convivial. Anne didn't need to acknowledge the strange phrasing. Victor Bonnaire didn't accept her visit here. Not at the institute, and likely didn't condone her hanging around with his daughter.

'Shall I get Madeleine to...?'

'No need. No need. It can wait. Just paperwork. I um... quite forgot you are all on your way out to dinner. Don't let a busy old fool spoil your appetite.'

'Not a problem.' Anne kept her tone light, if not her barb. With luck Bonnaire wouldn't realise he annoyed her. Unwise behaviour when she needed his permission to visit Madeleine at work.

'Hope you found a decent hotel.'

For a second Bonnaire's comment did not connect with her. 'A decent...'

Did Madeleine not tell her father Anne and Bill were staying with her? Many questions flitted through Anne's mind as to why. The only one which made any sense was perhaps Bonnaire would not be happy to discover Bill, an unknown man, stayed with his daughter. Not even for the purpose of accompanying his wife and therefore chaperoned. How old-fashioned was Bonnaire? Best to give a non-committal answer.

'We're set up well.'

They exchanged a few more pleasantries before Anne hung up the phone, determined to tell Madeleine of the call. Only as she did so, did she wonder… Was it possible Bonnaire attempted to catch her in a lie?

Why did Anne not admit to staying with his daughter? The woman was up to something. No way did he believe her visit to the institute casual. Did someone send her? Yes, Anne might be a spy… for a competitor, maybe.

Although the idea crossed his mind, Bonnaire struggled to reconcile the notion. The pixie-faced girl – as he always thought of her – didn't belong in any espionage novel he ever read. Madeleine spending time around a married couple might be a welcome idea, but… Anne. No knowing what manner of strange ideas the woman put in his daughter's head. Still calling herself Travers. To think her husband tolerated such behaviour. Nothing changed.

No, Anne was not the best influence on his daughter. The pair of them always too interested in science. He'd hoped Madeleine would step into the administrative role he foresaw when she joined him at the institute. Alas, she liked to be more involved than he desired. Constantly checking reports so that he had to take care that she didn't find those that he didn't want her to read.

If Madeleine became aware of everything going on in the facility, she might never speak to him again.

He didn't like uninvited people on-site and Anne… Bishop – he refused to call the woman by her maiden name. She had a way of seeing through a lie. She might glean more from a number of well-placed questions and watching for his reaction than from searching any of the unlocked rooms in the institute. Hard to oversee her movements personally, yet keep away from her, though.

'Damn woman,' Bonnaire muttered pouring fresh brewed coffee.

She had blocked him in a corner by nothing more than her relationship with Madeleine. A rebuttal would alienate him with his daughter – often an awkward kinship – and might make Anne ask more questions. Might raise Madeleine's suspicions, too.

Cooper especially wouldn't like strangers on site. Not that they would find their way into his laboratory. Bonnaire even needed to announce to Cooper any intention to examine his work. Cheek of the man, but sometimes necessary to pander to these twisted intellects. No. One thing he didn't need to worry about; Anne Bishop would never breach Cooper's lab because neither he nor Cooper would let her. Still, might be best to warn Cooper of unexpected visitors.

Time enough later. Drink first. No way would he waste excellent coffee.

Paul yawned and stretched, glancing around to make sure Cooper hadn't wandered out of the second lab into the outer room without his knowledge. To think the other night he had knocked on the door and tried to entice the professor to share a drink. Foolish of him. What had he been thinking? No chance Teddy Cooper would stop treating him as nothing more than an assistant and a second-rate one. Paul helped with at least seventy percent of the work in the lab so far, and only a quarter under Cooper's guidance. Paul was responsible for half the cataloguing and proposals put forward, which, fine… Didn't amount to much, but he wanted credit where due.

Speak of the Devil and run the risk he might reply, his grandmother used to say. The door to the second lab opened and Cooper emerged. He didn't so much as glance over and, moving to a table, he gathered up another tray of test tubes, no doubt intending to disappear back into his lab with them. What did the man do in there? Since Cooper's return, all Paul did was catalogue a thousand crystals, some of which he'd never heard of or seen the like. A few were so peculiar he joked they must be of alien origin, startled by the expression to cross Cooper's face. Paul took greater care handling them since.

Waste of time. Cooper wasted Paul's time. So why stay? Paul didn't like working there at all. His day contained only one highlight: to catch sight of Madeleine Bonnaire. If not for her, would he leave? Who was he kidding? He had no other option but to stay. Without this job, his future looked bleak. Bleaker than employment with Cooper, as unbelievable as it seemed. Would his day be any better if Bonnaire teamed Paul with any of the other professors though?

The scientists here… were competitive, sure, but they took no pride in accomplishments so great they might change human evolution. Or so Bonnaire boasted. While Paul didn't trust Bonnaire, he did believe him, so accepted that major experiments went on here. A fact backed up by the continued success of the organisation. The people here displayed a peculiar… smugness, lacking self-esteem and dignity. Cooper should fit right in, but he didn't make many attempts to. When asked to join in with anything, he threw the busy and working hard argument into the fray.

Paul cleared his throat, waited. Cooper ignored him, didn't hear. Paul coughed louder, making Cooper at last stare over, with what appeared irritation changing to surprise. Might it be…? Did Cooper forget all about him?

'You've not eaten.' Paul gestured with a lift of his chin to the plate of covered sandwiches of which he'd consumed less than half.

His risk of tapping on Cooper's door before lunch proved fruitless when he got no reply. Despite his dislike of the man, Cooper appeared gaunt these days, though why remained a question to which Paul had no answer. Overworked. Must be. On what? Paul itched to peek into the second lab, fought to stay seated on his stool. Connecting with the man was more important. He at least needed to make Cooper understand that taking care of his health was paramount. If Cooper grew sick, his illness might jeopardise both their jobs.

'You need to take better care of yourself. Your coffee's cold, too.'

'I don't mind. Drank plenty in my day. You learn to when you're on the track of a breakthrough.'

Paul risked a question. 'Is that what you are close to, a breakthrough?'

Cooper regarded him, gaze hard and chilly. He slugged back a mouthful of coffee and pulled the cover off the sandwiches, grabbed one, and bit off one-third in a single bite. He chewed and swallowed, causing Paul to hold his breath, certain the food would refuse to go down. Cooper might choke, Paul unsure whether he wished for it.

Didn't happen. Cooper recovered, snapping at the bread, devouring without savouring the flavour. If he kept eating so fast, the man would suffer indigestion.

'My progress isn't the issue. You made any headway with these crystals?'

'Still over half or more to catalogue.' No one would think so to view the crate, as, though sizeable, the box didn't appear capable of holding so many. However, plenty of the crystals were tiny.

'That'll keep you from under my feet.'

'What are these for, anyway?'

'Not your concern.'

'But if I knew, I can give you some input, add my ideas to yours. To others.'

Cooper snorted.

Paul bristled. 'Do I need to remind you how helpful my input has been so far with the temperature unit?'

Funny little box thing Cooper brought back with him from one of the few times he stepped away from the institute. He complained the reading needed to be constant, but the gauge fluctuated. Took Paul several hours, but he traced the source. The idiot used insufficient wire, incapable of carrying the right voltage and which, over time, broke. Lucky the gadget didn't catch fire. Although an easy fix, he hadn't told Cooper, and the man didn't ask. Cooper considered himself above such errors; any he made were more a case of impatience, of believing simple tasks beneath him.

However, the question niggled whether the man only pretended he needed Paul's help. Paul didn't like the idea, so cast the notion aside... for now. As for whatever Cooper wanted the unit for, Paul found no evidence. Pressed, Cooper got what Paul now recognised as a stubborn expression on his face and refused to speak a word.

'Work your way through this lot, and we'll see about you

doing something more significant.'

So intent on examining Cooper was Paul, he almost missed what the man said. 'You... you mean it?'

'Sure. I have enough assignments to be going on with. Glad to hand one of our larger projects over.'

Paul hesitated. Sounded better than likely. There must be a hidden reason. 'And I will receive full credit for my percentage of the input?' he asked before giving the wording any thought.

Cooper glared. 'What are you accusing me of?'

'N-Nothing.'

'I should think not. You act as though I'm holding you back, but perhaps you should do something about your attitude. There's no time to hold your hand. I must get on.' Cooper glanced at the clock and blinked as though surprised by the hour. 'You can go.'

'No. It's fine. I'll work on a while.'

Cooper grabbed another sandwich and disappeared into the second lab. Paul returned to examining the crystals, his concentration shot.

He didn't trust Cooper. The man's promise rang hollow. He needed to understand the man's motivation. For now, best to do as Cooper said.

As though in answer, a strange whine made Paul crick his neck as he twisted to stare over his shoulder at the door leading into the second lab. The sudden strange eerie wail now vibrating around the room.

Nosy upstart. Wanting to know more than he had a right to. Little did Paul Larousse understand that Ted gave him the job of examining and cataloguing the crystals so that if someone discovered the missing one, the blame would fall on Paul. Not all were for Ted's lab, so his need for one sample was a real problem solved by instigating Paul as a patsy to shoulder the responsibility. As far as Ted cared, Paul was welcome to smash the rest. Ted now owned the one he needed, and, with care, had cracked the crystal into two pieces, the why was no one's concern. Not even Bonnaire's, despite what the idiot man believed. Not as considerable an imbecile as Larousse though. How much of a brain did his assistant possess if he didn't realise Ted filtered all the rotten jobs his way?

Or perhaps he did, and all of the questions were Paul's inept way of complaining. Young men these days; weak and pathetic. Ted recalled all his years of acting as someone's understudy. Yes, he, too, had his work stolen, accredited to someone else. Such occurrences came with the territory, and if one wanted a sniff of promotion, well, back in the day, a young man understood when to keep his mouth shut.

Ted sniggered at the irony. People would call him a fool if they learned of these tests. Enough people told him to stop wasting his life for him to realise none of them understood. They would call his situation here an excellent one, but they would tell him many other projects deserved his attention, those with which even he understood he might yet make a name within the scientific community. None interested him the way his special project did.

Funding was the reason he slogged for Bonnaire. After the experiment reached its conclusion... Then, and only then, might he work for the man for real. If Ted succeeded, he might make further use of a man like Bonnaire. So many regulatory bodies oversaw experiments. So many precautions. Many who complained men like himself should take more safeguards in his time. Yes, Bonnaire, with his proclivity to allow risks was worth exploiting. So few people were truly brave.

A chill inched up Ted's arms, and crawled over his back and kissed his neck. His hands shook, scattering items on his desk, jarring the tray on which the vial of black liquid stood.

The tube toppled, and Ted puffed in relief as he snapped up the cylinder before it fell. Not that the tube would smash. Unlikely the top would come off either.

Ted replaced the container where it belonged; in the box with the cushioned lining. He should have done so first thing. Actually, he couldn't even recall taking the container out. He frowned, puzzled, and wiped a hand over his brow. Did he sweat again?

Exhaustion. Must be. The longer hours wore him down. His nerves bested him. Nothing to fear. He couldn't let his anxiety stop him now when so close. Thoughts of precautions were mere apprehension that he would reach the finish line only to fail.

Ted pulled goggles over his eyes. He threw a switch. A strange eerie noise filled the lab. Within the isolation unit, light directed from two sides shone through two crystals meeting at the midpoint to where a drop of black fluid lay on a suspended platform. He ran the sequence to the first time limit, the second, and the third. Nothing happened at any stage until he went over the last margin and the sample smoked.

First killing the power, Ted spun away, pulled off the goggles, and chucked them down on the table. He rubbed his hands over his face.

He'd been so sure. The whole basis of his work to date revolved around light refraction. He must be on the right track, he *knew* it. He needed a light-bulb moment. A spark. If only it were that simple. An ignited match, the flame set to the fluid...

Could it be...?

No. Ted dragged his fingers through his hair and stared wide-eyed at the results of his experiments so far. Still... what if he had latched on to something?

'One more experiment.' He made the promise aloud to harden his resolve.

One more and he would put the liquid away until this mania passed, or he came up with a real resolution.

Despite the pledge, the flutter of excitement disturbed his already uneasy stomach. He swallowed against a sick feeling, determined to follow through on what his gut told him was his best chance. The crazy notion, born from Gothic novels and horror films, might cause more harm than good but he wouldn't listen to any self-recrimination. If this proved to be madness, he accepted it. Too often he let his own fear dictate his actions, but no longer.

As Mary Shelley's creation gave life to a dead man by electricity, Ted would test whether the power produced a spark of animation in what remained of his black pool.

A simple study to begin with.

He set up a small battery with electrodes and put them into the isolation box via the outer compartment. The liquid subjected to light through the crystals now resembled tar. He slipped his hands into the gloves and took hold of a fresh sample. Extracted three drops, hesitated, and took another two. He gathered up the electrode and battery unit, checking the reading. The charge, a small one, but all he need do was cross the wires and touch the liquid.

Steadying his hands, Ted undertook the task. He jumped when the wires sparked. A small waft of smoke puffed up, but the fluid lay in the tray's base, like a dirty raindrop.

Pressure built behind his eyes. Although he hardly believed it, he wanted to cry.

Ashamed of the notion, Ted increased the charge and tried again with the same result.

Several seconds passed in silence, Ted unmoving.

'My father was right. I'm a disgrace.'

Though his father would have meant more personally, Ted's thoughts settled on the scientific community. His mind far surpassed most in his field and yet he'd flittered away the level to which he might have risen, at least in the eyes of his father. Not including his years on this earth or a childish whim.

Wait! What if he used light *and* electricity?

He extracted another fresh sample, considering how fast he needed to move to flip the switch on the outside of the containment unit. He then had to place his hands back in the gloves, to administer the power. A few tests performing the procedure without switching on anything satisfied him that he could do so within the required time.

This time he allowed the light to run for up to a third stoke, applying a spark for a second at each juncture.

He hit the kill switch. Waited.

Nothing. The liquid now lay in the trap, appearing like a lump of melted liquorice.

Might be he needed to adjust the timings, choose better when to administer the jolt. Would take time to figure out, each test damaging more of the precious black liquid.

Ted sighed. Perhaps Paul still had the whisky. He struggled with the sudden and undeniable urge to consume the entire bottle.

The black liquid blipped. Ted jerked back.

Nothing moved.

'This isn't real.'

He stared into the box, one hand still in a glove, afraid to shift. Almost too afraid to breathe.

So slowly he almost believed he imagined the outcome, the black puddle drew together to form a blob.

CHAPTER FIVE
A Cold War

ANNE TWISTED her glass of wine in a tight circle. Though delightful, the Bistro was a little too glitzy to warrant the title. Mirrors lined one wall; the upholstery was black, the edges of the tables and chairs fringed with gilt, the bar inlaid with copper. The meal little short of spectacular made up for the excessive glamour.

'Forgive my father. I'll be your escort, so it's not like I'll be taking you around under the watchful gaze of an armed guard.' Madeleine's lips twitched and twisted in apparent disgust. Though Anne mentioned the call before they left the apartment, Madeleine had waved away the details, only asking Anne for more information once they finished eating. 'Some of our work requires clearance, as is the nature of all research.'

Anne inclined her head in understanding and agreement. She didn't mention Bonnaire's comment concerning a hotel, as she wanted to speak to Madeleine alone about that without Bill... If she spoke to her about it at all. She didn't wish to embarrass Madeleine any more than necessary, but it would be nice to know whether her friend concealed anything from Victor Bonnaire and why.

'But it's not like you're anyone walking in from the street. Either of you.' Madeleine included Bill in the statement. 'And I know why my father called. I should sign a few papers, and he didn't get them to my desk on time. No way do I want to work late while you are visiting. No doubt he's unhappy I dared to leave when I should for once.'

'We appreciate the feeling.' Bill exchanged a knowing glance with both women.

'I'm sure they're waiting for me.' Madeleine slumped back.

'Forgive me, but would you mind if we stopped off on the way home? I can show you my office. That's hardly offensive, and signing will only take a few minutes. If a light is still shining in the gatehouse, we can call in for a nightcap with my father before heading back. He's bound to want to see you at some point. Getting it out of the way will leave us the day free for your real visit.'

'Makes sense,' Bill said.

'It does,' Anne agreed. Particularly as they had another day to explore the area tomorrow, their tour of the institute not scheduled until the day after due to Madeleine's busy itinerary and Bonnaire's apparent insistence. 'I confess an itch to inspect the building where you spend so much of your time. Even if I must curb my scientific interest.'

Madeleine's laugh was bright enough to make the crystal tinkle. 'Yes, I rather thought you might. It's why I suggested it. The papers are important but it's not my problem they arrived late.' She sighed. 'I guess I'm still trying to prove myself to my father.'

'And signing them so late at night will demonstrate your dedication.' Anne nodded in understanding. 'Alas, women still walk those extra miles to appear equal.'

'That's unfair.' A small frown creased Bill's forehead.

Anne reached over and laid a hand on his arm. 'And we need more men like you to keep saying so.'

'A toast to Bill.' Madeleine lifted her glass and Anne followed, struggling not to laugh when Bill became flustered.

Odd, but now they stood in her office, Madeleine realised how much she longed for Anne's approval. Her friend, having peered around with a keen gaze, at last nodded.

'I like it. I expected… I don't know. Something clinical. This is more traditional with enough touches to make me feel a capable feminine professional works here. It's very you.'

'I'll take that as a compliment.'

'As I intend it.'

Madeleine scrawled a pen across the last of the papers, having signed most while holding her breath awaiting Anne's endorsement. She straightened, gathering the pages and shuffling them into an envelope.

'Now we'll drop these off with my father on the way out.'

Enough lights blazed up at the gatehouse on their way in for Madeleine to tell Anne and Bill her father would be up a few more hours. Some nights he didn't sleep well and used the time for reading. When he switched on lamps instead, he prepared for bed. Since her mother's death, he didn't like to sit in the dark, a sentiment Madeleine understood, and one that had taken her many weeks to shake, whereas her father never had.

They walked through the entrance vestibule with its double glass doors, having checked out with the security officer. Madeleine had her hand on the outer doors when she pulled up short.

'Paul!' Shocked to walk almost straight into him, his name came out sounding too shrill. Worse still, he looked almost as stunned. Madeleine reeled in her wits. 'These are my friends, Anne and William Bishop. Anne, Bill, this is one of our assistants, Paul Larousse.'

She tried not to meet Anne's gaze as they exchanged introductions and shook hands.

'Paul... Why are you here at this hour?' Although she didn't mean to sound accusing, she surely did.

'Working late.'

Madeleine blinked, and opened her mouth, about to ask whether Cooper worked him too hard, but the question struck her as inappropriate. Wrong time. Wrong place. Wrong company.

'I understand you all do.' Anne's comment sounded innocent enough, but her expression said she noticed Paul's unease as much as Madeleine did. 'This concerns business, so why don't you talk? Madeleine, we'll meet you by the car.'

Anne took Bill's hand, and they walked off, Anne glancing back once over her shoulder with a grin and wink.

Well, really! Madeleine almost shook her head, but Paul might have noticed, even though he appeared distracted and agitated enough not to pay attention. Was his anxiety owing to his attraction? Speaking of which. Madeleine's reaction took her by surprise. Her unguarded response to seeing Paul out of his lab coat, jacket open enough to reveal how his t-shirt stretched over his chest...

Madeleine swallowed, cursing her foolishness. What would her father think of her? What would Anne? Fine, Anne might be more forgiving, but neither of them was in their teens, and Madeleine would be the first to declare herself too old to react to a man like that.

'Walk with me to the car?'

Her question startled him, but no more than a second or two passed before he gave her a nod and fell into pace at her side, steps slow. As they neared the slight run between the hedges to the wider field used to park vehicles, Madeleine stopped. She glanced back at the building's ornate façade, the one Anne had called rather too grand for science, though she also said it made it perfect. Determining they stood out of view of the guard, and, for the moment, of Anne and Bill, Madeleine gathered her courage.

She gazed at the man now staring at her in clear puzzlement.

'Paul, I'm not one to dither, or to play games. Do you understand what I'm saying?'

His frown only grew. This wasn't going so well.

'I wondered... That is...'

Oh, for goodness sakes. Anne would laugh if privy to this little spectacle.

'I thought perhaps you would like to join me for dinner sometime.'

'I... Well, yes, I suppose. If what you mean is... '

They would be at this stuttering chess game all night. Madeleine paced forward and planted a kiss on his lips. A chaste exchange of affection, as far as the French and kisses went, but a kiss nonetheless.

'That is my meaning.' She stepped back and waited.

Maybe he would now ask if the chance of a relationship was inappropriate. Damned if she knew, but Paul was the first man to attract her in a long while and not purely owing to his appearance or fitness level. His appalling attempts to make his feelings known – not as bad as her own but close – should have put her off. Yet something about Paul's character, his sense of justice, of right and wrong, and his humble brilliance made her want to get to know him.

His stunned expression took a while to transform, but the

smile to follow proved warm and inviting, made him handsome in ways more complex than desire.

'We'll talk tomorrow?' Madeleine made it a question, and received his nod before she walked off, hurrying to catch up to Anne.

Whatever would Anne make of her expression? Madeleine touched fingers to her face only to find her cheeks hot. She had better not blush.

'This is unexpected.' Bonnaire ran a hand along his nape. How did it come to pass that Anne Bishop now stood in his house uninvited? Most unwelcome. He glanced at his daughter who, after dropping a folder of the documents in his clutches, now warmed her hands by the fire.

Bonnaire tapped the envelope, peering from Anne to Madeleine and back again. Madeleine. Anne. The documents he'd left on her desk. Could it be...? No, his Madeleine wouldn't take Anne inside the institute without his permission, not even to her office. The visitors must have waited outside while his daughter went in. Only way to know for certain would be to view the visitor's book, but perhaps ignorance was bliss. Still, his Madeleine marched the woman and her husband into his home. Unpleasant emotions flourished, fuelled in the presence of this... this other woman.

As for Bill... William... He appeared to be an upstanding chap, should know better than to marry a woman of such free will. Women lib? Bonnaire withheld a snort. From what he recalled of Anne, it surprised him she married at all. The expression in her eyes hadn't changed, but appeared more forceful. Self-assurance – that was what he struggled to place. He witnessed an unhealthy level of confidence, the kind he too-often saw in his daughter's eyes. Not that those things were plain for all to view. Madeleine's beauty and Anne's innocent features deceived men, he supposed.

How did the man handle her? Or perhaps he didn't. No. The man was smitten. Bonnaire understood the danger. Pity Eloise didn't live longer; they might have had a son.

Eloise. What would she think of their wilful daughter? Perhaps if he hadn't tried to make her happier with her lot, she would be alive to tell him. Bonnaire quelled the thought.

That way laid madness. With Cooper's help, things would be right next time.

'Professor?'

Anne speaking snapped him back to the present. He glared at her as she stared back.

'Forgive me? Did you have a question?'

Whatever went through the professor's mind, Anne didn't want to know. The need to speak fast, now he opened the way for discourse, overcame her.

'Not a question. More a wish to express my gratitude. I can't tell you how delighted I am to view your facility. I'm sure there's much I might learn—'

'Yes, yes.' Bonnaire waved down Anne's enthusiasm, his tone revealing he found it nothing more than an irritation. 'Much we can teach the right people, I'm certain. I'm pleased to indulge my daughter and to allow your visit.'

'Indulge me?' Madeleine whispered, but her father appeared not to hear. Or he ignored her.

'Although I'm sure you um…'

He's searching for a word to be insulting without appearing to be. The thought silenced anything else Anne wanted to say. She peeked over at Madeleine. A frown set up residence across her friend's forehead.

'I'm sure you unduly concerned yourself,' Bonnaire said, calling Anne's attention back to him. Whether she missed a few sentences, escaped her. The notion he insulted her remained. 'I'd rather you…' He glanced over at Madeleine. 'Well, won't it be lovely for the two of you to spend the um… time catching up? Chatting. Shopping. Perhaps, Bill?' He made her husband's name a question. 'Bill might appreciate seeing one of our more military applications.'

'Father, those come under the heading of restricted projects.' Madeleine's tone asked what her words didn't: What was Bonnaire thinking?

'Quite, but as you said, Bill Bishop has suitable clearance…'

'As does Anne equally in their own country.'

That last bit of information seemed to floor him. His mouth moved, but no comment emerged. At last, he gathered himself. 'Yes, well, we're all allowing enthusiasm to take over our wits.'

'Possibly, but I think this is an appropriate note on which to call it a night.' Madeleine muscled past her father, pulling Anne and Bill along in her wake. 'I'm sorry we disturbed you.' She tugged open the door, shooing her friends to the exit. She paused. 'We can arrange another meeting, one not so late.' She glared at her father. 'You might be more alert and able to "indulge" me with a sensible discussion.'

When Madeleine thrust them out into the darkness, Anne was sure her friend said, 'Dimwit,' under her breath.

'I'm sorry that went so badly,' Anne muttered.

Bill's expression spoke of a man perplexed, and he seemed unable to gather his thoughts or his reaction well enough to say anything.

'Not as wrong as you think.' All three crowded into Madeleine's car, Anne and Madeleine in front, Bill in the back. Madeleine glanced over. 'That made my decision for me. You'll be viewing the institute as planned and, as much as I can, you'll be getting a full guided tour. Sorry, Bill, but I need you to clear your wife's schedule. I'm throwing open the doors and welcoming in liberation.'

From the rear seat of the car, Bill grinned.

CHAPTER SIX
Secrets and Strangeness

TOO MANY times Paul caught himself staring out of the window, pen still, the task before him forgotten. Yet another day in the lab and impossible to concentrate on his work. Stupid of him. Idiotic to make Teddy Cooper his priority. Best thing to do was to think of something else.

Madeleine.

The kiss.

So overwrought had he been, pity he'd not savoured the chance to enjoy it. Sure, the shock that the woman of his dreams shared some of his feelings sent everything else into retreat, but the distraction didn't last. Couldn't.

Madeleine Bonnaire sat in her office a few floors above, and he'd give almost anything to see her, but what would he say? No way could he claim to be in a romantic mood, and the last thing he wanted was to discuss Teddy Cooper with her again. God... What if he ruined any chance with Madeleine? All because he worried over a man likely to put him in a specimen jar if something knocked him down in the street. Hard to say why he felt that way, but he did, unable to shake the notion.

Speaking of, the man appeared. Whistling. What the hell? Cooper was never so jaunty, not so happy in... Well, forever. Cooper nodded to him, odd in itself. Despite his cheerful attitude, the man showed signs of being ill.

Without a word, Cooper headed to the back room, leaving Paul to grind his teeth.

Why would the institute hire Cooper? Not all the scientists on site were French, but the majority were. Again Paul wondered about Cooper's prize project. What did the man do in the back room?

Something more interesting, clearly. Either top secret research assigned by the upper echelons or... something of his own.

The thought iced Paul's blood, though he couldn't explain why. Warning fingers stroked the outer reaches of his mind. The man's questionable and unstable health might be down to personal neglect and extended hours, but another more nagging possibility formed. Might Cooper be experimenting on himself?

Paul ceased his work to stare at the locked door. The time had come for him to see into that room.

'This is Professor Fournier. Professor, this is a good friend and a visiting scientist from England. I told her all about your progress in microscopy.'

Madeleine introduced the professor to Anne in French and Professor Fournier answered the same.

'*Heureux de vous rencontrer.*' Fournier held his gloved hands up in plain apology. He broke into English. '*Pardon moi* for not taking your hand to shook.' He slipped back into French. 'But I am always ready to talk.'

As willing as Anne was to listen. Madeleine explained a little of Fournier's work as, though classified, the non-specifics had been mentioned in national news. A part of Fournier's project comprised collaborating with other counties, scientists, and institutions of scientific exploration and learning, so word spread. The man also spoke reasonable English if Anne preferred to converse that way. But luckily Anne's French was more than up to the task. The results of an excellent education.

'If you're willing, I'll leave you in Fournier's capable care,' Madeleine said. 'When you're done, wander along to my office and we'll take a tour.'

Anne thanked Madeleine and, happy to listen to Fournier, she allowed him to lead her to a prototype of his latest equipment.

Cinema and television made picking a lock appear so simple. Though Paul tried with several implements while Teddy Cooper took part in some meeting, the blood pounding in his

59

ears shot Paul's concentration. The man never stayed in these meetings as long as he should, so the opportunity was limited. Every time Paul believed the catch was about to give, some noise made his heart stop. A feverish glance over his shoulder and sweat broke out on his brow. Breath suspended, Paul gazed at the door. His fear of Cooper returning to find him on his knees attempting to force the lock became so strong that Paul easily imagined dying of fright.

One thing of which he was sure within twenty minutes of trying, no way would he ever make a career as a thief. Neither his skill nor his nerves would withstand it. As his attempts became more forceful, he feared leaving identifiable scratches around the lock, tell-tale marks Cooper would undoubtedly spot.

Paul gave up, returned to his workbench, taking steady breaths until his pulse eased, and did his best not to convey his guilt when Cooper entered mere minutes later.

God, that was cutting things close.

For once, he was glad Cooper didn't so much as spare him a glance. Paul might as well be invisible most days. Paul sat in an uneasy silence until the familiar wailing noise shattered the little composure to which he still clung.

Just what exactly *was* that sound? How he was going to enter Cooper's lab to find out, he didn't know.

'*Merde!*' Anne cursed as she opened the door to Madeleine's office and almost walked into a man standing there. Madeleine and her secretary attended a meeting, so Madeleine had left Anne the run of her office until she returned.

Anne sucked in a cool breath and placed a hand over her heart while she recovered. Worse things had startled her over the years, but maybe Bonnaire not wanting her here overly disturbed her. Paul Larousse had a trapped-in-the-headlights stare of a condemned animal. Or like someone had already run him over.

'*Monsieur* Larousse.' Anne inclined her head in a quick nod of acknowledgement. 'If you're searching for…' She hesitated over what to call her friend, knowing Madeleine and Paul had kissed, and opted for, 'Madeleine, I fear she's not here.'

His gaze swept past her and flittered over the room as if

60

he didn't believe her. 'I was, but maybe I might have a word with you?'

Anne dithered, but, in no more time than she took to blink, she stepped back, beckoning Paul into Madeleine's office. She let the door close but chose not to invite him further inside or to sit.

'What can I do for you?'

Though his peculiar behaviour made her cautious, Paul looked to be more in fear of her than she was of him. Surely, he wasn't this scared of Madeleine. Her friend had kissed *him*, after all, making her feelings clear. Maybe Madeleine's advance was more unwelcome than she believed. Perhaps Paul wasn't open to a relationship with someone who was also a colleague. He might view Madeleine as a dangerous prospect – the daughter of his benefactor. Or maybe he didn't like forward women, a thing Anne struggled to comprehend.

She studied his expression for a few seconds as he sidled his way along one wall, putting distance between them. Something else went on here. Something more troubling. He moved, one foot to the other, as though he found keeping still intolerable. He fisted his hands, released them, only to fist them again. Someone needed to speak first.

'*Monsieur* Larousse?' She waited until his gaze flicked her way. 'I presume you're here for a reason?'

'Yes.' He became preoccupied with the carpet, gaze lowered, a young boy standing in front of a principal, begging not to be caned. 'This will sound forward of me. Presumptuous.'

Anne stopped breathing. She couldn't imagine what went on here, but if Paul wanted to ask her out instead of Madeleine, she didn't wish to know. She remained uninterested, married, and would never betray either her husband or her friend. One part of her longed to laugh. She opened her mouth to tell him she'd heard enough, when Paul interrupted.

'I came to ask Madeleine, but you may be more open to my cause.'

Fine, so whatever Paul wanted she had no clue. 'Sounds interesting.'

Maybe because of her tone, the pink in Paul's cheeks bloomed. Teasing this man proved priceless. She expected him to slide into another round of broken sentences, but instead, he said, 'I think Professor Cooper is up to something. I need your help to break into his lab.'

Anne spent the next ten minutes listening to Paul, during which she stayed silent. At the end, she agreed with him.

'Very well. I'll see what I can do.'

'Do you have faith in Larousse?'

A long enough pause as Madeleine considered the question. 'Yes. I wouldn't be interested in him if I didn't.'

'Then why so sceptical of his request?'

Anne had told Madeleine of Paul's concerns – worries igniting Anne's instincts. She wanted more information about this professor, but she couldn't make those kinds of demands, not even of Madeleine. She was a guest here.

The woman fell back into her seat as though deflated. 'I'm not. And it troubles me.' She took a moment, seeming to search for a way to explain her thinking. 'I... don't like Cooper. I don't like the way my father regards him. More so than many other scientists here. I could respect my father's decision if I understood *why* the man is exceptional. Although he *is* exceptional. Of that much, I'm certain. What I don't like is someone keeping me unenlightened as to how. Also, intelligence... No, being smart isn't the same thing as being intelligent. Knowing how to do a thing isn't the same as weighing up whether one should.' She made a helpless grasping gesture. 'I'm unsure I'm making myself understood.'

'I think you're doing well enough. What else can you tell me about Cooper?'

Madeleine eyed her, not with suspicion, but with reserve. 'I'm sorry, Anne. As much as I would like to tell you, I don't have the right. I've broken so many rules by allowing you in the institute, and though we scheduled today I crossed lines there, too. I let you into areas of which my father would not approve. And I told you details I should not. Not that I don't trust you. I do, but I also carry the guilt of disobeying my father, although I'm angry with him and my actions. I've used you to retaliate.'

No surprise there, as Anne had thought. 'I quite understand that, too.' She resisted saying more, remembering too well how Bonnaire made her feel the other day. 'How about

62

we take Paul at his word? You investigate his claims, with or without me – I'm prepared to back you any time – and you decide where to go from there. You can then tell me more if you feel there are grounds. And whatever we do, I promise it's in confidence.'

Unless a matter of national security, or to keep others safe, Anne would keep her oath. She didn't say so, though, swallowing her remorse. Her recent dream refused to leave her and stopped her from wallowing too deep in guilt. As much as she loved Madeleine, a sense of impending peril persisted.

Her friend took so long to consider her words, Anne contemplated insisting. If Madeleine rejected Paul's concerns, Anne couldn't shake the sensation she would need to investigate alone.

'Fine.' Madeleine sighed. 'We'll do things your way. I'll let Paul know, and tonight we take a gander in Cooper's lab.'

The last light of the day waned, casting sweeping shadows on the walls. Anne should have flicked on a lamp by now, but she sat in the dark, refusing to be afraid of the gloom, not wanting to think why. She hated to push Madeleine into doing something underhand. Yet after speaking to Paul about Cooper, and adding that to Madeleine's opinion of both men, Anne felt it right they help Paul break into the laboratory. Now she waited for Madeleine to finish up and return to her office. They planned to meet Paul in the coffee room, and, if he confirmed Cooper was out, Madeleine would unlock the second door.

A small pulse of pain nudged Anne's temples. Did she do the right thing? This holiday was to celebrate her anniversary with her beloved husband, and here she allowed something to draw her into another mystery. It was like Pemberton always said; 'Once you join UNIT, you never leave.' Which was doubly true of the founding members like her.

Before she contemplated the path of the universe and her place in it any further, the door opened, startling her.

'Anne!' Madeleine sounded breathless. 'Why are you sitting with the light off?'

Unwilling to explain, Anne leaned forward and switched on a lamp. 'Bit of a headache.'

'Because of all this drama, I dare say.'

Anne nodded. Although true, there was more to it than she wanted to discuss. If she talked to anyone, it would be Bill.

Madeleine bustled around the desk to join Anne on the other side. 'I'm so sorry about all this. I can't believe Paul brought this to you.' The woman came across as more than vexed.

'It says a lot about Paul's feelings,' Anne pointed out. 'He wanted to check with me to see how you would react.'

'He should ask me himself, not drag you into this.'

'Agreed, but I understand his caution.'

Maybe her pressing the issue made Madeleine pause, but the woman glanced over and relented.

'Fine. So can I. I can still be annoyed. Now, are we going to do this?'

'This is your institute. I agreed to tag along.'

'And to search for any interesting mysteries to solve.' Madeleine flashed a familiar grin, too fast gone. 'Oh, this is ridiculous. You are right about one thing. This is my organisation, or as good as. My father goes on about me taking full control one day, so I may as well do so now. I can go where I want.' She dangled a set of keys. 'Well here they are.'

A passkey to all the rooms was one of the few non-privacy stipulations, as she had explained to Anne. She and her father, and anyone they deemed necessary, could investigate any of the private rooms in the facility. This included housing and working areas, with good cause. If those in authority needed access, they wouldn't hinder the police or fire service. The true reason for the clause, though, was that they didn't want someone to blow up half the building, a narrow escape that had occurred a few years before.

Fine, bit of an exaggeration but not by much. They didn't want any of the experiments taking place to be something of which they wouldn't approve. Not that they often took advantage of the stipulation. A few cases since they opened the institute took place, times when their entering had proven to be necessary and a good thing. Such as the time they saved a young scientist from suffering extensive burns, which, if his experiment went ahead, would have been the result. His assistant had raised the alarm and Madeleine responded without hesitation. So, Anne understood the need for the keys.

'Did you have to sign them out?'

'I'm supposed to have done, but no. Fortunately, Dubois is on tonight and he's a bit softer than some of the guards are. I pretended to need something else and signed that out instead.'

For the first time Anne noticed the file Madeleine carried and now lay on the desk. Although she kept her tone light and tried to sound carefree, no way could Anne fail to hear Madeleine's discontent. The woman had the right to march along the corridor and enter Cooper's second laboratory with little more than a knock, regardless of whether he was inside. She didn't want to though. Anne shared Madeleine's suspicions on this one.

'Shall we go?'

Madeleine made the question sound as if she had given Anne one final chance to back out. A moment whereby Anne could forestall everyone's involvement.

'Right behind you.'

Madeleine hesitated but gave Anne a nod, leaving the lamp burning. With a careful glance into the hall, Madeleine stared back once, and then stepped out. Anne followed, head high, refusing to appear as nervous as she felt.

'Why are you so nervous?' Anne asked.

Madeleine gave her a sideways glance. 'And you're not?'

'Doesn't matter how I feel. This *is* your institute. You're not wrong. You may go where you want to, so why the nerves?'

'Fair enough, but what if I'm doing this for the unjust reasons? What if I'm allowing a subordinate to fulfil a more nefarious wish? Might I be giving Paul access to information Cooper should keep secret until he's ready to reveal his results?'

'We discussed your feelings earlier. Paul isn't the jealous or thieving sort. His concern strikes me as genuine.'

'Me too, but considering my personal dislike of Cooper it makes this situation all the more uncertain. I won't lie to you, Anne. I'm grateful to you. For your support. Your strength. Your tenacity.'

The unexpected and deep compliments fell upon Anne as dull blows, causing her equal measures of pleasure and pain, but she refused to leave her friend's side.

CHAPTER SEVEN
Running Scared

RELIEF BROUGHT a sense of weakness to Paul's legs when the door opened. Anne and Madeleine, thank goodness. Although Anne had said she would help, until that moment Paul hadn't known whether to believe her. Now terror filled his belly with the realisation he'd likely killed any chance of a relationship with Madeleine. Her gaze was brutal, worse than he'd imagined. Bruising; his nerves were already fraught with hiding out in one of the staff rooms clutching a cup of coffee long since cold, waiting until the women appeared.

'How long have you been here?' Anne's expression conveyed concern. Only then did Paul realise how distraught he must look.

'Almost an hour, though I've been going back and forth. I thought Cooper would never leave.'

'Well, I checked the security books, and he left forty minutes ago but I thought it best to delay in case he returned.' Madeleine's voice, hard, abrupt, threw punches, as though he accused her of keeping him waiting for no good reason.

'Good thinking.' No better comment came to his mind. 'Are you happy to go ahead?'

'Hardly happy, but I'll accept there may be cause for your unease.'

Difficult to tell who she was more annoyed with – Paul for bringing it to her attention, or Cooper if found guilty. With Anne standing there, and no sensible reply coming to mind, Paul maintained silence, gave a nod, and fell into step behind them.

They entered the outer lab with no incident, completing the walk without bumping into anyone. Although a few worked late, most had left. Cooper might be aware Paul stayed behind, though the man should have no reason to check whether Paul signed out. Despite the logical assumption, Paul fought to shake the premonition Cooper knew everything.

Nerves. Worry over finding nothing. Of Madeleine losing her trust in him. Paul crossed a line the unknown representatives he worked for would take unkindly. Bonnaire would fire him. So might Madeleine if his fears proved misguided.

'Knock first,' Madeleine whispered, and shrugged when he stared at her. 'To be safe.'

He nodded and tapped on the door to the second laboratory. When there came no reply, Anne turned the key, locking the first door to the outer lab. She left the key in the lock so no one else could enter. Madeleine withdrew a second key from a pocket and moved to the inner door where she stood hesitating. Seconds passed. She was going to change her mind. A glance at Anne told Paul she thought the same.

'We go in together.' Madeleine spoke to Paul. 'Anne, you're to follow when I say.' Madeleine turned the key, and Paul twisted the knob. He thrust the door open before he or Madeleine lost their nerve.

The door swung back, greeting them with a well of darkness so black walking into the room would be like stepping into an abyss. No light from the outer lab penetrated. Behind him, Anne made a small sound but, to peer over his shoulder, Paul would need to take his gaze from the black rectangle, and he couldn't do that. Madeleine's breathing grew ragged and a slide of his gaze revealed a drop of sweat running down the side of her face. They were all jittery. How strange. To think Teddy Cooper inspired so much fear.

A minute must have passed before he recalled the torch he carried, switched it on, and stepped inside before fear overwhelmed him. The first wide, circling scan with the beam revealed nothing unusual. Cabinets. Shelves. Tables. Microscopes. Various other apparatus. Wiring. Boxes with dials. Test tubes. A Bunsen burner. The basis of most labs anywhere.

Hampered by the restricted circle of light, Paul glanced towards the light switch. Would someone come running if they saw the bulb go on?

Idiot. The windows in the room were high in the walls. Besides, the flashing from a torch would more concern a passing security guard. Although, if one came calling, Paul had a reason and a right to be in the lab with Madeleine at his side. Still, he was glad Anne had locked the outer door.

He flicked the switch, blinked, momentarily blinded by the overhead lights. When his vision cleared, a dark shape in a shadowy corner drew his gaze. Hard to discern much, as if the black surface repelled light, the notion enhanced by the concealing filing cabinet that stood in the way.

'What is it?' Madeleine moved past him, making him jerk as he reached for her, only to pull his hand back.

He wanted to stop her though he didn't know why. A series of impressions flashed through his mind. Hazy ideas that made no sense, the strongest telling him discovering the truth would do them no good. The warning refused to emerge. No words left his lips. He did nothing as she lifted a hand, and the blackness slid towards her.

Imbecile.

Paul choked on a laugh, inwardly chuckling at his own stupidity. The black shape was only a cloth over an isolation box, though one with a few additional attachments. To think he entertained such a foolish superstition, imagining the blackness rising like an engulfing tide.

'Any clues?'

Madeleine's question wrenched his gaze back to the device. No idea. Although… Yes, whatever this contraption did, it had to be the source of the strange, often heard noise. Nothing else in the room was out of place or looked capable, but why put the apparatus there? As though it was discarded and useless. If that *was* the project which so occupied Cooper, why not put it where he might more easily work? The chosen spot implied the machine was unimportant, or Cooper wanted to make it appear so.

Or the machine wanted to hide. Ridiculous.

An inanimate contraption didn't have wants, but a sense of someone watching caused Paul's logic to war with his anxiety. To shake off the agitation, he approached the gadget. As he drew closer, shadows appeared to gather, causing him to glance around and to rub his skin free of sudden goosebumps.

'Anne? Come and see this.'

The other woman came in at once, in answer to Madeleine's call. She walked directly to the corner of the room, studied the mechanism, tapping the readouts, staring at dials, gaze following the emerging cables, one of which led to a generator. In the box itself hung two crystals with other bars and wires holding them in place at either end, some of which were now brown, burned out. A frown drew lines on Anne's face, her expression making Paul's nape crawl. He shivered, casting a glance over his shoulder. No one had entered the room. Course not. They'd locked the outer door.

'Two crystals,' Madeleine murmured. 'Paul, didn't you say you were cataloguing crystals?'

'Yes, though I'm unsure what for.'

'So am I.' Madeleine appeared to consider the thought. 'The consignment was for several projects, but I don't know why my father...' She shook her head. 'No, never mind now. Are you done with the cataloguing?'

'Almost.'

Madeleine gave a slow nod. 'I suggest you make finishing up your priority. I'll try to check the original inventory to make a comparison. I want to know whether Cooper brought these items into the institute, or he's used equipment belonging to us for unsanctioned experiments.'

'Or if someone sanctioned this experiment at all.' Anne spoke up.

Madeleine's eyes widened and she hesitated, but at last nodded. 'Sanctioned without my knowledge.'

Shocked, Paul stared at Madeleine, but she either didn't notice or didn't care.

'I believe these create a beam of light which pass through the crystals,' Anne said. 'Meeting here.' She tapped the glass of the containment box, pointing to a raised central platform. 'But for what purpose or what type of light this produces, I can't say without tests.'

For several seconds all three stared at the box, mesmerised. A sound alerted Paul to the fact he stood where he didn't belong. Although he wouldn't need to talk his way around questions from a security guard, if discovered and word got back to Cooper, there'd be more than a little explaining to do. Even Madeleine didn't want Cooper to know they snooped, as her words now confirmed.

'We need to cover this,' she said. 'Leave everything as we found it. I don't want Cooper to know we're investigating him. Not until we've a clearer idea what's going on here.'

All three worked to set the cloth in place, backing off, peering around, and edging toward the door. Together they hesitated before filing out, Paul last, hand on the light switch, reluctant to plunge the room back into the dark.

He sweated though he felt chilled, unable to shake that sensation of surveillance. Madeleine's words, 'We've got to get out of here,' snapped him out of it, though he didn't like the way she sounded or the way she scurried out and left him alone. Power to the overhead light bulb fluctuated. Paul hurried into the other room, flicking the light off on his way. Closed the door, twisted the key. He took a step back, staring at the wooden panel, hair all over his body on the rise. The shadows at the base of the door appeared to lengthen. A trick of the gloom, it must be, but it didn't stop Paul stumbling away. Out of the lab, he locked up the second door and broke into a run, in pursuit of the women.

Although Paul's switching off the light threw much of the room into darkness, a shaft of moonlight flooded the room from the windows high in the walls. The shadows, which so spooked Paul, continued to shift and flow. Moments later, Ted stepped out into the centre of the room.

So, Anne Travers was on site. How and why – questions for another time. He was safe. For now. The evening, the night, his to enjoy. Ted breathed in, hearing, smelling, tasting, feeling, and experiencing everything through his new senses.

So, Paul, a snoop. Didn't surprise him, but Madeleine? Paul didn't know his place. Best he learn, fast. Else, Ted might give in to the temptation coursing through him, to remove the irritation. Getting rid of Paul wouldn't be easy, would need to resemble an accident. Better yet…

No. Although the desire to use Paul as part of his experiments burned strong, doing so would complicate matters. Might be the end of Ted working at the Repositorium and, he hoped, making his way to higher purposes. The way his own investigation advanced, he would likely surpass anything this place offered him. They should beg him for his services, not treat him like this, regulating him to this. A man at the whim of an old codger. Having to lie. To cheat. To steal. To experiment on himself.

Although, if he hadn't, he'd never have harnessed the power he now possessed. Maybe he followed a pattern, a greater purpose in the universe.

Ah, but his mind wandered. There were more immediate questions to pursue.

What to do about Paul? A lucky man tonight. If Bonnaire's dim-witted girl hadn't shown up, Ted wouldn't have resisted testing his new strength, overpowering the man, using him as a laboratory rat. The image of Paul waking up, strapped down, the fluid introduced to his blood stream with the right electrical circuit, made Ted laugh. Imagine Paul tugging on his bonds. His eyes bulging, moans spilling out, and the inability to scream or shout through his gag. The man terrorised because his small mind wouldn't be able to understand what happened to him. Almost worth it, but it would only bring about a similar transformation, and Ted wasn't into sharing.

He glanced around the lab. At least no one found the samples, too preoccupied with a machine they couldn't comprehend the use of. Never would. Except, maybe, Anne. She was another matter. The woman couldn't know of his being on site or she would have dragged that meddling Brigadier Pemberton into a business neither of them had a right to mess with. To think Bonnaire warned him there were strangers in the facility, but not told him their names. So far, luck stayed on his side. Anne still didn't spot him, and her visit was for one day only.

The equipment. If Madeleine or her father queried the use, Ted could dream up an explanation, but no story he thought of was likely to get past Anne. She was the real threat. Only good thing in this scenario was having Bonnaire on his side.

For now he had to bide his time. If they got too close, interfered, then he'd deal with them. No one would hinder his great work. If nothing else, Anne Travers' presence told him

71

he'd done the right thing in hastening his experiment.

'There may be cause for alarm, Paul, but until I speak to my father...' Madeleine said. 'Until I can throw more light on the project Cooper is undertaking, I cannot accuse him of anything.'

Her attraction to the man notwithstanding, the urge to put Paul on report simmered along Madeleine's every nerve. Instead, he pushed and he pushed all the way back to her office, tagging along uninvited. Wanting her to do something more proactive. Pressurising for an answer until her patience snapped the moment she stepped inside, leaving Anne in the secretary's office with some feeble excuse.

Alone with Paul, Madeleine growled out her displeasure, tone low, aware Anne might hear every word.

'Not only did you drag me into this, but you tow a dear friend of mine into your... your...'

'Into my what?' If Paul tried to keep his tone steady, he failed. Anger smouldered in his gaze, radiated off his being.

'Into your fantasies for all I know.'

'You think that of me?'

What passed for genuine shock scrawled across his expression; he paled.

'I don't know *what* to think. Can you not see? You have me...' She stopped, not wishing to discuss what she thought she'd seen in the lab. What sent her running.

Waves of pain pushed at her temples. Many months had gone by since she last suffered a migraine, which now seldom bothered her at all, but she knew how to recognise when one was on the way. The migraines she experienced when she had them, interfered with vision, as this one did already. Best thing would be to get Anne back before the true headache set in, but Paul stood between her and the door, non-threatening but still an obstacle.

'For all I know this may be a case of a...' She hesitated but Paul held his ground, daring her to finish. 'A case of professional jealousy.'

Silence spun out.

'If you think so little of me why the kiss?'

The same question inched through her mind, but she was

72

too tired to consider the answer. 'Must you bring it up now?' On a night like this, when they hadn't even gone on a first date, he challenged her?

'Excuse me, but yes. I think it's relevant. If you distrust me so much, we need to discuss it. And what better time?'

'The worst possible time. My friend is waiting for me to drive her home. I'm tired and we're all fraught.' Madeleine grabbed her coat, noticing Anne's hung on the same rack and laid it over her arm, too.

Paul stepped into her path. His voice emerged low and level, determination ringing out. 'Do you think I would jeopardise the chance of a relationship with you if I didn't believe I had a cause? I don't trust Cooper for a good reason. Neither do you.'

An unreasonable desire to argue made Madeleine press her teeth to her tongue while she waited for her blood to cool. 'What do you want from me, Paul? You've brought it to my attention, and I will deal with it. But it's like you don't have much faith in my promise. I won't dismiss your concerns. All I am asking from you is patience.'

'Patience may be dangerous.'

The urgency with which he spoke called to something inside her. Didn't matter. She had to do this her way. 'So may rushing in.' Madeleine lay a hand on his arm. 'I'm sorry I'm being short with you. Truly. I suppose... Well, I suppose I hoped to find more.'

'Me too.'

He slumped under her touch; disappointment written all over his being.

'No master criminal keeps his plans for world domination out in plain view.' Madeleine sent him a rueful grin, pleased when his expression softened.

'Are we all right? You and me?'

'Yes.' She hoped they would be given time. 'I take your concerns seriously and will do what I can. I definitely want to check whether Cooper misappropriated anything.'

'It's not much.'

'It's a beginning.'

The temptation to give him a peck on the cheek as solace proved strong, but Madeleine resisted. 'Goodnight, Paul. Get some rest. We all need it.'

Maybe in the morning what they suspected would lead to nothing. A few stolen items would turn up. Nothing more.

Nothing dark, chasing her.

Eyes lowered so to avoid Paul's gaze, Madeleine stepped around him and moved to the door, holding it open. When he walked through, she locked up the room before crossing to the other door, Paul having headed out. There, Anne waited. Madeleine locked up the outer door, too, and led Anne out of the institute, pausing by the front desk to enter the security room to return both the folder she hadn't needed and the stolen key. Not until she sat behind the wheel did Madeleine speak again.

'You heard?'

'I heard enough.'

Madeleine turned on the ignition. 'I don't want to talk about it. Not tonight.' She slipped the car into gear and pulled out of her parking space; heading into the night, telling herself driving away had nothing to do with running.

Lying.

Truth. What a strange ideal. Harder not to lie to oneself more than to others. She was spooked, unable to banish the notion that something had chased her from Cooper's laboratory. Something connected to the odd contraption but not the assembly itself. The room felt... tainted. Wrong. The 'wrongness' crawled down her throat, burrowed beneath her skin.

The truth made her push Paul away, not his demands on her. Demands because he was afraid. Paul's fear inflated hers. Scared. She was scared, and she didn't like being scared. The best way to fight a fear was to confront it, but the mere thought chilled her blood enough to make her want to hide beneath the covers on her bed.

Cooper.

Madeleine stared at the road, sensing Anne's glances, ignoring her, disregarding everything but her driving. Speeding along. Chased. Running away.

The backs of her eyes prickled, forcing her to concentrate on good, steady driving, maintaining her speed, not going too fast.

'Madeleine?'

The sound of her name broke the spell, but Madeleine gripped the wheel harder to keep from shaking. She eased up on the accelerator so as not to spin out of control.

'Not now. Don't speak to me now.'

Didn't Anne sense they must run?

'I want to get home. I'm... afraid.'

Not more than a second passed before Anne spoke. 'I know. I am too.'

They sat in silence the rest of the way, sliding through the night, too many shadows creating strange shapes on the road.

CHAPTER EIGHT
Sins and Shadows

ANNE RUBBED a hand over her eyes, putting off the moment when she needed to address Bill's concern. He asked nothing, didn't need to. He'd accepted Anne's simple, 'Let me get Madeleine to bed,' without question or argument and she loved him for it.

Ready to talk, Anne met his gaze.

'Is she well?' he asked.

'Migraine. Can't recall when she last complained about one of those, though she had a few, back in the day.'

This headache was not so surprising: Anne's head hurt, too.

'I'd ask if you had a hard day, but I can tell it's more than that. What's going on?'

Not quite demanding, but Bill wanted the truth.

'Make me a drink, get me one of those headache pills, and I'll tell you.'

Anne sank into a chair, easing off her shoes. Her friend had complained of feeling sick by the time she lay down. Anne knew the routine well. An hour or so in a dark room, still and quiet, allowing the medication to do its work, was the only way Madeline might avoid strobes of light impeding her vision all night long. What Anne required was to talk and there was no one better than Bill.

'The day started well,' she told him. 'Not until the afternoon did things take a strange turn...'

Anne told him a strange story, but Bill believed her.

'You're saying the technology is known to you?'

'I'm not sure.' Anne's gaze fell short of Bill's eyes. Not

avoidance. More a case of her thinking too hard, focusing on something in her mind. 'Light beams through crystals. Does it sound familiar?'

Enough to make him shiver and recall a day some eight years ago, when he stood in a car park outside of a hospital. Back when UNIT was in its infancy, when they were all finding their feet with the unusual and unexplained. 'So much so I feel I should put in a call to the Brig.'

'And tell him what?' Anne sounded more inquisitive than sardonic, seeking a genuine answer. 'A thousand scientists might use similar technology for a million different reasons for all we know.'

'You sound like Madeleine, trying to convince yourself something isn't true.'

'Yes. I suppose it's a habit I used to share with her.' Now nostalgia warmed Anne's voice, though she also sounded forlorn. 'Simpler times.'

'So, what's our next move?'

'Our?' Amusement entered her voice.

'You don't expect me to sit back and do nothing? I am, technically, your superior, you know.'

Anne's smile was enough of a response. Even Pemberton didn't get to pull that one on her. 'No, I don't expect you to do nothing, but I feel for now that is exactly what you must do.'

'Why?' Bill took the seat next to his wife and lifted her legs into his lap, rubbing her feet. Not something he did often enough, but for now he fought the strange need to keep Anne close and safe. If her suspicions proved true, he had every reason to feel this way.

'For now Madeleine needs sleep. I can't ask a thing of her until she's well enough. In the morning, I'll ask to return to the institute. I'll demand her files on Cooper.'

'But you'll be subtle.'

'Naturally.'

Yes, Anne would phrase the demand delicately, but she would not take a refusal.

'Need I remind you we're due to leave day after tomorrow?' Bill said, softly.

'No need at all. Though if we need to stay on?' Anne made

77

it a question, to which Bill stifled a sigh.

'If there's a genuine reason, naturally we'll stay. We do still work for UNIT after all, and there is a French division, so, if needs be, I could rustle up the back-up.'

'I know. I was there setting up their scientific arm a few years ago, remember? NUIT, the *Nations Unies Intelligence Taskforce*,' Anne said in a perfect French accent.

Bill chucked. 'Anyway, right now, you need something to eat, and to get some sleep yourself.'

Paul stared through his car's windscreen out across the park. What was wrong with him? Everything he'd longed for he had: a kiss from Madeleine, her interest, a possible invitation to dinner, and all he thought of was the secondary lab. A back room looking as ordinary as any other laboratory in the building. One where his mind lingered, trapped in a haunting, waking nightmare. There must be an explanation. *Bound to be.*

Either Cooper was a bad man or misguided. Dangerous in both cases. To think Paul ever believed him and the professor would reach some kind of understanding. What an idiot it made of him. If Cooper promised anything, even if he came through, he did so for his own agenda.

Paul lifted the whisky bottle, which rested between his legs, tipped it back and took a sip.

Maybe he didn't belong at the institute. Surprised his father when he got the job, his old man staring at him as though he believed he had caught his own son in a lie. Later mumbling something about Paul having no business being there. Cooper peered at him the same way, too.

Paul took another slurp of the whisky bought as an offering to Cooper, a poor attempt to make friends, and where did that get him? A refusal and claim of feeling too tired.

'Tired. Yeah right,' Paul muttered.

Cooper gave Paul all the mundane, routine jobs. Label this. File that. Send this to another department. Fetch it back. All the while playing with that secret of his. The institute was careful with resources, didn't pay out for eccentric scientists to run whatever unusual experiments they wanted. Of course, the organisation flittered money away on some strange ventures, if the rumours were true, some of which paid off and paid well. It got them additional funding and some slack, but...

Could it be they'd given Cooper one of those peculiar enterprises? The man showed signs of being overworked, and stress and an involved project would explain his physical and his emotional state. If so, why didn't Cooper arrange for Paul to assist? To keep all the glory, that must be why.

Although, perhaps it wasn't Cooper who didn't want Paul's help. Maybe it was those above him. What had Madeleine said, a remark about the possibility of an experiment that she didn't sanction but someone else did? Bonnaire perhaps but, somehow, Paul didn't want to believe it. If true, it threw everything the institute stood for into disrepute.

The truth had to be Cooper didn't want an assistant and, well, he didn't think Paul good enough. Paul had seen it in his eyes the day someone introduced them, but Paul, so determined to hang on in there, to prove himself, ignored his misgivings. Deemed unworthy, he wasted his time.

'Damn you, Professor.'

One more sip and then he should screw the cap back on the bottle. Wouldn't make his situation any better driving drunk. He should be home in a bed, but after the sneaking about with Madeleine and her friend, he'd felt restless. Also annoyed because he should have been thinking about more kisses, not the bane of his life.

Madeleine Bonnaire. Finally, he'd moved beyond stuttering hello every time he passed her in the halls, wishing he had the guts to ask her out. Little had he expected her to make the first move.

The wind buffeted the car, bringing with it the patter of raindrops on the windscreen, light but bothersome side-driven rain. No wonder Paul had the park mostly to himself. The parking area formed a semi-circle down one side of its length, a known spot for men to bring their dates. That evening the weather became so atrocious, only the most miserable, the hardiest, or the most amorous ventured out.

Time he made a move.

Paul reached for the key in the ignition, but his hand dropped back when the lights of another car dazzled him.

Parked beneath an enormous tree and not wanting to draw attention, Paul waited. A couple of minutes and the people in the car would take no notice as he eased out on the road.

The moon came out behind the clouds and Paul blinked, recognising the vehicle. Cooper's car.

The man couldn't have a date, the idea was too creepy. Cooper wouldn't know how to treat a woman well. If the man inside even *was* Cooper. Hard to tell, and Cooper may have loaned the car to someone else. Unlikely though, Cooper was never so generous.

Paul sat frozen, unable to leave. The atmosphere in the car grew stuffy until he felt suffocated. Tension must be the cause. Time suspended.

He let down the side window a few inches. With luck, the slight movement would go unnoticed. Blessed cool night air rushed in. A minute later the noise of a car door opening stabbed the night, followed by a soft *thunk* of it closing. A light didn't come on inside though. Peculiar.

Paul held his breath until his lungs protested, while he focused on the outline of a man heading into the trees. Once the figure moved out of sight, still Paul waited. Only when certain he was alone, did he get out, fast. If Cooper stood out there, with luck he wouldn't glance back, for, unlike the light in the other vehicle, Paul's came on. He crouched, tense, waiting to see whether someone spotted him. He hurried over to the other car, back bent, strides loping. One look at the license plate told him the car belonged to Cooper. Where had the man gone?

Moving around to the driver's side, Paul studied the ground. Didn't take long to find where Cooper's footsteps pressed the grass flat. Staying low, Paul hurried after the professor, trying to follow his trail, attempting not to disturb anything further, to leave no trace.

He almost tripped when he stumbled over the first garment. A quick examination. Cooper's jacket. The man's favourite if his penchant for wearing it was any indication; Paul had seen it often. Plain beige and hard wearing. Practical. Nondescript. As ugly as the man. Paul left the jacket where he found it. Odd Cooper would leave it behind.

Minutes later, Paul discovered a shirt. Soon after, a pair

of shoes. This grew stranger by the second. Odder yet when he located the man's trousers. He spotted a pair of underpants and socks. Hankered down, Paul scanned the trees. Half a dozen times, a shape caught his gaze but each time he blinked the landscape changed. Too dark. Too many odd shapes. No way to tell reality from a trick of the eye. For all he knew, Cooper might be standing nearby, watching. But as the seconds ticked on none of the shadows rushed him. Gathering his courage Paul rose and carried on in a straight line, presuming Cooper would stick to the direction his clothes led.

Another ten minutes of searching, including some backtracking, and Paul considered giving up, chilled. In the shade of a tree, he gazed around, indecision holding him frozen. Why would a man come out to the woods and strip off his clothes on a wintery evening? Not for any good reason.

If Cooper intended to commit an assault, then why remove his clothes? He'd be vulnerable, and who did he hope to find to attack anyway? The nearest houses sat at the back of the woodland, some distance away. The only people out that night were in the cars, back in the direction of Paul's approach.

If the man came out to kill himself, Paul had little chance of saving him. By the time he returned to his car, raised an alarm, got the authorities out here, if he could even convince them, Cooper would have completed the deed. Besides, the man had better ways to kill himself back in the lab.

This was madness. None of it made sense.

'Right nutter.'

Enough of this. Enough of standing in the frigid air and drizzle. The dampness accumulated. The bitterness snuck in under his clothes. How Cooper withstood being out here naked was beyond him.

Paul took a step. Something to his right caught his gaze. He stopped and stared. Nothing. Just another shifting shape.

No. Paul froze. Blinked once, twice, a third time.

The black outline moved, fortunately away from him, but it carried the unmistakable form of a man moving into the clearing. Although he didn't wish to spot Cooper naked – bad enough having to see that weaselly face every day – the desire to understand pushed Paul on.

He followed, drawing up short within a few minutes. Only

a shadow moving from tree to tree beneath moonlight.

'I'm going mad.' The sound of his own voice made Paul flinch, forced him back into the shade, an attempt to become nothing more than a silhouette if someone happened to look.

After a few more moments, he glanced to where he'd last seen a shape. No mistake. The round outline of a skull sat above the square profile of shoulders, leading down to a torso with two arms and two legs. The apparition appeared to tip back its head, observe the sky. Man or imagination? It was like peering at a child's drawing of the bogeyman. All black but misty at the edges. Like smoke.

A revenant.

What made him think of that?

The figure flipped or folded. Or it didn't move at all. Hard to tell. Either way Paul's nerve gave out. His heart pounded as he backed up.

Don't run. Slink away.

In case the thing, whatever it was, spotted him. The moment he believed he had the trees between him and the thing that terrified him, he glanced back. Nothing appeared to give chase, but on such a dark night, he couldn't be sure.

Paul broke into a run, darting back to the car, trying to control his breathing, fighting not to make noise. His mad dash became a battle of speed versus sound. Despite this, the night came alive, too loud. The commotion might be of a hunt, or the wind, or branches snapping under a squirrel's weight. He didn't wait to find out.

The parking lot came into view, a cry barking out of Paul's throat, disturbingly like a sob. He staggered, and stumbled, put a hand down, pushed, and kept going. If something attacked now, would anyone in the cars help? Not so many vehicles there now, most having driven off. Should he warn those remaining? No. They wouldn't believe him, and he daren't waste the time.

As he pelted down the final slope to his car, he forced all thoughts for their safety away, focused on his own. Air rasped, ragged in his throat; his chest burned. He hurried to his car, giving thanks he'd taken a chance and not bothered to lock the door. He sprang into the seat, pulled the door shut, and fastened the lock.

The key juddered around the slot, until he took a moment to calm himself and tried again, turning the ignition.

As he clasped the wheel, Paul spared a glance at Cooper's car. Whatever he'd seen, it couldn't have anything to do with Cooper. He must have seen something else. If the man was out there and the strange phenomenon was real, he wished the professor all the luck available to him this night. No one stood a chance.

Paul drove away, half convinced he'd hear of the professor's death come morning.

The house perched on the outskirts of town, the last of a long row, separated from the rest because of the large garden surrounding the property. Lara stood in the grounds, scanning the house, which had been in the Moulin family – her family – for eighty years or longer. To her the time seemed so long it might as well be centuries. Her grandmother said it was no time at all, but the old woman was seventy-four. Eighty could be less than one lifetime but stretched far in Lara's mind. A mere pool, her grandmother called it, crossed in a blink. Lara struggled with how that length of time could be relative. Eighty years was forever.

Same as Christophe Legrand was taking forever to meet her where he said he would – out back in the deep woods lining the grounds behind the house. A border of trees separating her family's property from the local park. The idea always gave her the creeps, so she hesitated when Christophe proposed meeting her there so late at night. Impossible to refuse though. The older boy was so good-looking; his interest in her made her a lucky girl. Still, he better hurry because it was one thing meeting her boyfriend, anticipation warming her more than the thought of his arms around her, but it was quite another to stand out there so long she froze to death.

She pulled her cardigan more tightly closed, hugging herself, hands tucked under her arms.

She should have stayed closer to the house, but if anyone peered out, they might spot her. The moon was high, full, a bright beacon for prying eyes. Only here amid the trees did the darkness snake, entwine, reach out, and grab hold.

Someone grabbed her from behind.

A gasp escaped as she opened her mouth, Christophe's chuckle cutting off her scream. She would have sworn at him if he hadn't kissed the back of her neck. Still, she spun and slapped out at him the moment he let go.

'I hate how you do that!' Her voice sounded unbearably loud in the gloom. She cast another glance at the house, despite the fact no one would hear from so far.

No one. Lara swallowed, hard.

'Ah, don't worry. Bet they're all snoring.'

Lara shot him a look. Did he read her mind? If anything happened, no one at the house could help either of them. What could happen though? There were together out here. She was safe with Christophe, surely.

'How do you creep up on a person?' Lara wasn't about to forgive him. 'What do you want? To give me a heart attack?'

'At our age that'd be a fluke.'

'A person can die of fright, you know.'

'You sure?' Enough light shone through the canopy of trees for his teeth to flash as he grinned.

'Think you're so damn clever. Would serve you right if I went back home to my room. I should, too. It's too cold tonight.'

To prove her point, the wind picked up and tossed the branches, making the woods whisper.

He swaggered closer, reached for her hand. 'Here, girl. Let me warm you.'

Although that was what she had in mind, Lara hung back. Christophe, always so sure of himself, a trait she often admired, irritated her now.

'That's right. Keep me waiting alone and pretend like its nothing to scare me half to death.'

For the first time, the smile slipped from his face. His brow creased, a frown spoiling his handsomeness. 'I thought you liked fun. That you could take a joke.'

Was he puzzled? Annoyed? One she could stomach. The other... What gave him the right to be angry? A little self-doubt slipped in, dispersing again when Christophe became sullen, pushing his hands deep into his pockets, kicking at the ground.

'If you want to go back, go back.'

Each syllable pricked her heart, made it sound as if he

didn't care. 'And if I stay?'

His grin reappeared. 'Come over here.'

A thought sidled into her brain – a thought older than her years. If this went wrong, he'd claim she asked for whatever he wanted. Folks would say she was in the wrong, out in the night, when she should be in bed. No one would argue when she was the one who came out to meet him. Many would agree. A girl her age sneaking out, asked for what happened. A boy wasn't to blame when a girl made things so easy for him. That last came to her in the voice of her grandmother. Did the old biddy believe half the things she said? The stories she told? If so, Lara was happy to be a generation once removed.

She chewed on her lower lip while Christophe struck an unperturbed pose, certainty written all over his face, so sure she'd take the small number of steps until she reached him.

'Is that all you came for?' she asked.

The frown reappeared. 'Don't know what you mean.'

He did know, though likely not in the same terms she was thinking. 'I thought we'd talk.'

'Talk?' He spoke as though the word needed translating.

'If we're dating… I'd like to know more about you.'

'What's there to know?'

Yes, what to ask him? She already knew his grades were average, though not to hear him tell it. He excelled at sports, though had no particular love for the subject. Everyone raved that he made a good athlete, but Christophe said he saw it as an easier route through life than studying. Not as she blamed him. Still, he must have some hopes and dreams.

'What do you want to do when we finish school?' she asked.

'You mean for the summer?'

'No. School. Like when we leave and go out into the world.'

Christophe replied with a shrug. 'What does it matter?'

'Well… What you plan to do is part of who you are. Sure, any of us may need to do things we don't want, might be stuck in a dead-end job, but it doesn't mean you can't follow your aspirations.' Maybe that was too much. Lara sounded too old and Christophe stared as though she had grown a second head.

'God, you're weird.'

'Weird? You think I'm weird?' Shouldn't bother her as much as it did.

'Kind of. Pretty, but yeah. Many at school do.'

'They do?' Lara hugged herself, feeling small, her tone turning sarcastic. 'Thanks.'

'Look, you're odd, dumping all these questions on me. It's almost midnight and you're asking me what I want to do with the rest of my life.'

'I'm sorry. I wanted us to get to know each other, that's all.'

'So did I.'

'You do?'

'Course.' His eyebrows did a little dance up and down suggesting his idea differed vastly from hers. He took a step closer.

Lara grew cold. 'I... I think I'd better get back.' She risked a glance at the house again, fearing she stood too far away for someone to hear her shout.

'Come on, Lara, don't be a spoilsport. Not saying we need go all the way on such a cold night. I'm sorry you'd think so of me.'

What? Wait. Lara screwed up her face, confused. He sounded reasonable, but she'd not decided about going all the way. Not with Christophe, not with anyone, and here he stood put upon, yet still implying their getting together a done deal.

'Come on, girl. What do you take me for?'

If only he'd stop calling her girl. The thought irritated her enough that she didn't notice him move until he stood close, rubbing his hands up and down the outside of her arms, her forearms crossed between them, a bridge holding him at bay. His touch generated the heat of friction. The rubbing hinted at the warmth of his body and her traitorous desires. She wouldn't mind a little hug about now. A cuddle to fight off the cold, a reassurance that all would be well.

She hadn't wanted this. Simply longed for a boyfriend, in part because her father went on about not getting distracted with such things, not until she finished her exams. Christophe had said they didn't have to tell anyone about the two of them dating until then, if at all. The 'if' worried her, always had.

His mouth sought hers, but she wasn't ready for that kind of kiss, having only ever practised on the back of her hand. This wasn't how she had imagined her first kiss, there in the dark, in the cold, feeling scared.

'Christophe, stop it.' Lara pulled away, and slipped from his grip, no idea how. He was so much stronger than her.

'What are you playing at?' He sounded angry now.

'I'm not playing.'

'You came here for this. You agreed to meet me.'

'I agreed but not for this. It's... It's too soon. We've not even been out together yet.'

Something passed over his face she found impossible to interpret. They *were* dating, weren't they? Boyfriend and girlfriend.

'Going to run home and cry?'

Christophe's words mocked. He ran his fingers through his hair, an action that mussed his style, made him more appealing somehow, but now Lara wanted him gone.

'Lara...'

She didn't know what he intended to say, longed to hear an apology that would never come.

Run. Flee. Get home.

'I... can't. I made a mistake. I'm sorry.' Why apologise? The answer came: to keep him calm. To try anything to get away. 'I... We're not ready for this.'

He would argue, she was sure, but instead his next words confused her. 'This isn't how it's supposed to go.'

What did he mean? She took a step back. Another. A few more and she'd reach the edge of the woods. From there the run was clear across the lawn back to the house. If someone spotted her... She didn't care. All to the good. She'd take her punishment. Anything to feel safe again.

Anger rose, at herself for being stupid enough to come out here, at Christophe for creating the situation.

'You can't.' He moved two steps to her one.

Lara spun; Christophe lunged. In the scramble, she tripped, fell short of the lawn. The wind howled, conspiring to conceal her scream.

She rolled, slapping at him, while he fought to grab her arms. His wide-spread legs pinned her hips. A twig snapped, making both her and Christophe freeze, to stare into the darkness. Not a branch breaking. No accident. Someone stood out there. Her father? No. He would shout. Come charging in.

Cuff Christophe around the head and drag her back to her room, grounded for a month, a year, and she'd happily stay, spend all that time in the house.

Though those sentiments might change come morning, Lara stared, seeking a face she recognised, but the woods grew darker, obscuring. Still… she was sure…

The darkness took on a shape.

The weight lifted from her, Christophe rising, peering into the trees as if he saw it too.

Without waiting to see what he looked for, or what he might do, Lara elbowed her way out from under him, scrambled to her feet, and ran. Not once did she glance back until she reached the safety of the house, by which time the moon disappeared behind a cloud, creating of the world a shroud.

CHAPTER NINE
The Danger of Knowing Too Little

'MADELEINE, PLEASE. I need those files.'

'Impossible.' Madeleine gulped coffee, trying not to view the eggs she'd scrambled minutes ago, wanting to avoid this discussion with Anne more than longing for food.

Scrambled eggs on toast, a staple that often helped settle her stomach after a migraine. Better to stick to nothing but toast. Scraping the eggs to one side, she picked up a piece of the toast and bit off the corner, resolutely chewing and swallowing. Her tummy threatened to rebel, but she took another bite through sheer force of will.

'I wouldn't ask if not important. You know.'

'It's important to you, not me.'

Anne sat back in her chair, Madeleine too aware of her, too aware of Bill in the living room, giving them space. Allowing Anne the time to badger her into submission. The kitchen walls pressed in and left her skin tingling, too alive, and too conscious of everything.

'What scared you so much last night?' Anne asked.

'Nothing. Paul projecting his crazy notions into my mind. All these conspiracy theories are a riot when you're young, but we've moved past all that.'

'Have we? Or do you fear the possibility it involves your father? That there are projects at the institute of which you may not be aware?'

'That's ridiculous. I know what I said last night, but it came from the mood of sneaking around, which prompted these mad ideas.' Madeleine's grip tightened around her cup. With the other, she traced the grain of the wooden table – a straight line, no diversions.

Anne placed a hand over hers and squeezed. 'It's not a fear to be ashamed of. The man has faults, but you've always known of them. The idea Victor may keep you in the dark—'

The mention of the dark galvanised her; Madeleine shot to her feet. 'Fine. I'll speak to him and consider what you've said, but now, I must go, and I cannot take you with me. Not today. Your time at the institute is over. I've already broken enough promises and rules.' She sounded accusing, wanted to apologise. Didn't. Couldn't. 'Leave it with me. I'll call you if I find anything.'

Her sense of foreboding increased as she parked her car near her father's cottage, got out, and marched up the path. The crunch of gravel under the heels of her boots held an ominous tone, though she felt ridiculous for thinking it. Madeleine used her key to enter, though she called out as she did so, pushing the door shut. The wood resisted, more prone to warping with the passing years.

Not the purpose of her visit, but Madeleine had accepted her father's invitation to breakfast with a disturbing reluctance. Not because of her migraine – almost gone – and not because of a queasy stomach. Surprisingly, not having eaten at home, her stomach rumbled with hunger. Maybe she should share a meal with her father more often. The opportunity to chat and reconnect would mean less bizarre thoughts circling. His warm smile and gentle gaze…

No. She could not imagine her father doing anything nefarious.

After hanging her coat on a hook by the front door, she went into the dining room, glad to spot the table already laid. A murmur came from the television – possible to view from the dining table with the doors between open – gave the place a lived-in quality it sometimes lacked since her mother's passing. Often her father left the contraption on to hear another voice.

'Toast and eggs?' he yelled from the kitchen; the first question to bring her pleasure all morning. Toast and eggs were about the only thing her father didn't ruin.

Leaving her morning meal almost untouched didn't sit well with her, but her father would cook these eggs and that made them special. Despite his many accomplishments, the well-known belief all the French made gourmet cooks and connoisseurs proved erroneous, even the basics having escaped her father's skill.

'That would be lovely.' Madeleine took her usual place at the table without offering to help, aware he would feel insulted. She cooked him more meals than he ever made for her, but he would enjoy preparing this small repast.

Random thoughts. Not quite nonsense but senseless in the face of her underlying concerns. She had to remain calm. Not let her emotions show. Victor Bonnaire carried enough burdens without concerning himself with mere suspicions, but she needed to talk to him.

So much for keeping her expression worry free. When he walked into the room, Madeleine's jaw unhinged, her eyes widened, and surely, she created the perfect 'O' of surprise with her lips. She closed her mouth and blinked before he noticed. He'd shaved, but without the familiar care. He looked tired and older, somehow. Maybe he aged without her noticing before now.

No, she didn't believe so. She knew her father. The lines on his face this morning were of worry, not time.

He brought in the toast and placed it on the table. 'Eggs coming.' He avoided her gaze. Unsure what to do, she did the only thing possible: buttered the toast and divided it between the pre-warmed plates. Her father returned as she finished and as she licked a trace of butter from a finger. The habit was one her mother would tap her on the back of the hand for: *Use a napkin* – a once sour admonishment, now sweet. She would give anything for her mother to be here to tell her off for what the woman saw as a transgression in etiquette.

They ate in silence, Madeleine struggling to find an opening.

'You rarely join me for breakfast. You never drop in this early. Not anymore.' Her father's gaze shifted away from her on the end, and a memory surfaced in Madeleine's mind.

The times she dropped in like this when her mother still lived. Since her death, though, Madeleine didn't always feel welcome. Or maybe she noticed her father's grief. Staying away wasn't fair on him, but he should have friends of his own generation.

As if he followed her thoughts, he asked, 'How are your friends?'

'They're fine.'

'Leaving soon?'

'I'm… not sure.' He came across as a little too eager for them to be gone. 'I guess they may stay an extra day or so.'

'The weather's against them.'

The grey morning split open. Hard drops hit the windows. Did her father imply her friends should leave because of rain? Maybe he hoped that it would force them to.

'We've a lot to catch up on,' she told him.

'Yes, of course.' He nodded, hands wrapped around his cup as though around a throat.

Madeleine fought a sudden surge of anxiety. Never had she felt unsafe in her father's company.

'You took Anne up to the institute? Yesterday?'

She should feel no surprise the information filtered back to him. He doubtless told the guard to let him know as soon as Anne put in an appearance. 'You said I could.'

'Yes, yes. I um… would prefer under my supervision. I um… thought I implied.'

'Implied isn't the same as said. And you didn't stop by.' Her impudence appeared to take him by surprise. He sat, gaze darting, maybe searching for the right reply. She refused to seek forgiveness.

'Is there a reason you came this morning?' He sounded irritated, but also tired and resigned.

'Yes. I wanted to ask about Cooper.' His mood-inspired caution. One thing that drew her and Anne to a close relationship was their heightened instincts. 'What precisely is he working on?'

'It's all logged.'

'Is it though?'

'Why do you ask?' He answered fast enough, but his manner remained guarded.

'I usually receive a report, but from what I can tell Cooper isn't filing them. Larousse is, and he's doing the mundane jobs so can't fill me in on Cooper's activities. Something is taking up much of Cooper's time, something I'm not sure he's

92

chronicling.'

'He um… has several important projects. As do most of our people.'

'True, but it's not an excuse to get behind in his paperwork, especially without informing us of a problem. He'll make my job more difficult, next to impossible if he continues in this fashion.'

'Um… Quite so, quite so, my dear. He should at least get his assistant to do the reports on his behalf. You should have a word, my dear. Um… yes, a word.'

'I tried, the other night. Wandered along. Knocked on the door but there came no reply.' Heart hammering, Madeleine forced herself to continue. She studied her father's face for his reaction. 'The door stood ajar, so I pushed it open and called out. When I still heard nothing, I went inside.'

Her father frowned, hands still gripping a cup of coffee, which had to now be lukewarm. 'Door was ajar you say. That's… unusual.'

He doubted her. Thoughts winged back to the night before. Her taking the key, not signing it out. Her father suspected the truth. Might not be sure, but he knew she'd been in the security office. Knew she didn't really require the folder she'd signed out. Though hard to say why she was sure, her scalp tingled. Fine, maybe he didn't know the details, but he knew something. Didn't believe her when she said Cooper's lab had been left open.

'Yes.' Now caught in a lie, she couldn't change track. 'There wasn't much to see, so I intended to leave when I spotted something strange. Tell me, is Cooper doing anything concerning light refraction?'

'Light…?' Her father coughed. 'Why I… Um… No. No. I don't believe so.'

If he were about to say he didn't know of every project taking place within the institute, she would call him a liar to his face. This old affable friendly grandfatherly act was only part of his personality. Those watery old eyes were often sharp and cunning. The fact he didn't glance at her said as much. Although she would never want to play poker with him, her father had several tells.

'There's a strange box kitted out to send light through

crystals and I'm sure I saw electrodes. I don't recall such a device approbated for any projects we've assigned Cooper. In fact, it looked likely the professor constructed the equipment himself. Rather a crude design. I fear he may have stolen the crystals from our latest consignment. I wondered if some project exists, of which you are aware when I'm not. And as I'm more in charge these days than you are…'

Although her father still didn't look over, his eyes were calculating. 'Well… Um…well… There might be. Yes. Yes. I think I left paperwork on my desk I um… not got around to…' He coughed, didn't stop. 'Oh dear me.' He got the bout under control. 'It's the cold air does it. I'm not the man I used to be.'

So what? Maybe she should she feel sorry, maybe even sympathetic.

'I'll come up later and get anything outstanding to you, um, yes, I will.'

Silence fell between them, during which Madeleine determined her next course.

'Father, are you…?' Before she asked how many projects were in progress that she didn't know about, her father nodded towards the television. A female reporter stood against a background of trees, a microphone in her hand.

'Early this morning, the body of the young Christophe Legrand was found in the confines of the forest, called locally Parkland.'

'Terrible thing. Um…terrible thing,' Father said.

'The cause is not yet known, although the boy's death seems to have been sudden.'

'See, no known cause.' Her father snapped his fingers. 'Gone, like that. No knowing when or how we switch off.' He made it sound like she should feel guilty for troubling an old man who might die any moment. Sure, his health wasn't the best, but he had medication, was in no immediate danger.

Ignoring the implication, Madeleine suggested, 'At his age maybe an embolism.' Although likely wrong, if there were no signs of dishonest behaviour, the idea might be one logical explanation. 'The real question is why he was in the parkland to begin with.'

'Yes. Yes. Young people these days.'

Madeleine almost laughed. Young people any day, in any generation. By the time a person was able to live the way he or she wanted, they no longer wanted to or didn't have the energy. God, she felt tired. No reason her father should be the only one feeling old. The week when she should have nothing more on her mind than a new relationship and enjoying the time with her friend, why did this sense of doom prevail? It hung over her, over the institute, the surrounding area... Ideas so bizarre her eyes played tricks on her. Tricks, which transported her to the lab the previous evening, where, in the corner, between a filing cabinet and a table, the shadows appeared deepest. To where she could swear for a minute, a man's face loomed, his gaze watchful.

'Madeleine?' The scrape of her father's chair against the flagstone floor brought her around. 'Are you well?'

'Yes. Sorry. I had a migraine last night.' Caused by phantom images or creating them? 'I'm a little tired.'

'Explains everything.'

More than anything, she should demand answers, but the more one pushed Victor Bonnaire, the less information he volunteered. Papers on his desk... Her next course of action sprung to mind along with the determination to go through with the idea.

'Time's getting on. I better go.' She was over an hour late from her usual early start.

'Yes. Um... Yes, you do that. For the best.'

He mumbled as he walked her to the door. For the first time in ages, Madeleine didn't kiss his cheek as she left, pressing her fingers to her forehead. She struggled not to run to her car and speed up to the institute. Although her father might not follow right away, she needed to get to his office before he hid anything he didn't want her to see.

Madeleine nodded to colleagues in passing, distracted by thoughts of Paul, fearing what she needed to do as she hurried to her office. A lift of her head, a perfunctory nod, gaze drifting along the corridor, the sight of the person entering at the far end almost made her change her course.

Cooper.

He sauntered with his head down, an intense frown, heavy

95

lines creasing his brow apparent even from this distance. No side hallway to dart into and all of the doors led to rooms she had no excuse to enter. Simple dislike of the man and her guilt obliterated any notion of who worked in which. A couple were unoccupied, and a few locked regardless, but choosing proved impossible, her mind a blank, room numbers dancing in front of her eyes. Hell, she panicked.

Maybe he wouldn't look up.

No such luck. Cooper's gaze slid to her face, as though drawn to her like a crow to carrion. Madeleine swallowed despite trying not to, hoping he didn't notice the movement. Fighting to curb her unease, she kept walking, focusing her eyes ahead to the far door.

No use. His hard, cold, dissecting stare drew her gaze. His eyes flicked down, back up, crawling over her skin, making her itch. Why hadn't she worn the white coat donned by most of the staff? Hers hung on the coat rack in her office. She usually hated the stiff fabric but, for the first time, in her own clothes she felt vulnerable. Her confidence faltered, a drop of sweat trickling over her nape, beneath her collar. Felt like it ran down the length of her back, prickling, urging her to squirm. Maddening. Her grip on her briefcase tightened, as she performed the customary nod, along with a clipped, 'Good morning.' A few more steps, another few seconds, and she'd be past him.

He stepped in her way. 'Good morning, *Dr* Bonnaire.'

The emphasis of her title struck a blow. No way could she prove his contempt, but it pummelled her ears. Pity his rude behaviour wasn't so apparent she could make it a dismissible offence. Why had her father hired this man? She wished he hadn't. Wished they had never seen his name.

'*Professor* Cooper.' An attempt to copy the man's sarcasm failed miserably, causing his title to emerge on a hiss.

'Lovely weather for this time of year.' His glance towards a nearby window made her flick her gaze to take in the pouring rain. The sun could be high in the sky for all the difference it would make; did he think she wanted to discuss the weather with him? Talk over anything?

'Excuse me.' A step to the left cleared her path until he moved to block her again.

'We all work too hard, which is such a shame. It's easy to forget the days passing. Life moving on. Before we know it, our lives will be over. Gone.'

'Rather morbid thinking, Professor.'

'Not at all.' He treated her to a close examination of his less than perfect teeth. The grin flashed, gone. His eyes glittered. 'I am merely contemplating how much we all need to remember to live. I know you happened to work later than usual even for you yesterday.'

He knows. Of course.

Nothing got by a man like this. Her father now knew; she told him so, but her father had suspected her of something before then. Had Victor Bonnaire called Cooper after she left? Heat slid into her face, an immediate prayer rising: Please whatever ruled the universe, don't let her blush. Not in front of this man.

'I saw you talking to Paul Larousse.' Cooper lifted a hand as though he wanted to touch her, Madeleine battling not to pull back, not to show him she noticed. She let out a steady breath when his hand dropped to his side. 'Are… relationships within the institution allowed?'

Anger helped her locate her voice when dislike failed. 'Talking doesn't indicate a relationship, and if there was, there's no exact rule against such a thing. We have a husband and wife team on staff.'

'Still.'

Those teeth flashed again but, odd thing, she didn't recall Cooper, or his teeth, looking so bad. She stood too close to examine him without Cooper noticing but she shifted her gaze a little. Much about his appearance seemed changed. Paul was correct about one thing – the man looked ill. No way to tell whether he'd ceased his personal grooming, including brushing his teeth, but he no longer bothered to shave well. Showered? Madeleine breathed in, wished she hadn't. Cooper didn't smell bad exactly. Sour, though, and something else. Sweet, pungent, sharp. Like ozone.

A sensation stole over her. If he opened his mouth, he'd be nothing. A black chasm, a hole, an abyss. An eternity of nothingness.

'Don't you have work to do, Professor? I would hate to

keep you. I'm sure you're busy.'

'Work, yes.'

'Yes, Cooper. Indeed, we need to talk about that soon. I'd like to hear all about your latest projects. I appear to be lacking some reports. Which do you think...?'

'My work.' He interrupted her, but his unfocused gaze revealed his thoughts were no longer with her. Should she snap him out of the trance, or whatever he suffered from? Before she decided, his prejudices rose to the fore. His gaze adjusted, falling again on her face. 'I wouldn't think Paul your type. Your intellectual equal.'

'That's not—' Madeleine gasped, protest cut off as he clasped her arm. She tugged by instinct, but Cooper held on. She stopped pulling only because he appeared to enjoy the struggle. His gaze danced.

'You'd understand my work. Isn't that ironic?'

If it were, she didn't know why. Didn't want to know.

'But Paul...' He shook his head. 'Small minds. Dealt with too many of them. You. Yes, you. Now you might...'

Gone again, the light going out in his eyes, the man pondering something cosmic of which she remained clueless.

'You would be interested. Intrigued.' He spoke slowly, with care, consideration, and wonderment lacing his tone. 'We might get along, you and I, under better circumstances.'

She doubted that but was wise enough not to argue.

'But you shouldn't have done what you did, Madeleine.'

His eyes rolled upwards until he stared into her gaze, spreading coldness, blanketing her, his loathing moulding to her form. She hated the way he used her first name – too intimate. Her own words lodged in her throat. She tore her gaze free, staring beyond him along the corridor, but no one entered from that end. No one came to save her. Unwilling to turn her head away she strained her hearing, but no footsteps echoed from behind. They remained alone. Where was everyone? Would anyone hear her call for help?

Idiotic notion, especially there in her own institute, but the idea didn't feel stupid. As Cooper at last let her go, Madeleine stepped back.

'This...' Damn but she had to clear her throat in order to speak again. 'This conversation and your actions are inappropriate.'

'As were yours.'

'I've no idea—'

'We both know what I'm talking about, but I merely wish to leave you with the thought.' Cooper's eyes appeared to darken. 'Until later.'

That sounded like a threat.

Shock dulled her senses, but as Cooper walked by, drawing close, revulsion made her press back, flattening against the wall until Cooper passed and continued along the corridor.

CHAPTER TEN
Different Ways to Die

'**WHILE OUT** walking his dog, a local resident found the young man identified as Christophe Legrand. He was last seen alive by his parents when he went to bed the previous evening around ten.' Anne read aloud from the newspaper, cutting through the flourish the reporter put on the article, sticking to the facts for Bill's consumption. 'Why he left the family home and entered the surrounding woodland is yet unknown, as is the cause of death.'

'Drugs?' Bill suggested.

'Possibly.' She sifted through the information available, all the various physical indications. 'Nothing here. It's possible the family or police kept the details out of the papers. They must have rushed this through to get it into the second edition.'

The boy, found about five in the morning, made the third page. By the time the evening paper rolled out, no doubt the story would be on the front.

'Why the frown?'

'Pardon?' Anne looked up from the other side of the table where they lingered over lunch.

Although Bill had coaxed her out for yet another walk earlier, she was on edge, waiting to hear from Madeleine, so he had agreed to return to the apartment to eat. If they didn't hear from Madeleine soon, Anne was determined to ring her.

'I hate to be blunt, but people, even the young, die every day. A report of a death should not cause you more than a moment of empathy.'

Although Anne sometimes felt these things more than Bill did — his subjectivity a part of his duty — he wasn't wrong. She couldn't carry the woes of the world.

'Doesn't it strike you as strange?' Anne wondered aloud. 'In this quiet, sleepy place, a death occurs the same week we happen to visit?'

'Now we're harbingers.' Bill didn't sound happy, but his hard gaze softened and he relented. 'I'm sorry. I understand why you feel that way, but we don't orchestrate these happenings by our presence.'

'No, but they have a habit of following us.'

'A quirk of the job.'

'Unfortunately.' Although she agreed, Anne couldn't help feeling disturbed. She glanced at the telephone. 'I'll give it another two hours then I'll definitely call Madeleine at work. If she doesn't answer, I'm going there. I'm not simply going to sit here all day.'

They kept the master keys to all the rooms in a safe. A safe housed in the security room behind the lobby. No longer trusting any of the guards not to call her father the moment she asked for the key to his study, and seeing the worse of them, Faucheux, on duty, Madeleine slipped into one of the unoccupied labs. In a little under fifteen minutes, she set up an experiment to combust, and exited the room, leaving the door ajar. She hurried to the room nearest the lobby on the pretence of being unable to decipher a word on a report filled in by the scientist who worked within. A professor with notoriously bad handwriting.

He was squinting at the page, struggling to read his own scribble, when the fire alarm went off. Both he and Madeleine ran to the door, though she hung back while he scurried ahead. The security guard puffed around the corner shouting, 'Small fire in Lab four.' The alarm tied to a main board so the guard would know where it triggered. Although the institute had a sprinkler system, Victor Bonnaire didn't like it used because of the risk to vital experiments, so each room now came equipped with a fire extinguisher for use in the first instance. The guard would head straight for it. A rumble of thunder added to the commotion.

Madeleine circled around him and slipped behind the lobby desk, entering the room there. She spun the dials on the safe to the correct positions, grabbed the box housing the keys, and identified the right one with ease. After closing the lid, she replaced the box, slammed the safe door, and twisted the dials in less than three minutes. With a glance to check the way remained clear, Madeleine went out of the door, heading back seconds later.

A sense of dread brought her to a halt, an image flashing in her mind. A clipboard, the one she'd left behind on the floor of the room. How could she be so stupid?

Don't panic. Good advice. A fast turnaround saw her back in the room, dipping down to grab the clipboard, heading back out, no time to glance around, hoping no one spotted her. By now, enough people gathered in the corridor for a few to mingle in the lobby, but all had their backs turned. Madeleine hugged the clipboard, one hand in her pocket around the key, and sidled along the wall, working her way through the crowd.

'Do we need to evacuate?' The man who spoke sounded more worried for his experiments than for his life.

'No. No need.' Faucheux reappeared carrying a fire extinguisher and sweating. 'It's out now.'

People grumbled, less than pleased, cursing the fool who caused this, but dispersed without complaint, eager to return to work. Madeleine waylaid the professor she had spoken to earlier.

'I'm sorry. But you were trying to tell me what you wrote here?'

She made sure the guard saw her next to the professor, caught his gaze, and raised her eyebrows a little. The professor peered again at the paperwork, waited for his light-bulb moment, and came up with possible answers. Madeleine knew the word, likely never to forget now it served her purpose.

Faucheux stared back at the lab, scratching his head, puzzled. 'I thought no one worked in here.'

Madeleine stepped forward. 'Laboratory four? No. There shouldn't be.' She peered in. 'Is it safe?'

'Quite safe. Wasn't much of a fire.'

She made a show of stepping into the lab, casting her eyes over the desk, and gave a light laugh. 'Someone's idea of a prank.' She ran off a list of chemicals the guard wouldn't understand. 'Creates a localised bang, but it's pretty much all. Likely a dare between the younger associates. Seen it before in other labs, although it's not the type of behaviour my father tolerates. I'll put out a memo. Include a hint of a threat. I doubt it'll happen again.'

Not such a marvellous plan, but she seemed to have got away with it, never mind the emergency key to her father's study now lay in her pocket, with no way to return it. A problem for another day; she'd withstood enough excitement for now and she still needed to riffle through her father's files.

The day couldn't end fast enough. Paul rubbed at his forehead, still suffering the dregs of a headache brought on by too many stiff drinks. Enough, anyway, to make him late. With luck, Cooper hadn't noticed or didn't care. Paul failed to feel any guilt. Sure, he'd downed a few sips in the car while out by the park, but that was all. After seeing the menacing shadow, and making it back to his vehicle, no one could blame him for needing something to steady his nerves, but he'd resisted while driving. Hard to say why he kept to the road. The flight reflex refused to leave him in peace, so he'd kept going, following a random route for an hour back to his lodgings at the institute. Once inside, he stood for a while outside Cooper's door, and considered knocking. But even if not in his room, the man might have returned to the lab. No way was Paul going out again, not even to another building on the grounds. He wanted nothing more than to visit his bed.

Questions had continued to plague him. The time Paul had spent driving certainly allowed enough time for Cooper to make it back before him. Trouble was, when Paul looked that morning, the logbook specified he'd signed in minutes after Paul, Anne and Madeleine left (talk about a narrow escape), and, after that, he never signed out. So, therefore, he had worked all night.

Which meant Paul shouldn't have seen Cooper in the park. Unless he snuck out somehow. A window? Possible, but the ones in the second lab were small and situated high up in the wall. Cooper might have slipped out from another room, but he'd need access, and the large windows were wired to alarms. The parking was distant enough, though, for the guard not to notice Cooper drive away.

Maybe some other fool streaked, but Paul struggled to fight his certainty.

The car. The license plate. Cooper's face. Paul wondered if he had hallucinated it, his dislike of the man going so deep as to play tricks on his mind. Maybe he was the mad one, and he'd dragged Madeleine into the mess for nothing. The sooner he got away from Cooper the better, but there remained one layer of crystals to go through. Until he did so, he couldn't give the list to Madeleine to check against the original manifesto.

The cataloguing proved to be more a case of

104

separating and re-packing for distribution. Cooper demoted him to nothing more than a packing and stock boy.

There had to be more to life. Maybe he should speak to Madeleine about all this, but there he faced other problems. She already believed he might be guilty of professional jealousy. If anything he said led her to believe he wanted a relationship with her to further his career, she'd never forgive him. If she were truly to run the institute, she'd need to reassign him or fire him. Must do, and perhaps that was preferable.

Although it felt a little like going behind Victor Bonnaire's back, things were so peculiar, what other way would get him out of his predicament? Paul couldn't keep working with Cooper. The need to bring all of it up in conversation was real. Madeleine would understand.

If he trusted her.

What was the Repositorium anyway? A secret organisation, he got that. Private investor? Sure. Either Bonnaire was a rich man with more money than brain cells or he put on a good act as one. The place might be government run, maybe military – they housed and designed advanced weaponry on site – and it would mean they at least worked for their country. Something didn't sit right with him though. Some days Paul wondered which side the people here were on. He feared they were businessmen of the sort who sold to the highest bidders.

If her father were into anything clandestine, Paul hoped the daughter proved innocent of such knowledge.

Damn him as an idiot for taking Bonnaire at his word, believing every scientific breakthrough was for the good of all. Maybe he worried over nothing, without proof. If he found any, though, he had to contact the authorities and let them know what went on here. Although who those authorities might be, escaped him.

Paul wondered if any of the projects there explained what he believed he saw the other night. If he told anyone, they'd tell him he hallucinated or drank too much, or hallucinated because of the drink. Not true, though. Not until later, when he carried the bottle back to his room fearing Cooper was in the building, petrified he was somewhere else.

Upon leaving the park, he'd feared for Cooper's safety. The more he considered, the more convinced he grew that Cooper had some connection to the strange shape out in the woods. Now more than ever – after what he'd witnessed – he was satisfied things went on here of which he wanted no part.

What he saw.

What he *felt*.

Haunted didn't come close. Overnight, on an unforgiving morning, it would be easy to believe he suffered a waking nightmare. The sensation he would never see Cooper again remained strong. The man was involved with something out of control, killed by his own folly. A possible empty lab and no sounds from the second room supported the notion.

Would it be so bad to have imagined those events, or for them to be true if Cooper disappeared? Trouble was, if the man went missing, what would Paul tell people? Might someone imagine him guilty of something? If the man's mutilated corpse showed up, and Paul turned out to be the last to see Cooper alive… It wouldn't bode well. If he said nothing, and someone had noticed Paul in the vicinity and he kept it a secret, the situation might worsen. Better to hope Cooper couldn't have been the man in the park.

Despite Paul knowing otherwise.

An alarm jolted through his nerve-endings. What the…? Fire? Should he—

The inner door opened, and Cooper emerged from the second lab. So, the man had been inside all along. The clanging of bells continued, both men unmoving. No one knocked on the door or shouted for them to evacuate. An image assaulted Paul of a large blaze and everyone standing outside getting drenched. He should join them but until Cooper made a move, Paul took root. He glanced sideways at Cooper every few seconds. A flash of lightning made Cooper's skin grey.

Did the man sweat again? His skin carried a sallow sickly pallor. The dark circles around his eyes were almost mask-like, and... Paul was sure Cooper's eyes were darker than usual. Impossible. Must be the light. Previously, a distinguished touch of grey provided highlights to the man's temples, but Paul saw no sign of it now. Maybe Cooper dyed his hair now. Strange.

Cooper moved across the room. 'Stay there.' He barked out the order, opening the door to the corridor, and went out.

Paul, still unable to move, waited, tense, wondering if the professor would leave him to burn.

The bells fell silent.

A minute ticked by. Cooper slipped back in without a word, heading to the second room.

No. He slid. The movement so alien, it made Paul's skin pebble.

The soft leather of her father's chair sighed as Madeleine slumped back into it. Having found some overlooked paperwork, she was annoyed and a little disturbed but not distraught. Upon locating a locked drawer within a drawer and fuelled by the embers of anger, she'd lost all reason and worry about her father finding out. Having grabbed a letter opener, she'd used it to break the lock.

The documents she pulled out, stole the strength from her legs and she sank into her father's chair, no longer caring if he caught her there.

Files. Lists of experiments. Ongoing. In the East Wing. Not possible. The East Wing wasn't in use, not a wing at all, but another building and it remained closed. Due for refurbishment should they ever require the space, but, so far, Victor Bonnaire said it didn't warrant the expense. The building stood dark. No one ever entered. Not seen.

Why would they be? The structure sat on a corner of the estate, back of the derelict stables, and behind the halls of residence. There might be ways to make the building appear empty.

As she turned the pages, acid burned her throat.

'Nooooo.' The word escaped her, mournful, a little short of a howl.

The list in her hand detailed the supply of animals, something Madeleine detested. At the most, she sanctioned the provision of mice under protest, but, if what she read proved accurate, her father allowed experiments on a handful of dogs and apes.

Madeleine lifted her gaze, staring across the room, the floor about to give way over a pit. She didn't know her father at all. Damn him.

She sniffed, wiped angrily at her eyes. How dare he make her cry? She needed to confront him with this. Make sure nothing like this continued. Investigate all experiments of which she was uninformed, cease, and desist any illegal operations. Decide whether any of the rest deserved a place in the genuine function of the institute.

She had to get moving. Her father might appear any moment and she wanted to confront him on her terms. Before then, she wanted Anne's advice.

She rose from the chair, when she remembered the reason for breaking in. A fast shuffle through the files brought what she sought to the top. Cooper's file. The light seeped away as an approaching storm closed in making it difficult to see.

Madeleine flicked on a lamp and lifted the file, flipped back the cover, scanned the data. And froze on the spot. Though there was little information regarding his purpose here, one thing was clear.

Cooper was not the man's name at all.

CHAPTER ELEVEN
One Person Wishing to Change the World

BONNAIRE'S DAUGHTER was up to something. She had emerged from the security office during the guard's absence. Which made him wonder, why would she even be in there during a fire when she should be ushering people out, or determining the cause? Something was wrong. The conflagration put out too easily, while Madeleine Bonnaire did something she shouldn't.

Cooper returned to his lab, closed the door, and stood thinking, hands braced on the table. Maybe Dr Travers knew he was on staff, and had told Madeleine, but he'd kept out of sight thanks to Bonnaire's warning. Nothing for it. He needed to know. The storm would provide him with the perfect cover. At least this part grew easier.

Cooper took out a syringe and injected himself.

Each time the effect took hold faster. Not without pain though. Perversely, sometimes it felt as if his eyes boiled in his head, or his brain overheated. Couldn't be helped. No time to worry about side effects, physical or emotional. Although he didn't know why, he had a sense of the minutes running out on him, no time left.

You know that's right.

The whisper came, speaking into his ear. Cooper spun, gaze darting into every corner. Nothing there. Alone. He breathed easier, relaxed. Larousse hadn't bothered him all day. Most of the institute settled, the fire forgotten, secret tests locked up tight behind closed doors. He could almost hear people breathing within the rooms, his senses spreading outward.

His thoughts settled on Bonnaire's daughter. The interfering woman stayed away, despite his belief she would be around asking questions after her night of snooping. Stupid to have confronted her earlier in the day, but the struggle to resist proved pointless. The woman was almost as bad as Anne Travers. Bad enough when Madeleine Bonnaire came on schedule, once a week, doing rounds, checking work, poking her nose in, demanding paperwork. She made him feel violated. Wanting access to this room, his private lab. His space.

No one else would steal his find. He'd worked too hard. The compound belonged to him to use. No one else. Certainly not that fool, Bonnaire.

Cooper alone. Always alone. For years. Scared and isolated the first night he used the initial full-strength dose of the substance, a minute trace to test whether he suffered any ill effects. Aside from the strange cold and hot fluctuations, he'd felt fine. Earlier on, he'd taken more caution… Couldn't now that he realised what he'd stumbled across. The military applications alone were stunning, not that he'd let the likes of those men get their hands on his formula.

As the sensation of melting progressed, Cooper understood at last this was too much power for a man not to keep secret, his alone to use.

Numbers and letters amassed, creating a paper maze to navigate. Back in her office, Madeleine rubbed at her forehead, squeezing her eyes shut, and blinking where she sat in a solitary pool of light. When had it grown so dark? Her intention hadn't been to linger, but habit and necessity trapped her as it so often did. A glance at her watch told her she stayed longer than she intended but not as late as the lack of daylight made it appear. A peep out of the window revealed a storm gathering. Figurative or literal? Both probably.

She had to escape. No sign of her father, but she overstayed her welcome having stolen from him. Would her heart pound if she passed him on the way out?

Madeleine stood, collecting up the papers that could wait, slipping a few into a drawer of her desk, and locking it. She slipped on her coat, grabbed her bag, and sped into the outer office, pausing to lock her room, her secretary gaping in apparent surprise. A sense of shame made Madeleine avert her face, the hope rising she wouldn't blush. Guilt weakened her.

Signed forms in hand, Madeleine faced her secretary, passed them over and without pause headed out with a simple, 'I'll be gone the rest of the day.'

In the corridor, she quickened her pace until she was almost running. One more stop to sign out, a nod to the security officer, and at last she broke free, drinking in the sweet, cool air. The taste and smell of rain flooded her senses, though the storm had yet to break.

Although anxious not to encounter her father, she stood alone on the front stoop unable to move, the walls of the institute looming, familiar but menacing, the path to her car ominous. Something or someone out there in the dark. Cooper, though that was madness, the man unlikely to be anywhere but alone in that laboratory of his. Why think of him now?

Because she was scared. The man rattled her so much she wanted to leave permanently, abandoning her work, the institute, her father... All so wrong. Whoever Cooper truly was he had no right to affect her this way. Yet the fear...

She glanced back. Might it sound peculiar to ask the security guard to escort her to her vehicle?

'Don't be ridiculous.'

Would be wonderful when word got around, as it was bound to, that Madeleine Bonnaire needed a man to safeguard her on her own grounds. Cooper would laugh himself sick. No. She couldn't... *wouldn't* put up with it. She would walk to her car today and every day thereafter, the likelihood of Cooper trying to harm her mere nerves. Besides, not a particularly large man, Cooper had lost weight recently, looked ill, and she could throw a decent punch; she'd deal with the cretin if necessary.

'Enough of this.' Enough hesitating.

The storm rolled in, rain pattering against her face. Another irritation, promising more to come, these specks a mere warning. The sky gave off a heavenly show of Armageddon. Clouds roiled, boiled white, grey, and black. The storm leached more colour out of the day. Shadows crossed her path.

Despite her bravado, she fished out her car keys before she stepped on the track, glad the heels she wore weren't too high. She could run if she needed to.

Stop it! She needed to silence these ridiculous notions.

By the time she spotted her car, she was thoroughly annoyed with herself. Guilt, that's all this was. Cooper forcing her to steal from her own father.

Something grabbed her ankle. Madeleine gasped as she hit the ground, knees first, second her hands, pain blasting up both legs and arms. Her keys and bag flew several inches in front of her; she swore at the idea of the gravel scratching fine leather. She rubbed one stinging hand against another, pushed up from the ground, ran her hand over both burning knees, and raked the area with her gaze.

No one. Nothing attacked. Nothing broken, though hands and knees throbbed, and her left kneecap protested every step. Obviously, she'd tripped. On what though? Nothing on the path. Nothing wrapped around her ankle, although the sensation was still too real.

Mad. Wasting time. Where were her keys? Madeleine hobbled over, hesitated, glanced around, before she bent to pick them up, grabbed her bag, and limped to her car, all the time scanning the dark.

She pushed the key in the lock, turned it, put her hand on the handle, palm smouldering with discomfort, likely branded by grit.

Something caressed her neck. Not a hand but not a breeze. Gone as fast as it came, but though it no longer touched her, it drew a line of fire up her back. The darkness watched.

Cooper?

Couldn't be. How?

Defiant, Madeleine peered over her shoulder. Leaves rustled as the wind picked up. More drops of rain fell, this time heavier. Explained what she felt. The hum of her skin, the soft caress of the wind would soon turn to a gale. When she got home, bathed her sore patches, took a hot bath, maybe poured a glass of wine, she would laugh and put it all down to her imagination.

Cooper *was* responsible for this attack of nerves, though. For spooking her, threatening her, making her uneasy, and she wouldn't forgive or forget.

Turning back to the car, she pulled on the handle and opened the door.

The meagre light inside flickered, fading, swallowed as blackness flooded the interior. No longer wanting to enter, Madeleine retreated. The shadow followed, spreading.

'Oh, for goodness sakes.'

Madeleine chided herself. She had to be more shaken than she thought. It couldn't be anything more than the strange play of light with shade as the storm gathered. Imagine, Madeleine Bonnaire afraid of her own shadow. Imagining a cloud flowing, coming for her, spreading out like a pool of water. Seeping up from the ground itself, moving until it touched her shoes and appeared to flow over her tips of her footwear.

Madeleine had heard of people paralysed by terror. She never expected to be one of them.

I'm not scared.

This couldn't be real. She stepped back, growing dizzy, having done the same thing earlier in the day with Cooper, backing away, and seeking sanctuary.

Cooper was responsible. She didn't know how or why, but the certainty settled in her bones. She would speak to Paul. Speak with Anne. If she made it home alive. Not with her father though. She couldn't speak to him; he wouldn't understand.

As though the darkness read her mind, it backed up, veered off.

Madeleine didn't wait to see more. She ran to her car, flung herself into the driving seat, and slammed the door. Threw the lock, though there had to be many ways a shadow might seek a way inside, through the vents, through gaps she didn't know existed. Key inserted, she turned on the ignition, revved the engine, peered through the windscreen. Stared. Gaped. Shook off the on-coming paralysis and pealed out of her parking space.

Although she couldn't be certain, she was sure that for one moment she imagined the dark silhouette of a man.

If Cooper knew – and perhaps he did – the man would be laughing.

Cooper entered through the window he'd left open to a mere slit earlier, sliding over the sill like an approaching eclipse.

The difference this time was his ability to feel the shape of the wooden trim, an almost sensuous tickle passing through his being. The metal catch... not so pleasant, making Cooper pause before pushing ahead, though *push* was inaccurate, lacking as he was physical means. Movement required more mental acuity. Although his dislike of touching the latch puzzled him, he pushed it to the back of his mind until his discomfort increased. His steady glide became a tumble, the distance to the floor considerable. He fell as though he truly retained substance, so he landed in a splodge smeared over the floor tile like so much spilled milk. Spread. Stretching, extending out, growing thin.

It took a concerted effort for Cooper to draw together, to rise, to reform. Holding the shape of man but still a black shadow, he took a few tentative steps. All appeared normal once again, but the strange sensation – not felt before – of the sharp metal catch cutting through him gave him cause to worry.

He lifted his hands, seeing not with eyes but in a wider spectrum over every inch of his exterior. Dismay set in when the 'hands' appeared puffy, ill formed. He directed all thoughts to how his hands usually looked, to how slim his fingers normally were, and gradually the foreshortened stubby digits elongated and trimmed down.

Alas, the sense of worry didn't diminish. Something was wrong. Never before had Cooper needed to think so hard to hold the black mass in a human shape. Or any shape! Part of his newfound freedom was the ability to become anything he wanted. The choice to walk as a man was only one of his favourite constructs because it amused him.

Would he struggle to change back?

Sharp white fear pierced through his gloom, his intellect softening the blow. Never having struggled before, he should have no cause to do so now. Maybe the sensation was a good thing, another development. Yes, must be. Another advancement. Part of his evolution.

Cooper moved to the nearest chair and lowered his shadow form into it as if he were a man sitting. What if Paul walked in? Or Bonnaire trespassed? Imagine if Bonnaire let himself into the lab without permission, and found his adversary there like this. Maybe the old coot would suffer a heart attack and be done with it. Save Cooper from having to...

Having to what? The thought faded, sliding away the same as day eased into a premature night. Although uncertain where his mind wandered, Cooper fought a sense of uneasiness. He didn't feel like himself these days.

Why should he? He was better than he used to be. Stronger. Maybe the best thing to do would be to sacrifice his human form and with it...

Humanity.

All the ailments and woes. Like this, he could do anything...

Whatever he wanted.

Go places humans never went, down into the earth, maybe the oceans. He should test his need and capacity to breathe. Provided he didn't go too long without oxygen, he could use the change for the good of humankind. Slide into a patient...

Kill him from the inside.

And bring about cures no surgeon could with all his knowledge and scalpels and drugs. He might root out cancer from the source...

Put himself in its place. A little of him in everyone.

Cooper extended his senses, able to view the room in three-hundred and sixty degrees. Alone, naturally. Alone. Alone. Always alone. Aside from those in the building. Paul. Outside. In the other room. So close. Nothing more than a locked door between them. Easy to get to. Entice in. Dispose of.

The thought drifted away, Cooper tired. So tired. His mind wandered. Time to become a man again.

It took longer than usual to transform. His eyes stung, body ached. He pressed his fingers into his closed burning eyes, rolled his shoulders to ease cramps in his neck and back. His stomach growled – hunger, but he was not of a mind to attend it now, unable, unwilling to move.

Not ready to for his legs remained black, not yet formed. Cooper sat there, letting the minutes slip ahead while he became a thing motionless, not one type of being or another, able to bide its time, to sleep for centuries if need be. These strange thoughts worried him, yet they did not. He was too important. A scientific breakthrough. A miracle. He didn't know what he would do with this discovery, but he was determined it would be something to change the world.

CHAPTER TWELVE
Side Effects

'MADELEINE?'

Anne's welcome changed to concern as Madeleine hurried in, threw her bag on a nearby chair, and kicked off her shoes. She fought her coat like a straitjacket until Anne moved to help.

'Here, let me.'

Only when free of the garment did Madeleine collapse into a seat, shaken. Bill hovered nearby, but she didn't speak a word to him or to Anne.

'What have you done to your hands?' Anne asked.

'What? Oh.' Madeleine curled her fingers, winching. 'I fell. Excuse me.' Without pause, she was up again and heading into the bathroom.

Fell? Anne followed. The woman's palms were so scrapped they had to be alive with prickles and pain.

'I landed on my hands and knees. Need to bathe them.' Madeleine tried to shut Anne out, but Anne wasn't having any of it.

'Let me help.' The women stared at each other via the reflection in the bathroom mirror, protest written all over Madeleine's face. 'I can do this better,' Anne insisted.

Anne closed the door, searched for tweezers and antiseptic. For a time, silence stretched between them.

'Is this the extent of your injuries?' Anne coaxed out a small piece of grit embedded in Madeleine's palm.

'Yes.'

'Good thing, though you may discover some remarkable bruises.' Anne sat back. 'What's upset you? Not Paul? Did you argue?' She kept her tone guarded.

'What? No! Why would you say that? I told you, I fell.'

Madeleine pushed past Anne, heading into the living room, Anne on her heels.

'I didn't mean he was the reason, though it's interesting you thought so. I believe you. But you are a little more upset than you should be from a mere fall.'

Madeleine stopped, turning to face her. Her expression... Anne knew it well; her friend was deciding whether to tell her the truth. Bill glanced between them, wisely silent.

When she spoke, Madeleine sounded lost. 'I knew what to say all the way here, but now... with the light on, with the damage mended, it's all a little ridiculous.'

'I'm used to the ridiculous.'

Madeleine regarded her, gaze thoughtful. 'Yes. Yes, I rather think you are. More so than you've told me.' She stared at her hands as if inspecting them, then fumbled for the arm of a chair, and sat. 'I don't know. God... Paul. I can't help wondering if he's in danger. He can't be though. No one can be from a...' She trailed off, gave an uneasy smile. 'Never mind me. An unfortunate run-in with someone spoiled my day, and the fall shook me up. Final straw. I... did something, which broke my ethics. I guess it all added up, and the stress overwhelmed me. Caused me to jump at... At shadows.'

Although Madeleine tried to keep her tone light, maybe the expression on Anne's face and the regard in her eyes made Madeleine ask, 'What?'

Anne leaned over and patted her hand. 'I think you need to be more honest with me. Tell me what happened. Don't lie to yourself, or to me.'

Though positive it was the last thing Madeleine wanted to do, the woman curled her hands into fists and started talking. She went over the conversation with her father, of having an unpleasant encounter with Cooper, of breaking into her father's office, of feeling guilty and betrayed. Of falling and feeling spooked...

'So, you see, stress, like I said. I let my personal feelings affect my imagination. It's all rather ludicrous.'

Anne didn't feel the same way. Apparently, neither did Bill for he said, 'Not at all. People, especially women, ignore their instincts when they shouldn't.'

Although Anne refused to get Madeleine the wine she

wanted, she got her a coffee with a shot of brandy. Better for her nerves. Madeleine cradled the cup.

'So… these papers?'

Madeleine met Anne's gaze. 'I feel I should be the one to confront my father. But I need time to think. Please. Just let me finish my drink, enjoy a bath, scan through the files to see if I missed some details…'

'How will it change anything?'

'It won't, but let me gather my thoughts.'

Her friend didn't frighten easily, not the woman Anne once knew anyway. Wisely, Anne withdrew, sensible only to push Madeleine so far, so hard. Victor Bonnaire's involvement made Madeleine's emotions complex. Anne glanced at the clock. Mid-afternoon, though it might as well be night for all the daylight outside.

'Get yourself settled. We'll talk later.'

Madeleine drained her cup. 'You think my father will call?'

'If he goes up to the institute and discovers his desk broken into? Yes. He may even come round.'

Madeleine pressed a hand to her forehead. 'I don't know what's wrong with me. I'm not thinking clearly.' She gave Anne a sheepish glance. 'But then I've never robbed my father before.'

All three stared at each other, the silence shattered by the sound of a ringing telephone. Their gazes fell on it as though it were a thing of evil.

'If it's my father, I can't face it.'

Bill spoke up. 'If it is your father and there's no answer, he'll definitely come around. That's what I would do. Better one of us makes an excuse.' He walked across the room and picked up the receiver, barking out, 'Hello? One moment. It's Paul.'

Anne and Madeleine exchanged a glance, but Madeleine nodded and stood, more steady than Anne expected her to be. She took the call, Anne and Bill exchanging glances and trying not to appear to eavesdrop.

Minutes later, Madeleine hung up. 'Odd. Paul says our disagreement last night unsettled him so he took a drive during which he believed he spotted Cooper's car. He followed him to the *Parc terre*.'

'Parkland?' Anne asked.

'Yes. A strip of forest and greenery, mostly recreational. There Cooper got out and went for a walk.'

'Nothing too strange,' Anne ventured.

'True.'

'The Parkland you say?' Bill picked up the newspaper from which Anne had read earlier. 'I think you'd better take a peek at this.'

Victor Bonnaire grew tired of all the deception. He didn't know what was going on with his daughter, but things were bad between them. Never an easy relationship; couldn't be having a girl so well-educated and assertive like her mother. Interesting. Definitely made life interesting, but he wanted her smile along with a cup of coffee. For her to forgive him his foolishness and everything would be well. Wouldn't happen while he continued to refuse to believe Cooper was up to something he shouldn't be. Not that Madeleine would like the agreement he and Cooper made anyway. Their arrangement meant Bonnaire couldn't sound too accusing. Still, he had to have it out with the blighter, so he would. At the least, Cooper proved his carelessness.

Almost as careless as Bonnaire. He now realised he should have followed his daughter to the institute earlier that morning instead of dithering until the storm closed in.

Procrastination – his weakest trait. Understandable though. Cooper might not take kindly to his questions, so Bonnaire had waited. Sat in his kitchen drinking endless cups of coffee until he buzzed. Hours spent with thoughts circling until the day faded into a gloom as dark as his mood.

'Enough.' Bonnaire rose.

It may not be best to speak to Cooper alone. Where would the man be? Although he put in long hours, the professor might have left for the day. Of course, he lived on the grounds, but Bonnaire wouldn't bother him in his rooms. He would much prefer to speak to Cooper in the lab. That way maybe Cooper would take him seriously. Bonnaire experienced a little self-disgust and reproach at the hope.

He departed the gatekeeper's cottage, hopping into his car, and trundled up the long path to the institute's car park. A couple of cars passed him on the way, Bonnaire peering out at faces he recognised. He raised a hand, greeting both staff who preferred to rent rooms in town. Not like them to leave early, but rain lashed at the car providing an explanation. He pitied anyone out in it, unsurprised for once to note the absence of his daughter's car when he parked up.

'Sensible girl.'

Bonnaire first stopped at the front desk and asked if Cooper signed out. The security guard flipped through the visitor's book. 'As I thought, no. He must still be in the lab.'

'Yes. Yes, he must. Paul Larousse?'

'He left about half an hour ago.' The guard didn't need to consult the book.

Pity. He would have liked Larousse with him. Perhaps the man was in his room, instead of off the grounds. No way to know without investigating, and Bonnaire didn't feel inclined. Would take time. Besides, Larousse would ask questions, so maybe he wasn't the right choice.

It was Cooper making people second guess themselves. Bonnaire owned the institute. Cooper, causing Bonnaire to feel uneasy about asking questions was the same as making a man feeling awkward in his own home. Wouldn't do.

Without Larousse, only one obvious answer presented itself.

'Would you mind putting a notice up on the door to say you're otherwise engaged for a few minutes and follow me?'

'No problem.' The guard knew the procedure. He turned the key in the lock of the front doors and lifted the sign stating people coming or going must wait for his return. Then he gave Bonnaire a questioning glance.

Bonnaire didn't blame the man, not at all. The circumstances were unusual.

'I need you to accompany me. We'll need the passkey to lab six. If all is well, you can wait outside the door while the professor and I exchange a quiet word.'

The guard answered, 'Yes, sir,' but a slight lift of one eyebrow said he wondered what the man had done. No point wasting time to reprimand the man's idle curiosity.

Bonnaire knocked on the door of the outer lab, and when he

received no answer, he marched right in. A swift glance around revealed nothing out of the ordinary, so he crossed the room. He rapped on the inner door, and waited before knocking a second time and calling out, 'Professor Cooper. It's Bonnaire. I'd like a word.' Again, he lingered but, receiving no reply, he looked to the guard to open the door with the passkey. The door swung open revealing a black hole. The illusion lasted long enough for Bonnaire to feel as though he were being drawn in.

He performed a mental shake. What nonsense. He reached out and fumbled along the wall seeking the light switch, refusing to give into the temptation to snatch his hand back, fearing something sharp would sever his fingertips any moment. Perhaps the teeth of a creature from some nightmare. More likely, a trap left in place by a genius.

Apparently, his daughter's unease was contaminating. Still, even without a light on, he should be able to spot something due to the brightness coming from the room behind him. As he flipped the switch, it took a moment for the bulb to bloom, darkness, and light locked in conflict.

The brightness won to reveal a normal room.

My daughter is driving me mad.

Bonnaire stepped inside. The guard peered around, though he didn't step over the threshold.

'Seems he's out.'

The man might well sound puzzled. Cooper was not in the room, but where did he go without signing out? He had no business elsewhere. He might have snuck out, but why? Bonnaire found it hard to imagine Cooper shinnying over a windowsill, even if he bypassed the alarms, which was unlikely. He had to be in the toilets or the coffee room. As he might return any moment, the best thing to do was use the time well.

'Wait there a moment.' Bonnaire moved to close the door but decided at the last second to leave it ajar. Odd notion but he imagined the bulb exploding above his head and the light going out. Leaving him trapped in the dark, with every strange creation his distraught nerves might conjure into being.

He toddled around the room, peering into a few unlocked drawers. Paused to uncover and stare at the box his daughter mentioned. Nothing in the room made it obvious for what purpose someone might use the apparatus, and he spotted no sign of Cooper's private assignment, though from his request it had to have something to do with it.

The area beneath the clean work surface was swathed in darkness, making it impossible to see anything there. With a grunt, Bonnaire got down on one knee, too old for crawling about on the floor, and tried to peer under the desk. Impossible. The light in the room seemed to dim.

A frown edged its way across Bonnaire's face as he struggled back to his feet. He took out a handkerchief and wiped his brow of sweat caused by the effort, then glanced back at the overhead lamp fitting. He waved a hand in the air, the light sending a silhouette on the wall, a strange multi-digit creature waving back. Bonnaire's outline, the shape of his body, stretched out to the right, but it cut off beneath the table. Surely, he should be able to see more of his shadow.

As though the darkness understood, it withdrew, flattening itself out, elongating at either end.

Old eyes. Bad light.

Bonnaire rubbed a hand over his face. What did Cooper do in here? There appeared to be none of the projects Bonnaire set him except, perhaps, Bonnaire's own, if the box was part of that. Madeleine might have a point. Surely Cooper didn't fob off *all* his chores on young Larousse? The younger man held promise and might one day be in charge of his own lab if his work to date had any basis. Still, some tasks Bonnaire selected for Cooper were not for Larousse to study or to oversee alone, and some not at all. The purpose of an assistant was for the man to… well, to *assist*, and to learn during the process.

Bonnaire took a step and something crunched beneath his shoe causing his gaze to follow a line of spilled liquid and broken test tubes. The destruction made Bonnaire blow hot. This would not do. Cooper might not be guilty of anything more than carelessness, but Bonnaire didn't run a lazy establishment. The professor needed telling. He huffed his way out of the lab, had the guard lock up and then made his way along the corridor, heading for the stairs to his office.

On the way, he stopped by the toilets and the coffee room. No sign of Cooper. Where was the man?

Head throbbing again, Madeleine tried to ease up on her frown. Didn't they say frowning gave a person wrinkles? Not that she cared much about such things, but anxiety did no one any good.

Cooper out by the Parkland, seen by Paul, and now here... in the paper...

No, it couldn't have anything to do with the professor. Nothing to do with her father.

'Madeleine, are you all right?'

Engrossed with the article and files, Madeleine jumped, not having noticed Anne enter the room. She gave her what felt like a strained smile, confirmed by Anne's worried expression. Where was Bill?

'So, it's us girls? Time for a cross-examination, eh?'

'Enough, Mads. You've spent plenty of time examining your father's files. We're friends. Nothing you can say or do will shock me or disappoint me. And I won't judge your father. I'm here to help you.'

'I'm not sure you can. We may have a situation on our hands. My hands.' Madeleine realised she rearranged things on the table and forced herself to stop. She hated repetitive actions, aware she did them when anxious, and she didn't want Anne to pick up on how nervous she felt. 'To tell the truth, I'm not sure what I'm saying. I feel I'm going mad.'

Anne sat in the chair across from her, movement slow, sliding across a threshold. Or maybe Madeleine projected her own imaginings onto her friend. Did she do right dragging Anne into this?

There's no one else.

'You can talk to me, you know. In complete confidence.'

'That's the trouble. I know I can, but I don't believe it's fair of me. And there's your husband.'

'Bill?' Anne sounded surprised.

'Oh, I know he's a good sort but what we do here includes work for the military and other organisations. I wouldn't blame Bill but if he felt a threat existed...' Madeleine trailed off, having said too much.

'If there's a danger to the national security of any member state of the United Nations, then I'm inclined to report it myself.' Anne's tone turned grave. 'But, Madeleine, my dear, so should you.'

Did Anne slip a warning in at the end? Madeleine rather thought so. 'I don't know what I'm saying. I...'

She hesitated once more, reluctant to talk. Speaking about what she'd found would make it real. There'd be no ignoring it. No going back.

'My father lied. By how much I don't know.' She drew the pages out from under the paper and handed them over, those concerning animal experimentation first. She studied Anne's expression as she read, a look of disgust passing over her friend's face.

'He promised me this would not happen. Or at least we'd keep such experiments to a minimum and to rats and mice. He said he would allow nothing like this without consulting me first.'

'I understand your anger, I do. I can also see why he lied. Not that I approve,' Anne added, as Madeleine grimaced, unable to conceal her dislike. Anne fell back in her seat. 'Bill says it's like I want to save every living thing sometimes. Maybe I do. I'm saying you and your father have extreme points of view. I'm on your side but I can understand his.'

'Hate the sin not the sinner?' Madeleine asked, making Anne wince, sorry at once. 'Oh, ignore me. I'm so angry and upset with him and the joke is, if I took this to my father, he'd be angry with me. I'm the one who cracked open his desk drawer.'

'I take it there's more?' Anne eyed the papers Madeleine had yet to hand over.

'I wish I could say no.'

'This is between me and you. I promise to do nothing more until we're both sure there's a good reason to.'

Madeleine failed to vanquish the smile stretching her lips. 'Trust you to be sensible.'

'You're entirely sensible, just cautious.'

'You wouldn't think so if you'd seen me running from my shadow.' Madeleine shook her head at Anne's widening eyes. 'I'll get to that in a moment. Believe me, I'm so angry with my father I'm struggling to make sense of all this. First, read this.'

She handed over the evening's newspaper. Anne had said

there would be more detail of the boy's death and there was. Anne's understanding of the language would be enough for her to skim the main article.

'Did you know the young man?'

'No, but reading between the lines, Christophe Legrand was healthy, wouldn't you say?'

'It says here he's a top athlete at the school.'

Madeleine caught herself nodding, looked to the window. 'Anne, the situation we face may be worse than I thought. Paul saw one of our professors near the local woodland, as I've told you.' She stopped, unable or unwilling to say more.

Anne, perhaps sensing this, diverted the conversation's course. 'Tell me a little more about the area.'

'Locals sometimes call it the Parkland, sometimes the Fields because the land is more like open forest, extensive. There's a natural boundary formed by nearby woods, which separates some wealthier houses from the park.' Madeleine flicked her gaze back to Anne and gave a quick nod to the paper in her hand. 'The woods are where someone found the boy.'

'Did he live close by?'

'Close, but not close enough to warrant his being out in the forest.'

'So, he was…?' Anne awaited Madeleine's theory.

'Who can say? But a boy his age, young man, it's not a stretch to say he met with someone who lives in one of the many houses lining the woods.'

'A girlfriend?'

'Or a boy.' Madeleine shrugged. 'Love would make more sense. Unless the autopsy reveals drugs or excessive alcohol, love, or what we sometimes mistake for love, is as good a reason as any for him to be wandering about on a cold night.'

Anne's gaze continued to drift over the article. 'It doesn't say why he died.'

'No, but…' Madeleine made a vague gesture with her right hand. 'The autopsy and these things take time.'

'But you would like to read the report?'

'Indeed.'

'Didn't you say you had a contact…?'

Where did Anne pick up a snippet like that? Madeleine

tried to recall what she might have said. Or what Anne read. Gave up. What did such secrets matter now?

'Yes. There is someone. I don't like asking.'

'Yet you intend to try.' The paper rustled as Anne folded the pages. 'Is Paul in danger, do you think?'

'I don't see why he should be. I don't think he's seen as a threat.'

'It might be worth speaking to him in person to see if he can think of anything else.'

'I believe Paul's told me all he can.'

True, but what Anne said made sense. Why protest so much?

'Even though he works with this mysterious professor?'

Did Anne still dig for the man's identity? Madeleine didn't know what to tell her, not until she spoke to her father. Maybe not then.

'In no story I've read does the bad guy share.'

'Until the denouement,' Anne quipped.

Madeleine fought a smile despite her depression.

'And you trust Paul.'

'I do.' The lack of hesitation surprised Madeleine. 'Paul's not involved.'

'You have a point, but Paul being at the same forest,' Anne gestured to the report, 'seems curious.'

'Not so much. It's a well-known romantic spot. Paul... Oh, I don't know why he went or what he was thinking.' *Or who he was seeing.* Heat flared in Madeleine's face, but telling Anne made no difference to the outcome. 'I can't say whether he met someone, but I believe not. I think he was so upset and angry by my shutting him out, maybe that alone drove him to...' *To see someone else?* Madeleine didn't believe that; he'd had feelings for her for too long.

'You're still keeping things from me.'

'Damn you, Anne, must you be so astute? Fine. What you need to understand is this isn't about Paul. This professor... He's not the type to have a romantic interest. He is... how to say, not the sort. Paul was as curious as I am as to his presence there. Though it pains me to admit it, I can appreciate why. Paul expected the professor to meet with someone. It's what most everyone goes there for.'

Madeleine broke off, glanced into Anne's eyes, away. Something made it easier to go over all this without meeting her gaze, not because of embarrassment but because she felt stupid.

'He did not. He got out of his car and headed into the park.' Should she tell Anne how spooked Paul said he felt? No. Surely not. There was no reason to. 'Paul followed but lost him and returned to his car. Worried, and when the professor did not show in his rooms, he tried to track him down, to check if he was in the lab.'

'Was he?'

'According to the security log.'

'But Paul's not so sure.'

'No. And it's an unusual coincidence. The man does something contrary to character in the vicinity of, and on the same night, where this boy dies.'

'But the boy may have passed away for any reason. In which case, I believe you know your first course of action.'

Madeleine met her gaze, knowing what she would say before Anne spoke.

'You must call in this favour and discover how the boy died. Unless there's something untoward...' Anne didn't finish, without need.

'You are right. Forgive me, Anne. I am letting Paul's own uneasiness get the best of me. But I cannot ignore what he said.' Madeleine was too aware her own gaze was furtive. 'It doesn't make sense, but Paul claims to have stumbled across the man's discarded garments. If this man controls a creature that kills, it still doesn't explain his behaviour that night. And with what else I found in my father's desk, it's made me afraid.'

'Madeleine, please, I think it's time you tell me which professor we're talking about.'

'Cooper. Only he's not.' Madeleine blurted it out, surprised she did. Oh, what the hell? Enough of her father's secrets. Madeleine slid the rest of the pages across the table, giving in.

'It turns out my father's been hiring people unofficially. Not many. There are three names, but Cooper is one and—'

Madeleine broke off as Anne shot to her feet, eyes wide, staring at the page. The chair she sat in wobbled, threatening to tip, at last settling. Before it did, Anne yelled for Bill who came at a run. Anne thrust the paper at him, Madeleine a silent witness to the man's expression changing from one of concern and puzzlement to outright horror.

When he spoke, he conveyed a blend of emotions. A toxic soup in one word. 'Copeland?'

CHAPTER THIRTEEN
Scientific Sacrifices

RATTLED BY his visit to Cooper's lab, plus the climb up the stairs, Bonnaire was still wiping sweat from his brow when he entered his office. All the stress was getting to him. The need to keep things from Madeleine was taking its toll. Had to be, for him to imagine such strange things. His daughter and Cooper proved to be thorns of different varieties. One thing of which he was sure, he would keep a tighter rein on the man. They needed to talk.

God, he trembled. Bonnaire staggered around to the far side of his desk and fell into his chair. Elbows on the desktop, Bonnaire put his face in his hands, and took steady breaths until his pulse slowed. Didn't take long. Good. No medication needed, though he patted his pocket to make sure he had his pills.

Right. First things. He needed to remove any proof. Should have cleared out his desk before now.

Bonnaire stared at the drawer where he kept the most incriminating evidence. Nothing could disguise the cracked wood. Heart pounding, Bonnaire fell to his knees, wrenching the drawer open, heart racing again, skipping beats. He grew breathless.

'*Non non non!*' he shouted into his empty office, pleading to some deity he wasn't sure existed that the unthinkable hadn't occurred. As he gazed into the hollow space, his world narrowed until his head became light. He fought not to faint.

Couldn't be Madeleine. She couldn't! Not his girl. She wouldn't steal. Not from her own father.

She would, though. If she possessed the gall to break into his desk, and if she read…

A long low moan eased out from deep in his throat, rising and growing, until it changed, becoming a wail.

The animal experiments. She would never forgive him. He could only thank his stars he hadn't left any information in his office pertaining to why Cooper was on staff.

Bonnaire lost track of how long he knelt in his office, but by the time he closed the drawer and rose, stiffly, to his feet, less than five minutes had passed. Strange how it felt someone froze him in place for hours. With nothing left but to confront Madeleine, or wait for her to challenge him, Bonnaire stumbled to the door, stepped out into the corridor, pausing to lock up his room.

How did she breach his office? The question floated through his mind, but he failed to hold onto it. Didn't matter. The fact his daughter knew some of his lies…

Bonnaire closed his eyes and leaned his head against the wood, wanting never to move. Unable to remain there forever, he pulled himself together and walked away. What a fool, leaving such evidence on the premises. As much as he wanted to blame Madeleine, he made these decisions, acted careless.

He hired people like Cooper.

Speaking of…

Bonnaire hurried down the stairs and walked the final stretch, heading out when he bumped into the man. He skidded to a halt in shock. Cooper straightened his tie as if he'd recently put it on, otherwise appearing reasonably turned out. Bonnaire peered behind him, gazing down the hall. The door leading to the lab was shut, but Bonnaire had stood in that room less than fifteen minutes ago. Time for Cooper to get by him but… he'd checked the toilets and the tearoom. Where had Cooper gone?

'I came by looking for you.'

'Oh?' Cooper sounded mildly interested. 'I didn't hear you knock.'

Did he hear an accusation in the man's tone? Bonnaire would not have this insubordination. He would not! 'I knocked but when there was no reply I entered. I tapped on the second door, too, but when I again received no answer, I used my passkey and went in.'

'I see.' Cooper straightened a cuff, all his movements

suggestive of a man settling into his clothes, only having just dressed. 'I believed my laboratory to be private.'

The accusation was real, made worse by Cooper's almost toneless delivery.

'It is, but I had an urgent need to speak to you. The... condition in which I found your laboratory takes precedence. You must understand, Cooper, I am most aggrieved not to find much evidence of scientific pursuit of the type I um... I hired you for.'

'I do not leave such work out on my desk for all to see. I thought you of all people would appreciate my discretion.'

'But you leave broken test tubes on the floor.' Bonnaire struggled to tell whether the man stared right through him or into somewhere deeper, perhaps searching for his soul.

'You called on me when I had occasion to use a bathroom. I've cleaned my work area now.'

He's lying. Bonnaire didn't know why he felt so certain, but he was. His skin itched with the absurd certainty Cooper was privy to Bonnaire's inspection of his lab all along. Impossible, but... the man knew everything, and he hadn't stepped out into one of the washrooms. Not at all. For Bonnaire not to see him in all that time and for Cooper to be here now... Even allowing for the minutes Bonnaire spent in his office, the timing was tight for him to have gone elsewhere, and why use a toilet on another floor without cause? Not the reason Bonnaire refused to believe the man though.

'Is there anything else?'

Although the man's voice remained monotone in pitch, Cooper challenged him. Bonnaire wanted to rise to the challenge as he always did with everything throughout his life, but now was not the time. He couldn't even bring himself to ask whether the crystals had helped, whether the box was part of the main and private experiment Bonnaire hired him for. He shook his head, allowed Cooper to walk off without a word, and stood there staring after him. How did a man respond when he failed to understand the dispute?

Back in his room in the halls of residence, Professor Theodore Copeland released his grip on the tube in his pocket, afraid of snapping the glass. His breath caught as he eased it out, checking for damage. Holding it cupped in his hands against his chest, Copeland stood in the centre of his room, waiting for his heartbeat to calm. Damn Bonnaire for annoying him and making him almost lose his precious formula.

All evidence so far collected declared his initial conclusions and suppositions right. The creature, discovered eight years before, changed matter on the molecular level, its reaction to light something he stumbled upon by accident. First UV. Ultraviolet radiation, of which without the protection of the ozone layer most living organisms of the earth would face the possibility of cancer and mutation. The light gun he'd created back then concentrated various forms of illumination into a beam at a wavelength relatively harmless to humans, barring extended exposure. That wavelength caused the shadow creature pain, even death.

The shadow creature.

An incredible being he helped to disarm. A being chased across Scotland by UNIT. He had still used his full name back then and helped to modify the weapon's power source, adding modifications of which he'd never let on. What Brigadier Pemberton hadn't realised, when he had levelled the gun at the creature he hoped to eradicate, was that the weapon first suctioned a little essence of the beast. Only when the hidden compartment filled, did the weapon release at maximum strength. For the first ten-seconds or so the most Pemberton did was to cause the creature pain as part of it ripped away. Altered enough for containment, the extracted part essentially died, though Copeland hadn't been sure about that until recently.

'Like removing a limb,' he muttered.

Exactly like. As he had hoped, his plan to discover much through tissue collection eventually proved successful.

'And you never knew I got one over on you.'

Pemberton would be spitting mad if he ever learned of the deception, but the thought only added to Copeland's joy. He didn't like the man from the moment they met, and Pemberton had certainly taken an instant dislike to him.

There'd been a small risk the creature might escape in those seconds, and that it might harm Pemberton, but nothing Copeland couldn't blame on a malfunction.

Did his actions make him evil? No. Sacrifices had to occur for scientific advancement.

The shadow creature was a thing without substance. Copeland had supposed the blackness would rise and dissolve like vapid smoke. Dead. Passing through the light gun appeared to kill it, but the collection process also altered its consistency in unexpected ways, turning it fluid.

Copeland had since changed the liquid to another substance, one he'd tested first on his own blood samples and then by injection. He couldn't be more delighted with the result. What worried him now was his own clumsiness.

Bonnaire's fault. Only not. Hating to admit it, Copeland saw no choice but to accept that his reactions continued to slow, making him clumsier of late. A side effect? Had to be, though he'd been a little butterfingered for some months, maybe as much as a year.

No. Coincidence. Exhaustion. Now… He wasn't so sure, but some side effects were expected. This was not the time to allow himself the luxury of doubting. Though his collection method worked all those years ago, recently allowing him to develop a formula, he couldn't know if it did all he hoped. Either the sample or his preparation might be at fault, and he'd had no chance to cover the depths of the possible and hoped-for uses. Not yet, but he would in time.

Copeland fell into a chair still holding the tube. Never had he stumbled so much over his own feet. Never had he reached for things only for them to appear to slide away from him. Maybe his depth perception was faulty. His hands… He held one up in front of him. Not as steady as they once were but not shaking. The slight waver could be age or stress.

He'd taken so long to become fully human again, had needed to dissolve and try to reform several times, hiding under the desk when Bonnaire entered his lab. After the doctor left, Copeland had still required three attempts before he turned human and hurried to dress, meeting Bonnaire out in the hall not five minutes the change.

Why did the transformation take so long?

Calm down. Get a grip.

Maybe he needed help but who to approach? Bonnaire? Larousse?

Anne Travers?

God, he wanted to. If she was onboard, together they may have developed something wonderful but her position in UNIT would never have allowed such a thing, fear ruling UNIT's decisions.

People always killed what they feared.

It's good to kill.

No! Copeland jolted in his chair, and rubbed a hand over his eyes. Where did these aberrant thoughts come from? He was overtired. Hunted. Misunderstood. Anne... She'd not helped him eight years ago, but maybe she would help him now. Maybe he could force her.

Before all the liquid ran out. Before he was no longer able to make more formula.

A grin twisted his lips, stretching wide. When he first heard of such beings, they'd ignited his imagination like no other find. Legends put aside, to rest, until science merged with the myth, his work dragging him into a mess he tried many times to regulate to hobby status. Stories which even found their way into the Quran – pitch-black sapient beings created from fire. What would Anne think of those?

The plan hatching was misdirected and malformed, but he saw no other way. They wouldn't let him alone. They would hunt him down. He couldn't live in the shadows forever and he couldn't stop now. To be a Shadowman was a marvellous thing. Impossible to give up.

CHAPTER FOURTEEN
Pitch-Black Sapient Beings

BASTIEN NOYER was not a man of whom Madeleine said she liked taking advantage. Anne understood why the moment she met him. Not only did he break the law and his own ethics, he allowed a stranger to accompany Madeleine as an unwanted witness. Anne tried to make herself appear insignificant, but no one fooled anyone. A fact *Monsieur* Noyer made plain the moment they were alone behind locked doors – a clear indication the man didn't take chances. He treated Anne to an excess of pronunciation almost comically delightful.

'There is one reason and one alone why I am doing this.' Noyer waved a file in Madeleine's face in the manner of a significant form of punctuation. 'If you are asking for this information, then it is for a serious reason.'

If you are ask-king for this infor-may-sea-on, then it is for a ser-e-oust rea-sea-on.

Anne blinked away her amusement not wishing to offend. He then launched into a sequence of French so rapid he lost her, though she caught a few snatches. Even without those, she would have realised he said nothing complimentary.

He finished with, 'Is there any way you can tell me what you know?'

'Not at this time,' Madeleine said. 'It's little more than supposition. And it would be polite to converse in English for my friend's sake.'

Anne kept her expression blank. Madeleine knew Anne understood, but perhaps gathered how difficult it was for anyone to follow Noyer's lightning diction.

'Supposition has you worried?' He spoke this time in English. He tossed the file to Madeleine. 'You may read it once then I am removing it and putting it back where it belongs. And this never happened.'

Madeleine wisely remained silent, but gave a nod. She opened the file, laid it on her kitchen table, and leaned over it. Anne glanced at the clock, having sent Bill for a walk, not wanting Noyer to feel too pressured or suspicious. Plenty of time before Bill would wander back. He'd asked why naturally enough, accepting her assurance that she would explain when able. Her husband trusted her but, in time, would require answers. A smidgeon of guilt caused Anne to read a line without taking in any of the information on the page, making her read it again.

'This isn't possible.' Anne spoke before her friend, but the lines woven into Madeleine's forehead spoke of her friend's frustration.

'Anne's right.' Madeleine lifted her head to gaze at Noyer.

'You think I don't know? It is the real reason I am letting you inspect the file. I am stumped. So odd the mortician's cause of death, I did something I have not done in years. I checked his findings.'

'And?' Madeleine sounded scared of the answer.

'The boy asphyxiated, outdoors, but with no signs of a cause.'

'No pre-existing medical conditions?'

'None.'

Madeleine and Anne both continued to study the report, but Madeleine asked what Anne wondered. 'Is this... murder then?'

'As yet to determine. My recommendation is of possible suspicious circumstances. In the morning, this will pass to people higher than I. They will... how you say, re-examine my findings.'

Findings of findings, being that Noyer already took it into his own hands to go over the conclusions of his underling. Now the death would be under the jurisdiction of the police, though a pathologist's work didn't end with a report. When determining a cause of death many components needed consideration. Noyer's extensive background suited the work – his involvement with police would double his guilt over speaking to Madeleine like this. The first item he would consider was location, and the boy definitely wasn't found anywhere he needed to be.

'Injuries?' Anne spoke aloud though unsure whether she questioned Noyer or simply wanted to churn over the meagre information on hand.

'You can read for yourself.' Noyer sounded entirely put out. Although he did them a favour, Madeleine shot him a dark glance prompting a reply. 'Forgive me, *Douceur*, it has been a tiring couple of days.'

Douceur? Sweetness? Anne wanted to ask Madeleine the details of their 'friendship' but refrained.

'*Non*. No injuries. Well, a few scrapes from where he appears to have slipped and thrashed on the ground, but no others.'

No injuries and the thrashing around suggested natural causes. 'Is it possible he suffered from an unknown condition?' Anne asked.

'I have not seen his full medical files but his doctor says it is unlikely. I found nothing, although unless I know what I search for...' Noyer made a seesaw gesture with his hand. 'We are still waiting on some test results, but so far our investigations show him free of disease. His heart showed signs of stress, I would say owing to death, but not of long-term conditions. We collected evidence, some fine hairs on his clothes, long, blonde ones, and believe he was out seeing a girl. But there are several blonde girls in the area and we have not yet narrowed the field.'

Noyer hesitated. 'His tracks stop someway behind a house and it is likely the girl who lives within is the one, but they are questioning everyone so as not to single out a person at this stage. It may well be he went to meet a girlfriend, but I do not believe she caused his death. Nothing a girl of similar age could do matches my findings so far. Love can be vindictive, but such young love is more often subject to tears.'

Ignoring his Shakespearean comment on romance, Anne murmured, 'Nothing beneath his nails.' Not a question, she was merely deliberating. Noyer seemed to understand as he nodded at her for several seconds. 'Tears and rips in his clothes?'

'None not caused by a tumble in the woods.'

'So, no clear signs of attack, but you still believe he suffocated?' Although Anne still mused to herself, Noyer once more performed that persistent nodding gesture. 'No reason to think someone moved the body?'

'*Non*. Not after death. He walked, even ran, some distance while alive but under his own…erm…' Noyer searched for the word. 'Water vapour.'

'Steam,' Anne filled in the blank.

'Yes. It is my opinion he died where he fell. But his trail… that is odd.'

'Odd how?' Anne refrained from winching, realising she had taken over the investigation.

'Haphazard. Backtracking.'

'Running from someone?'

'Possible but no other tracks to indicate a chase.'

'Might someone have poisoned him?' Madeleine closed the file. 'Some toxins take time to work. Maybe he ran for help but became disorientated.'

'I would expect to find more evidence that he staggered.'

'Of course.' Madeleine sounded put out with herself.

'And so far all toxicology says no, though we are awaiting a few more results.'

'But you don't believe they'll find anything.' Madeleine stared at Noyer. Being she'd known the man for some time, Anne only guessed she studied his reactions.

'No. And I am seldom wrong.'

'But you could not give them an opinion on how death occurred?' Anne read that in the file, but she wanted Noyer to elaborate.

'I… believe some form of smothering took place.'

'As you say in your statement, but…' Madeleine's gaze held steady, a stare he returned.

Anne watched the calculation speed through his gaze and recognised the moment he relented. Either his feelings for Madeleine were strong, or he was desperate for some clue. Possibly both.

'I checked the victim's eyes, and they were bloodshot.'

That certainly indicated suffocation or smothering.

'Nothing blocked the airways. I detected nothing in the deceased's system to show a cause. He was not near water, so

I ruled out drowning but, upon inspection, his lungs are fine. Clear. Healthy. No bruising around the nose or mouth.'

'No evidence of toxic gases?' Although it would be in the report, Anne couldn't fail to ask.

'None. Unless it is something undetectable to our present level of science, I believe none of our known gases to be a cause.'

Carbon Monoxide, Hydrogen Sulphide, solvents... Anne didn't bother to list them. Noyer would have considered any she thought of.

'No smell of almonds,' Anne murmured.

Noyer frowned. 'Cyanide? No. Although I'm surprised you mention it. It's not a substance that comes up too often.'

'So, what killed him?' Madeleine persisted.

Noyer gave her a hard look. 'I don't know. If I didn't know better, I would think someone put him in a room and sucked out all the air. But then there would be signs of him struggling to escape. There is none. It's as if... As if someone cut off his ability to breathe or took him out of this world into another where oxygen didn't exist.'

'That's not in your report.'

'What would be the use? They'd think me mad.'

'This is why you answered my call.'

'One reason.'

There came that moment again that spoke of a shared history that made Anne glance away, perhaps to give them a moment of privacy. A history about which she would not enquire.

'I also don't like coincidences and for you to ask about a case that is so peculiar...' Noyer took a step in Madeleine's direction, a gesture Anne may have believed almost menacing if not for the anguish on his face. 'I don't like a crime I cannot solve. You know something and I need to know what.'

'But I don't. And if I did...' Madeleine's words ran out.

'What, *Douceur*? You cannot tell me because it would break a confidence?' Noyer gathered up his report and marched towards the door. 'I will give you forty-eight hours and then I will have no choice but to tell the police you made inquiries.'

'You won't do that.' Madeleine followed him across the room.

'And why is that?' He spun to face her.

'Because you will open the path for me to say you gave me access to confidential information.'

'Which you would not mention.'

His reply appeared to stump her. 'What makes you think so?'

The two stared at each other, making Anne feel awkward to be in the room.

'So,' Noyer paced a few steps, 'we are at a stalemate. Unsure if, or who, will tell on whom. No, you are right, my sweet Madeleine. I will say nothing, but you are no more able to let a murderer walk free than I. Investigate where you must, but if you know the cause...' He gestured with the folder. 'Then I need to know. And if I find out that it is something you are responsible for then no threat will keep me pointing the police to the institute. My conscience would not survive anything less.'

Madeleine nodded. 'Neither would mine. I didn't mean what I said.'

'I know.' Noyer gave her a rueful nod. 'We are excellent at hurting each other. But we are good at being there when needed. You must pursue this.'

'Care to explain?'

A folder slapped down on his dining table, one Bonnaire recognised. Shocking enough Madeleine and her friends turned up on his doorstep again. His daughter using her key and letting them all in without knocking this time was the height of ill-manners.

'What have you done?' he asked, though he knew. He'd spent a night and part of the morning wondering whether he should contact Madeleine or wait until she came to him. Cowardice kept him imprisoned in the cottage, aware this confrontation was coming, unable to run, unable to walk toward it.

'What have *I* done?' Disbelief laced his daughter's voice.

While it might have surprised her, did she forget he founded the institute? 'The institute is mine. Mine. Everything that goes on inside is up to me.'

'Your idea built the foundation but there are investors.

141

You signed part of the place over. To me. It's not *yours* alone, and if it were it doesn't give you the right not to distinguish right from wrong. To work without a moral compass. To lie to me.'

'And what gives you the right to steal, um?'

'To uncover the secrets you wish to conceal, you mean. Do you know who Copeland is?'

Her question confused him. He'd expected Madeleine to protest about the mere handful of cats, dogs, and monkeys they sacrificed over the years. 'I don't see what... He's... Um... He's a gifted man.'

'Brilliant, one might say. Exceptional.' Anne stepped forward.

'How um... would you know?'

'I've worked with him before.'

'Really?' Bonnaire cleared his throat. 'Well, then you know how lucky we are he's onboard.'

'Lucky or unfortunate.' Anne paced around the table toward him and, to Bonnaire's dismay, he took a step back, uncertain which of the three menaced him more.

'Where... did you um... meet?'

'I can't say. As you know from your own paperwork, Copeland listed quite a few facilities where he's worked. He's not been honest about them, used false names for several. Seems like dishonesty is a trait you share, though on this occasion I approve. At least he's maintained his discretion. What he hasn't told you is in at least one of those places they let him go, and some of those where he wasn't dismissed, his superiors didn't always approve of his methods.'

'Oh that,' Bonnaire scoffed, catching three combined expressions a second later and realising that perhaps his reaction was not the best. 'Look, he um... told me of a few of those instances. Not with any specifics, of course. Didn't give away any secrets. Explained how too often those in charge shackled his hands. I wanted to free the man, that's all. Release his full potential.'

'His free potential to do what?' Anne stepped closer. So close that with a single step he could strike her.

Not that he'd hit a woman no matter how she aggravated him, but a glance at her husband said best thing was not to

142

even entertain such a notion.

'I wanted him to...' Bonnaire glanced at his daughter. 'Never mind. I wanted one thing, he another. We agreed one project to be a pay-off for the um... other.'

'How?'

'Well there's this gun—'

'This isn't about a gun, though I've an inkling what that may be. What else was he doing for you?' Anne insisted.

'Well... the specifics escape me, I um... admit. There are several...'

Madeleine approached. 'What was he doing for you, Father?'

'Medical based work, I assure you. For the good... of women, if you must know.'

'How?'

'I left that to him.' Bonnaire rallied around. Who were they to demand this? His daughter had a right, perhaps, but the other two...

'To achieve what?' Anne persisted.

'Medicines to help women. Look, I must protest. This is um... the institute's business.'

Anne took that step, closing the distance, and by the light in her eye Bonnaire couldn't help wondering whether *she* might strike *him*. 'What women? How?'

'They're um... to make them... um...'

'Make them what?' William Bishop spoke up for the first time, a hard unwelcome edge to his tone.

'Happier!' Bonnaire let out the truth in a frustrated rush.

'What do you mean?' His own daughter now advanced, the three of them essentially boxing him in. Anger hardened his nerve. 'I wanted something... Madeleine you have to understand. I always hated seeing your mother so unhappy, especially toward the end.'

A series of expressions ran over her face. 'The end? You mean when she was dying?'

'That and before.'

'Mother regretted some things in her life, but she wasn't unhappy.'

'No, well... um... Depends on one's point of view. I just wanted to make women like you and your mother... Look, it's delicate territory.'

'Explain yourself.' Madeleine slowly and precisely pronounced each word, tone clipped, gaze ablaze.

'I wanted to help women be more content.'

For a second he believed Madeleine had stepped back, but it was more like shock dealt her a blow and she fell back a pace.

'Content?' She blinked rapidly, gaze searching. 'God, I don't know you at all.' The words whispered out like an accusation.

'And how was Copeland going to help?' Anne asked.

At first, Bonnaire thought she asked after the medical implications with genuine scientific curiosity, but one look at her face told him the truth. Anne and Madeleine were both furious.

'But don't you see, this is precisely what—'

'I suggest you shut up now,' Bishop advised.

'You did it all,' Madeleine accused. 'You funded Copeland's work. You got the crystal he wanted added to the list, and if someone noted the loss, you would have let Copeland blame it on Larousse. It's the only thing that makes sense. There's no other reason the consignment should have gone to Copeland's lab.'

'How was Copeland helping?' Anne's anger spilled over into her voice. 'What method?'

'The method is beyond me.' Bonnaire turned his attention to Anne rather than deal with his daughter's accusations. 'It's all to do with altering forms on the molecular level. Dangerous stuff, I understand. One with many wide-reaching applications. Both his and mine.' He passed his gaze over all three. 'Look, he's years away from perfecting anything. It's not as if I took no precautions. It's not like he will have a breakthrough overnight.'

'Oh, Father.' Madeleine shook her head. 'I've known for some time your best days are behind you, but I never took you for a fool.'

CHAPTER FIFTEEN
A Trick of the Light or Eyesight

THE CHILL from the flagstone floor seeped into Madeleine's limbs. Maybe if she sat still long enough she would freeze? Inside she was already an icicle. If she were an ice queen, her father transformed into a queen's impish sidekick. His back bowed, his brow drew down, and his eyes appeared sunken in dark hollows. Guilt drew an unpleasant mask over his face.

After spilling all, he kept saying, 'I didn't know. I didn't know,' leaving Madeleine to bite back the retort, 'You should have done.'

Someone should hold her father responsible but, if true, much of the blame was not his alone. She should have kept a closer, more watchful eye on what went on at the institute, not followed so blindly. Try as she might she could not heap all the culpability at his feet. She'd sensed something wrong with Cooper... Copeland, she corrected, and done nothing about it. The worry of an underlying 'wrongness' to the institute had haunted her for months and the simple fact was, she hadn't asked enough questions. Hadn't harassed her father enough.

Because she didn't want to know the truth.

Madeleine pressed fingers to her brow as another headache loomed. Not now. She had no time to be ill. She needed to be on standby for when Anne needed help. Not that she wanted Anne involved with this, not now she understood the truth. If anything happened to Anne or to Bill, Madeleine would never forgive herself. The thought nibbled at her from the inside. She carried enough guilt and couldn't stand to carry any more. Her father's fault, but equally hers...

Anne stepped into the room. Madeleine straightened at

once. 'Time to go?' She projected a business-like tone.

'Not yet. Why don't we go for a walk?'

'A walk?' Unable to conceal the little snap in her voice, Madeleine frowned at the outside view then back at Anne. Ah... So, Anne wanted to talk. Although she would rather avoid the moment, Madeleine glanced at her father, the man oblivious to their presence, let alone what they discussed. She reached across the table and clasped his wrist. 'We're just going to step out for some air.'

Took him a moment for him to give her a nod, but whether he took in any of her actual words, she couldn't tell. Madeleine rose, following Anne, pausing in the hallway to don a coat, hat, scarf, and gloves. The wind nipped her cheeks as she stepped out.

Without waiting for Anne, Madeleine walked around the side of the house to where they would gain shelter from the wind. There she stopped, knowing Anne caught up by the sound of her boots on the paving stones.

She tried to conceal her feelings by focusing her attention on the problem. The ruse didn't work.

'You mustn't shoulder all this.' Anne voice broke through, silenced the wind.

'I should have done something.'

'What would you do?'

'I don't know, but I should have known.'

'Even then—'

Madeleine spun. 'I should have known my father lied!'

Anne stepped back a pace, making Madeleine take stock of herself – hands fisted, eyes wide, lips pulled back into a snarl, a second away from growling like a wild animal. This was to what her father reduced her.

'How dare he? How dare he!' Madeleine hugged herself. 'How dare he falsify papers and take Copeland on staff without at least telling me and explaining himself?'

She flinched when she felt Anne's hand rest on her shoulder. Her friend spoke not a word, but her comfort opened a floodgate of sorrow.

'Where do we go from here, Anne? I had my life mapped out, or part of it. The institute was to be mine. The only other thing I wanted was a relationship, and I was beginning to like

Paul. What future might we have now? What future the institute? And what trust can I ever place in my father again? And before I can deal with any of that I must stop this thing.'

'No. *We* must stop whatever Copeland has done. You're not alone.'

'Why, Anne? Why you and Bill?'

'Because if I connect this strangeness to the case we covered years ago, for all I know the whole of humanity may be at risk.'

'What do you mean?'

Anne never really talked about her work, and now Madeleine had to wonder just what that work was.

'I'm only telling you this because the situation may be urgent and because I trust you not to divulge anything I tell you,' Anne began. 'Not unless we're both in a position where we believe it's necessary,' she added before Madeleine voiced the objection that lay on her tongue. 'We encountered a... creature, for want of a better description, several years ago. It appeared like a shadow, with the ability to slide down walls, through small spaces. It appeared to feed in some manner and for that purpose went after the youngest... food source available.'

'Animals?'

Anne avoided her gaze. 'No.'

'Children?' Madeleine couldn't conceal her shock. 'That's terrible.'

'Yes, it is and yes, children, but not always. If there were none, it would choose from those available. It... infected – again, not a perfect description – a young NCO and during a transfer where the people I worked for planned to transport him to a more secure facility, this creature... melted the capsule in which he was being moved. Again, melted is the wrong explanation. It altered things on a molecular level.'

'And it escaped?'

'No. They used a gun, a light-gun Copeland helped to construct to eradicate it, or so we believed.'

'Why do I feel there's so much more to this story?'

'Because there is. And it ended in one of the creepiest adventures I've experienced, but there's no time to tell you it all even if I wanted. What you need to know is that the case involved this shadow being and—'

'There's a shadow involved now, so it's all connected with Copeland at the heart.'

'It would appear so, though I cannot say for sure.' Anne paced. 'There's something... different about this. I need to speak to Copeland. We need to know what he's been up to.'

Finally, Madeleine felt she could do something productive. 'Then let's all head up to the institute now and see whether we can catch ourselves a crazy professor.'

'There's nothing here. Nothing except for the box, anyway. And I suspect it's only on site because he didn't see a way to remove it undetected.'

Having first checked the security book and then with Paul, who confirmed no one had seen Copeland that morning, they'd entered the second lab to find it much as before. Only this time they performed a closer inspection.

Anne ran her fingers along the outside of the box, feeling a strange hum. The contraption still drew power, but the fact she felt it indicated crude work. She traced the cable to a socket low down beneath one workbench and disconnected it.

'Might we not determine more if we work out which crystals he used?'

Paul's question was not a terrible one, but glancing at the stones in the box revealed the problem with that. They had burned out, become blackened husks. Either Copeland fulfilled his work and needed them no longer or he was out of luck. Though Bonnaire had arranged for the acquisition even he didn't know what they were. Anne compared Paul's almost completed list with that of the original manifesto. Many of the crystals listed as Unknown Origin including the ones Copeland stole. If he knew what they were when others did not, Anne suspected the unknown origin to be not of this world.

'I fear we'll discover it's one of those things that only Copeland is aware of. Unless we find documentation or can trace his sources, we're floundering. And we'll waste time.' While sure she gained all the details she needed, Anne required time, the one thing she sensed running out on them. 'We need to know where Copeland has been since...' She glanced across at Bill. 'Since I last worked with him. All those he had contact with. If there are things he doesn't wish us to know, he'll have tried to hide them.'

'What about his rooms? Is he staying on-site?' Bill asked.

'Yes.' Madeleine rose from the chair at the desk, pushing back paperwork with a huff of disgust, having clearly found nothing. 'We can go there now.' She hesitated. 'Paul, you may as well accompany us.'

'I... I... I don't think we've um,' her father began. 'Sunk so low as to break into a man's room.'

'We need not break in, Father. We can get the emergency key from security and this time I won't need to go about stealing it as I did the one for your office.'

Bonnaire flushed, but no one took any notice except Paul, who appeared to be realising he didn't know all the details.

Anne followed Madeleine, Bill and Bonnaire in tow, Paul maintaining a polite distance. Without hesitation, Madeleine headed for the room behind the security desk, bringing the guard to his feet fast. He moved to step into her path, blanching under her challenging stare. The man gazed across to Bonnaire to seek his help, a slight shake of his head and a downcast gaze Bonnaire's only response.

With minutes, Madeleine returned. The group walked across the courtyard over to another building where many staff lived on site.

'I'm not sure what I imagined, but this isn't it,' Anne said.

The building looked bright and warm. Although unsure why, Anne struggled with the idea Bonnaire would skimp when it came to housing his staff.

Madeleine sniggered at Anne's comment. 'There's a game's room with snooker and a chess board, and a communal library set out rather like a club, complete with reading areas and log fires.' The amusement vanished from her tone. 'Apparently my father stinted on nothing except his ethics.'

Anne did her best not to wince. Although she'd not brought this down on her friend, Anne couldn't shake the notion that part of the blame belonged to her. Maybe thanks to the strange dreams that plagued her on the way here. Maybe because of some other reason. She'd never expected to cross paths with Copeland again. Small wonder she felt such unease.

She followed Madeleine up a flight of stairs to Copeland's room.

The moment the door was opened, Bill pushed past both women, going inside first. Anne almost rolled her eyes, but she let him check the situation, walking in only when he called.

Her jaw fell open at the sight that met her eyes.

Drawings covered the walls. Anne stepped closer taking it all in.

Sketches, though it was impossible to tell whether Copeland made them. Some were articles cut from newspapers and magazines. Other pages torn from books. She pushed aside her natural instinct to object at the sacrilege.

Stories from many places all over the world. All displaying different shadow people.

'I'd think they were… I don't know. Ghosts maybe? If I believed in such things.' Madeleine's voice filled with wonder and question. She stood before an image of a hallway lined on either side by what appeared to be shadows of people. If a light source existed, and people stood in the hall to cast the shapes, they should have overlapped, but these didn't. 'Do you think the photo is a fraud?'

'It's a possibility, but I don't think Copeland would waste his time for long on things he believed fictitious,' Anne said.

Although as taken with the images as Madeleine was, Anne noted how Paul edged closer to her friend, a man trying to protect the woman he loved. Sentiment tugged at her lips though she fought the smile.

'Not all these stories can be based on fact.' Bill sounded troubled.

'Not all. Or not on facts as we know them. Remember that's all the unexplained is – truths not yet uncovered.' Anne concentrated on reading material Copeland ringed in red. One circle caught her attention. 'It speaks here about figures inhumanly tall, able to expand and contract.'

'Exactly like a shadow.' Madeleine crossed over to her to read the article. 'The perception of the height, length, or size of a shadow is determined by the light placement and distance between that which cast the shadow, and the surface on which it appears.' Madeleine moved her head as she scanned the page.

'God, they talk about the shadow being camouflage. It's as if they're talking about aliens.'

Anne and Bill exchanged a glance but remained silent.

'Hell, they *are*,' Madeleine exclaimed as she read on. 'Beings from other worlds, or other dimensions... All this time and I didn't realise how crazy Cooper truly is. A madman right in our midst and I didn't see.'

As much as Anne wished to correct Madeleine's assumption, she didn't need Bill's unwavering gaze to remind her of things about which she couldn't speak.

As Anne scanned the evidence, another image held her transfixed. A dark shape leaning over a man, as he reclined in bed, black except for white holes where its eyes should be. Her dream returned, with it the sensation of shrinking under the gaze of some unseen beast, crawling closer until it stood taller than she. Holding her frozen, descending until nothing existed but the dark and the flash of its eyes.

'Doctors seem to connect the appearance of shadow people with sleep paralysis and neurological disorders.' Paul shocked Anne out of her sinister thoughts. The man stood reading from many pages scattered across the room's only table. 'Although clearly it's not what Professor Cooper... I mean, Copeland, believes.'

'The man is mad.' Bonnaire ran a hand across his brow. 'I must apologise. I'm um... so sorry, my dear. I made a dreadful mistake.'

'You think hiring a man you now see as demented is the mistake?' Madeleine rounded on her father.

Before the issue became one of Madeleine's righteous anger with her father, Anne broke in.

'A neurological disorder may apply sometimes, but it doesn't explain a shared psychosis.' She tapped another article pinned to the wall. A report of a shared experience between a husband and wife who stated they both saw a strange shadow or smoke-like being in their bedroom at night.

'Such things are um... a trick of the light or eyesight.'

'Not always.' Anne looked to Bonnaire and, as though something in her stare took the strength out of him, he sank on the bed, turning pale. Instinct told her to push. 'Tell me, what spooks you?'

Four people stared at the institute's director. Hesitation flittered through his gaze, but they waited and he said, 'I was in Copeland's lab and I thought…' He shook his head. 'But no, it couldn't be.' He met their collective gaze. 'I thought I saw shadows gathering under his desk.'

'I too thought I saw something in his room.' Madeleine looked ashamed of the confession.

'And me.' Paul didn't sound embarrassed, busy peering at yet another document. 'It says here sometimes shadow people can be dangerous.'

Victor Bonnaire blanched, but Bill said, 'I can't speak of that, but I can tell you some of the things Copeland was involved with were beyond dangerous. If he's meddled with what we think…'

Paul Larousse and Victor Bonnaire stared at the others and in unison asked, 'What are you talking about?'

CHAPTER SIXTEEN
A Deeper Longing

ANNE DECIDED she needed to talk to the girl, Lara Moulin. She couldn't approach her through the authorities, though, and her parents, as to be expected, kept an eye on their daughter. As were all the parents in the vicinity. Lara's name emerged from a vague report – namely, as the most recent girl in a long line of girls seen in Christophe Legrand's company. Journalists used the term flirting. Also, someone found Legrand's body out back in the forest close to the Moulin's property. Didn't take much to add up the numbers, but Lara's father met Anne with the same fury she suspected he used with any reporters and the local police.

'If Legrand was out there, he was up to no good. No doubt stalking our poor girl, you sad excuse for a…' There followed a line of profanity, though the embarrassment was his; the man became red in the face under Anne's unwavering gaze. Fortunately, his French was not garbled like Noyer's, but Anne could have done without understanding most of the bad language.

'You realise your animosity makes you an ideal suspect should the cause of death prove not to be natural?'

Various departments still argued over that fact and the rumours of something having killed the young man in the woods led to speculation. While *Monsieur* Moulin was not a suspect and not likely to be, so far no coroner could come up with a means by which a human brought about the Legrand boy's death. Moulin was not to know this.

'Forgive me. I… It's been a difficult week.' The redness faded as he stood towering over her, appearing to digest her words. 'You say you're here to assess my girl?'

'This is traumatic for many in the area. I'm simply assessing whether anyone requires trauma counselling. While it appears Lara and Christophe were not an item...' Anne paused conspiratorially and gave Moulin a strained smile. 'Young women can be more easily flattered than older ones. I am sure Lara is—'

'She's a good girl.' Moulin's expression brought a rumble of thunder to mind.

'I'm sure she is. Doesn't mean Legrand was a decent boy. Someone found his body close to your home. Lara may experience some misplaced feelings, even if not involved. Guilt for example.'

'Guilt?'

'If Christophe planned to see the girl, with her permission or not. If his intended destination was this property, clearly he did not have your consent. He might not have had Lara's. Likely didn't.' Anne kept her speech formal. 'Either way, he never made it here before someone attacked him or he was overcome by some ailment yet to be determined. There's a chance Lara mistakenly believes if he'd not come, or reached here before he collapsed, something may have saved him. She could even think she should have been the one to rescue him. The truth is whatever overcame him worked fast and I wish to make certain she knows she is not responsible.'

'Well, of course she's not.'

'You and I know that, *Monsieur* Moulin. But we are experienced adults.'

'So, you... want to talk to her?'

'A few words. Thirty minutes alone, at most.'

'Alone?' A frown appeared on Moulin's face. 'Where did you say you were from?'

'Central Youth Bereavement and Disaster Counselling. A new structure bridging local authorities with education departments. You're welcome to sit in. I cannot speak to Lara without your permission, but women of Lara's age are more open with other women. Reveal more when not under the watchful eyes of their parents.'

She waited, striving to put across the impression they had plenty of time, heart racing. He might wish to check her credentials, or the local police might turn up if only to check on the family. If they suspected him, could be a real possibility but, for now, they weren't seeking a human culprit.

'Her mother's gone shopping.' Moulin stared beyond Anne, down the road as if wishing his wife to magically appear.

Anne remained silent, stood her ground. All the better for her – the wife might be more difficult to get by than the father – but only if Moulin hurried up and decided. She wanted to ask when he expected his spouse to return, but decided it was best not to.

'Come in. I'll tell Lara you're here.' He hesitated in the hallway. 'Where do you usually do this kind of thing?'

'A lounge or kitchen if you prefer, though I sometimes talk to people in their own rooms where they often feel most comfortable.'

'Very well. Wait here and if she'll speak to you, I'll shout.'

Anne gave him a nod and bided her time, the perfect image of patience as she stared around the narrow but long hallway. White walls. Grey carpeting. Black banisters. Photos in black frames lined the walls, family members all.

'*Madam* Bishop, please come up.'

As she ascended the stairs, the rows of pictures continued. With a glance, she witnessed Lara's progression from baby to a teenager. The Moulins appeared to dote on their daughter a little too much.

'Lara, this is *Madam* Bishop.'

A pale, thin girl stood in the doorway to her room. Anne held out a hand. After a moment's hesitation, Lara shook it, Anne saying, 'I'm pleased to meet you.'

When the girl didn't say anything, her father sighed. 'Lara, where are your manners?'

'I'm sorry. It's good to meet you, too.' She did not sound happy. More bewildered, which was understandable.

'You don't mind having a small chat?'

Lara glanced at her father, before shaking her head.

'I'll leave you two alone.' He grunted but stepped away, lingering. 'Lara, if you need me...'

'I'll call.' Lara nodded, opening the door wider, allowing Anne to walk in.

An overly pink room met Anne's gaze. Not that she detested the colour but this... for a girl of Lara's age felt wrong.

'It's hideous.' Lara's voice carried a hint of strength not previously present.

'It's...' Anne meant to say it's not so bad but didn't get the chance.

'You don't need to pretend to like it. My parents don't want me to grow up.'

Explained a lot, namely Lara's interest in a young man like Christophe Legrand. Photos of him showed a good-looking teen who believed himself handsome, the perpetual smile more for himself than the camera.

'*Madam* Bishop...'

'Anne, please.'

Lara gave a slow uncertain nod. 'Won't you sit down?' She gestured to the only chair in the room – also pink – and Anne sat, grateful not to share the bed.

'I should tell you I'm fine. I don't need to talk.'

'May be true, but it won't hurt.'

'What do you want to know?' Lara plucked at a fluffy half-bald cushion on the bed, its condition suggestive of a nervous habit.

'As I explained to your father, if you're feeling any sense of unease over what happened...'

'Unease?' Lara stared straight at her. Gone was the young fragile girl. 'I had nothing to do with Christophe's death.'

'No. I simply meant if he made his way here to see you...'

'I've said if it's true I didn't know it.' A hard edge crept into Lara's voice.

Something felt off here. Anne planned to spin the same tale she fed the father, try to coax the girl into telling her what happened on the night. Something told Anne conciliatory talk would make Lara hostile. Anne met Lara's gaze.

'Is there anything you wish to tell me?'

Lara's eyes narrowed. 'What kind of counsellor are you? Did you take an oath of some kind? Is what I tell you between only us?'

'It's most definitely between us. Is there something you want to say you can't tell anyone else?'

The girl wanted to talk. The quivering lower jaw and brightness in her eyes gave her away, but she dithered. 'I shouldn't say. You'll use it against me... or against...'

'Against who?'

'I don't know.' Lara gazed to the window as though she saw outside, which from this height and angle was impossible. 'Against whoever or whatever went after Christophe.' She flicked her gaze back to Anne. 'You tell anyone this I'll deny it. Say you tried to make me believe untrue things. Say you wanted me to give a statement.'

Anne gave the girl a single nod, not bothering to argue the implications of that scenario, none of which were important.

'Christophe got what he deserved. I agreed to meet him but he…' A rosy hue appeared high on Lara's cheekbones.

Anne took a not-so-wild guess. 'Things got out of control? He wasn't who you believed him to be?'

Lara nodded, eyes blazing, though she didn't look at Anne as she went over the events of that night. 'I wanted to talk. He wanted to…' She bit at her lip. 'I refused. He called me a spoilsport. Said I'm weird. God, I'm an idiot.' She shook her head in clear self-disgust.

'You're not. You're young. And some people have charm. Some expect to get what they want. It's alien to them when they don't.'

What she said seemed to speak to the girl. 'Yeah. Yes. That's how he was. I told him no. Said we'd not even been out on a date. He acted all…' She searched for the word.

'Aggressive? Insulted? Aloof?'

'All those things, I guess. I was so stupid. He wanted me to apologise to him. I ran away from him and he… He tried to grab me. I fell.' She stopped talking, a frown furrowing her forehead. She curled cushion fluff around a finger.

'Lara, what happened? What did you see?'

'I don't know. A shape. A man, I thought my father at first. But it wasn't him. I know it wasn't because I heard his voice when I made it back home. My father, upstairs in his bedroom. Both my parents talking. The thing that went after Christophe, it was weird.' Lara stopped picking the cushion, her whole focus on Anne. 'You're after it, aren't you? It's why you want to know. You can't.'

Although Anne understood, she wanted to hear Lara say it. 'Can't?'

'You can't hurt it. Whatever it was, I'm sure if it hadn't

157

distracted Christophe I wouldn't have got away. It saved me. If you find it, I want you to thank it for me. You can't hurt it. Because you shouldn't.'

Bill stared out into the woods. 'Where do you think he might go?'

'What do you mean?'

Upon her return from visiting the Moulin girl – though she learned little more than what they thought they already knew – Anne had told him how speaking to the young girl upset her on many levels. The boy attacking her, and the hatred Lara now felt for him, bothered Anne. As did the endorsement of his murder shining from Lara's eyes. As Anne said, a person Lara Moulin's age shouldn't be so scared. So vengeful. Bill agreed but said he understood Lara's feelings.

'Whether Copeland is with the creature, he's human. He has needs. So where might he go and still be able to hide the creature?'

'Is he?'

Bill frowned. 'Anne?'

'A theory of mine.'

'Which is?'

'I don't believe we're searching for two entities. I think we're hunting one.'

'You mean...' Bill struggled to digest what Anne said. 'You think Copeland *is* the creature?'

'Not the shadow creature.' Anne gave an infinitesimal shake of her head. 'Not as we knew it. I think this is something else. I think Copeland... I don't know, but the shadow's behaviour is so different to before, and with Paul believing the professor experimented on himself... Let's say I think Copeland's become a shadow of his former self.'

Despite the seriousness of the situation her lips quirked. Bill closed his eyes and groaned. He'd best keep things on track less they fall about laughing, though any laughter might come with a touch of hysteria.

'Even if you're right, Copeland's still partly human, isn't he? At least sometimes. If we go on the assumption that he has needs the same as anyone else, at some point he'll search for food. It's cold out and getting colder. He may need to hanker down.'

'I'm not sure about any of that.' Anne threw down her pen. 'I don't know how he's changing form, whether he requires a dose of some formula he's invented and it wears off, or if he can change at will. I have no clue as to his needs. Weather may not affect him. Hunger... It's hard to guess what he consumes. If he has no mouth, no stomach... I'm sorry, Bill. This is beyond my abilities.'

Bill fought the sense of dismay that came over him upon hearing Anne's words.

'Given the chance to understand what Copeland has done, and what he tried to do, maybe then I can help him. But right now, I can't.'

'Trying to do?' Bill put his back to the window, though the thought that a monstrous shadow might be out there watching made his shoulder blades itch.

'Bill, I don't think for a minute Copeland planned to become this... thing.'

'He is rather obsessed with these shadow people.' Bill reminded Anne of all the documentation found in his room.

'Yes, but he's too great a man for us to draw so simple a conclusion.'

'Too great a man?' Bill did nothing to hide his distaste, his tone harsh. 'We are talking about Copeland here.'

'I'm not referencing his personality. I'm referring to the scientist.'

'If you're right – and I know you're not telling the whole truth about why you think you are – he may no longer be that man. He may be insane.'

Anne looked down, making Bill believe his accusation. She hid something. Not... professional. More personal. He was sure. Anne would withhold nothing she considered essential, but if something affected her, maybe she would for a short while. Her instincts were often spot-on in ways he didn't entirely understand.

'It's possible this damaged his mental state,' she said, 'but he's not exactly rampaging.'

'It's because he's gone to ground.'

'Is it, though? And is it because we've forced him to? He'll have watched. Will know we've been in his lab and his room

159

by now. I think the most important thing…'

'Yes?'

'He needs resources. A laboratory.'

'And he can't use any here.'

'Precisely, so where would he go? Where might we find him?'

Anne as good as repeated Bill's earlier question but still with no answer. 'Maybe there's somewhere else,' Bill suggested.

'Perhaps, but unless Madeleine or her father know of it, it's a dead end. Copeland's obsession with these apparent myths must evolve from a deeper longing.'

A deeper longing? Was Copeland capable of such a thing? Aware of his biased thoughts in part from his personal experience of the man and the way Old Spence viewed him, Bill tried to understand things from Anne's perspective. She believed Copeland brilliant and that might be so, but did it explain why he would do something so hideous to himself? Still, she had a point.

'If there is a reason… Might it help us get through to him?'

Anne sat bolt upright. 'I'm lacking sleep. Thank you, Bill. You are right. Not only might insights into Copeland's motivation provide us with more information, when we find him it may help me talk sense to the man.'

Bill said nothing but apparently didn't need to, his intent likely written across his face.

'I'm not trying to make excuses for him.' Anne met Bill's gaze. 'I'm saying he might not be responsible for his actions. If he is the creature, he's no longer fully human. There's no way to tell what it's done to him.'

'So how do you expect to reach him? What makes you think he'll listen to you?'

'I don't know he will. I only know I must try.'

'Fine. We'll do it your way, but I'm telling you, Anne, I still want a way to defeat him. Kill him if need be. Subdue him at least. I don't want you trying to save his life until we find a way to overcome him should it prove necessary. I'm sorry, but I mean it, Anne. I want to take all the precautions we can. I will help you if I can, but I will not place you or anyone in harm's way.'

'But wouldn't it be better if we can do so without further

bloodshed on any side?' She scanned the papers she held in her hand, the few scientific notes they'd located. 'There's nothing here, and I don't believe we'll find it in the institute. I need help to track down the information I require.'

She didn't need to complete the thought: she was tempted to call Pemberton.

'If we try to bring anyone else into this…'

'Now who's not talking sensibly?' Anne said, clearly irritated, though not necessarily with him.

'There will be all sorts of diplomatic complications. You cannot tell Brigadier Pemberton any of this.'

'Coming from you after a speech about saving everyone, it's a surprise.'

'I'm not saying don't call him in, but he'll do this by regulations. You've worked with him longer than me; you know what a stickler he is. If we had a more flexible commander…. But we don't. Once local authorities step in, they'll oust us out and as ironic as it is, we're the only ones who may stop Copeland.'

Anne opened her mouth but said nothing for a few seconds before admitting, 'As mad as it sounds, I believe you're right. Either you'll manage by force or I'll manage by persuasion.'

Persuasion? Bill doubted it but he recognised the right moment to end an argument with his wife.

CHAPTER SEVENTEEN
The Attack

'**ARE THERE** any local storage facilities in the area?' Bill asked Madeleine.

Her expression of puzzlement swiftly cleared. 'There's a thought. And yes. Three within a twenty-mile radius.'

'The nearest?'

She told him. Bill gave the address consideration but shook his head. 'Too close. We'll start further out.'

'Wastes time.'

'True, but I trust my instincts on this one. When we get there, we won't know which of the units may belong to Copeland. And I don't have the resources I usually would.' Bill sagged, the joy of his light-bulb moment fading because it became yet another problem to overcome.

Madeleine sat in her chair tapping a finger against the arm, a sure sign of her brain cells at work. 'The local gendarme?'

Bill shook his head. 'They'd want to investigate. Would confiscate anything they found, and everything would come out. The institute's connection to Copeland, the story of what he may have done.'

'I don't care about the institute's future at the moment.'

'I appreciate you don't, but bringing the institute down won't help solve this.'

'He's right,' Paul Larousse broke in.

Something had changed him, subdued him; Bill had just about forgotten he stood in the room. Maybe what Paul claimed to see in the woods was the cause. Bill had yet to see the Shadowman – Copeland in his altered state, if Anne were correct – and he didn't look forward to the experience.

Paul grimaced. 'Draw attention to the institute and the

next thing you know there'll be mob rule. People at the gates with pitchforks and burning lanterns demanding to burn all the monsters we're creating inside. Maybe the scientists responsible, too.'

Madeleine opened her mouth, but said nothing.

Bill got back to the problem playing through his mind. Any storage facility in the area would likely only have padlocked doors, and he could break into those. The issue was one of which room. He couldn't open them all without attracting attention. They had to get into the facility itself, past security, if there happened to be any. Or another set of more secure doors and, for all he knew, there might be surveillance at the location. He needed his wits here. To rely on his resources. Assets of which he had many, but breaking and entering weren't generally on the list.

'One other man might know whether Copeland stores anything elsewhere.' Bill gazed at Madeleine. He waited while his words sunk in. Her eyes widened at the suggestion and… did he spot a flash of anger? She gave him a nod.

'Let's go speak to my father again.'

'You don't know what you're asking.'

'Believe me, Father, I know too well.' Madeleine leaned over the table and stared into his eyes. 'Copeland likely killed the boy. In fact, I'm certain. If Anne is right, and he is the shadow, he chased me in the car park of our own facility. What if he's out there?' She pointed to a window, behind which dusk fell. 'What if he's out there watching us? He can creep in through any gap and murder us as we sleep. I want to stop this before things get worse. Anne wants to talk him down. I support her. Hell, one death is more than enough and there may be real scientific advances to Copeland's discovery. But if we don't do all we can to contain this, none of it will matter. Word *will* get out because I'll make sure. Not that I think I'll need to. The news will leak. Our own security guards know something is wrong with the way we're acting. Maybe another scientist wonders about Copeland. Someone will talk, investigate, and it will mean the end of the institute, or our careers, yours and mine, and all the scientists on staff. We'll be lucky not to face criminal charges.'

'But... But...' Her father's hands flailed as if he tried to snatch an answer from the tabletop. 'I didn't know. This isn't what he was supposed to do!'

To watch her father flounder was hard, but she couldn't afford to back down. 'Father, we don't know Copeland's full capabilities. We don't know how strong he is. He can pretty much come and go as he pleases. What if he breaks into a nuclear facility and causes a meltdown? Oh, not that I think it's his agenda,' she added when her father tutted at her – a familiar sound he often used when he thought her ridiculous. 'But it's the threat of a man who is little more than smoke. He can do anything he wants.'

'And why would he want to murder us?'

'Maybe not us. Maybe not me. But maybe Anne. They share a history. With people she knows. He's a threat to the innocent. He's proved so. I dread to think what he's capable of to those he deems less than virtuous. Anne's husband is waiting for me outside. If you don't give me what I need, I will leave and call him in here and I'm sure he'll get the information out of you in any way necessary. Anne is his wife. She may be in danger. Copeland is a threat to my friend, and it makes him an enemy of Bill's and of mine.'

Her father stared at her, his gaze imploring, but he eventually nodded. He rose from the table, moving like an old man. Madeleine pushed down the shock of how much all this aged him. Her father moved across the room to an old bureau less ancient than he looked now, removed a key from his pocket, and unlocked a drawer. From within he took out another key. Pausing, he scribbled a note on a piece of paper and returned, handing both over.

Madeleine glanced at his writing, stared at her father. 'Thank you.' She moved to leave.

'I really didn't know. What I wanted... Your mother was happy. She really was. But she wanted more than I could provide for her. Times change and I'm sure...' He paused, Madeleine waiting.

Let that be the end of it. She had heard enough.

'The formula he told me he was working on, it wasn't meant to do what it does. All I wanted—'

'Enough. I've heard enough.' Madeleine leaned on the

164

doorframe for support. 'Don't you get that your excuses will never be enough? Never be reparation. So enough, Father. Just... no more.' She took a step, lingered. 'Stay safe.' Without waiting for a reply, she hurried out and got into Bill's car.

'Where to?' he asked her.

'Where you surmised. Good deduction. I have the entry code to the outside and the number of the storage unit.'

'Key?'

She held it up.

'I can drop you back. Go alone.'

'No. I'm tired of sitting behind a desk. It's good to be moving. To feel as if I'm doing something practical. Now let's go see what we can find.'

Bill glanced across at Madeleine as she flinched yet again. Every time the car hit a bump or a dip, she winced, as if she expected a blow-out any moment. She feared an attack, he was sure.

Hadn't occurred to him that Copeland might spot them, and... What? Attack a moving car? Would he do that? Could he?

'He can't know what we're up to.'

'You can't be certain.' Madeleine slumped in her seat, stopped flinching, but her hands curled into fists. 'Anne seems to think he's confused and may not be entirely responsible.'

'That may be true.' Bill flicked on the wipers as yet more rain started to fall.

'But doesn't that make him more dangerous? Aren't we better off if he's rational?'

'Hard to tell. I've dealt with enough rational threats in my time.' Some of those had been worse than the irrational ones, but he didn't want to tell Madeleine that. She was scared enough.

'He should be ashamed of himself.'

'Who? Copeland?' From what he recalled of the man, Bill wasn't sure what emotions Copeland was capable of.

'No. My father. I've never heard such nonsense from the man.'

No doubt. Nothing Anne had told him had led Bill to believe Bonnaire could act so reckless. Such an idiotic plan.

'Sounds to me as if he blames himself for your mother's death. I think he's feeling if your mother had been more content then maybe she wouldn't have fallen ill.'

'That's crazy talk.'

'Mad thinking, perhaps, but it's amazing what a grieving man can latch onto.'

For some minutes Madeleine did nothing but stare out at the forest through which they passed.

'I said to Anne that my mother's death made me wonder whether love was worth having at all.'

Though he'd had no intention to discuss matters of the heart or pick apart any universal truths about the human condition, Bill said, 'Of course it is. If anything, the bad stuff reveals that things like love are the only true importance in this world.'

'I'm not so sure.'

Bill had no clue what to say, remained focused on the road. Might be best if Madeleine said nothing more, though his instinct said she was going to.

'I overheard my parents talking one time, when mother was dying. Neither of them knew. People believe that death makes life worth living, but she was questioning whether death gave life no meaning at all.'

'She was dying. You can't trust those were her true feelings.'

'No, but I think they were, and I think my father knew and took them onboard. I've asked the same questions in numerous ways. I want to blame him, but maybe his desperate need came out of the simple desire to save his wife and daughter from themselves.'

Maybe. Did Anne know her friend felt this badly? At least Madeleine facing these things might one day help to repair the relationship she had with her father.

'I think...' Madeleine shook her head. 'Ignore me. It's just that I fear something worse.'

The next few seconds stretched out, time slowing. Bill didn't want to stop but he couldn't see a thing, and though by reaction he flicked on the headlights they failed to penetrate. A glance in the rear-view mirror revealed a grey day; ahead an unnatural night had fallen. Should he press his foot hard to the floor or brake? The Shadowman could get in anywhere, through any gap. Drift in through the car's vents. Bill spotted a path through the trees, applied the brake, and twisted the wheel. He transferred his foot to the accelerator as the car slid to a sideways stop and rocked, tyres squealing. At his side, Madeleine gasped, then squealed as the car left the tarmac and went onto rough road.

'What are you doing? We'll hit a tree!'

Bill feared so too, gaze intent on the narrow passage through which he drove. Clearly Madeleine had yet to recognise the threat but as he drove, saying nothing, grip white on the wheel, the woman shifted around to stare behind. Fast glimpses in the mirror showed him the black cloud gaining, and he had no doubt that if it caught up, whether by frustration or by fear, or Copeland no longer being human, they would die the same way as the Legrand boy.

The car fishtailed as he took another turn, the rear end clipping a tree, making Bill wince as he lost the security deposit on the hired car. The thought almost made him laugh, but if he started he feared he'd lose control. He aimed the car for an adjacent road, the turn sharp.

For seconds the car lifted on the driver's side, leaving Bill feeling light, almost weightless. He'd failed. The car was going to tip and that meant they were finished, but just as it seemed the car couldn't possibly fail to roll, it dropped so hard, Bill clicked his teeth together. Had his tongue been caught between, he couldn't be sure he wouldn't have bitten it off.

More rubber burned, but then the car shot forward. When Bill looked behind them it was like the threat had never been.

'We need to go back.' Madeleine twisted in her seat gazing back down the road.

'Can't.'

'But—'

'We can't!' He and Anne had discussed this. As much as Bill hated it, both he and Madeleine, and Paul with Anne, were two couples, each on their own. 'Just because Copeland spotted us doesn't mean he knows where we're going. He's no reason to suspect we're a bigger threat to him than he thinks.'

Took her a moment, but Madeleine nodded. 'You're right. I don't have to like it, but we can't turn back now.'

Bill was glad to hear her say so because he wasn't at all sure he could have resisted had she told him a second time to return to his wife.

'How do you do it?' Paul Larousse asked the moment he saw Anne... Travers, Bishop, whatever her name was.

He closed the door, having let himself into the room where they hid out while Madeleine and Bill went off to search the storage area. Although he and Anne wanted to go with them, it felt right someone stayed behind. If Copeland attacked, one of them had to survive. Apart, they stood more chance of survival, at least until the others returned with whatever research material they might find. Anne's husband argued if Copeland knew of the danger, and attacked, he was more inclined to go after those on the road. Paul didn't want to let Madeleine out of his sight, but he doubted Bill wanted to leave Anne. What the man said, about Anne being their greatest chance of figuring out what Copeland had done, made a great deal of sense. Although he resented that Bill Bishop seemed to put his wife's safety over Madeleine's, the man in reality placed the mission first and Paul respected him for that. He also hated to admit Madeleine would likely have more of a clue should she and Bill find anything, so Paul couldn't go in her place. If he had, it meant leaving the two women they loved alone... and despite both being strong and independent, Paul couldn't help feeling he wanted to protect the woman he cared about, so that idea didn't sit well with him either.

God! Impossible choices. Why was life sometimes filled with impossible choices?

'Sorry. What?' Anne reached for the bag he handed over.

Paul had dived into town to grab food for them both, having found nothing more than biscuits and coffee in the institute. Two bags he set aside for Madeleine and Bill's return.

'I said how do you do it?'

'Do what?'

'Sit back and let your husband head off into danger. Possible danger,' he corrected, not wanting to make either of them more alarmed. 'Yet keep so calm?'

Anne's lips curled. 'Who says I'm calm?'

'You look it.' Paul bit into his baguette amazed to realise

how hungry he was.

'I'm used to this. We've... had our share of adventure.' Anne picked at the bread, staring off into a past Paul found hard to imagine. 'And if you marry someone in the military or any dangerous profession, it's something you must learn to face.'

They both ate in silence for a while.

'Did you notice anything peculiar?' Anne asked.

'No. And I was careful not to be followed. For all the good it does.' Paul shrugged and Anne nodded. The institute was an obvious place for Copeland to search. 'You weren't wrong, though.'

'What do you mean?'

'You said word would get out. Lara Moulin, she was in town with a group of friends. Many of the adults are sneering, looking on, and while I was there, her father turned up and dragged her off home. I asked about all the fuss from the woman behind the counter when I picked up our food. Lara's been talking about how there's something strange going on, some kind of story about a bogeyman.'

Anne frowned. 'Why would she do that? She was grateful to Copeland.'

'I don't know for sure, but I think she's caught up in the notoriety. The teens are circulating all kinds of tales, including one about the evil in town stirring up supernatural forces.'

Anne set down her half-eaten baguette. 'So, pitchforks and torches.'

'If the authorities and parents don't get things under control. The boy's family, well they're all brimstone and retribution.'

'Great.' Anne finished her baguette, sitting quietly.

They sat in silence until Anne spoke.

'They'll be back soon.'

Paul followed Anne's gaze to the clock. Neither said it was a hope more than certainty.

CHAPTER EIGHTEEN
Shadow of His Former Self

'THESE BOXES will take weeks to go through.'

Bill cast an eye over the neat orderly rows. They'd taken a few down and set them on the central table but all appeared to contain papers. Madeleine removed her coat, rolled back her sleeves, and opened several boxes. More of the same things found in Copeland's rooms. Pages. Drawings. Stories. Reports. Shadow people from around the world. Whatever the true basis behind these, he was sure no one ever encountered a Shadowman like Copeland before.

'Some of this may prove useful in time, but it's not what we need.' Madeleine's frustration leaked out.

'No.' There might have been some scientific papers hidden among all it, some pieces important to Anne. If such information existed, they needed several days and more than two people to shift through the contents. Bill searched for something else.

'So, what *are* we looking for?' Madeleine asked.

'I'm not sure.' He'd know when he saw it, unhelpful if true. 'Something...' He scanned the room moving behind the boxes. 'Something larger.'

Like packing cases.

Bill moved behind one rack and found a pile. No sooner did he take hold of the lid from the first, than Madeleine appeared right there to help him. The first half a dozen held nothing but standard scientific equipment, some of it damaged.

'Mind, there's broken glass.'

'So I see.' Madeleine helped Bill lift a packing crate, the tinkle of glass an unsuitable merry tune to the task. 'Wait. What's this?'

The box she referred to appeared different from the rest. More of a suitcase than a crate. A memory nudged at Bill's mind. He'd seen something like this before.

'It can't be.' Bill shifted things out of the way until he cleared a space. The case's two catches were locked. 'I need...' He blinked at the screwdriver Madeleine waved in his face. He took it with grace. 'No wonder Anne likes you so much.'

He swore Madeleine Bonnaire flushed, but he turned his attention to breaking the locks, flicking them open, lifting the lid. He glanced into an empty tray filled with a sponge, vacant cavities designed to hold specific equipment. Unwilling to waste time pondering what the missing items might be, Bill lifted the tray and the lining beneath. He stared, surprised but not shocked. A grin threatened to split his face.

'Hello, baby,' he said, not caring how stupid he sounded. 'Found you at last.'

So this was how Copeland somehow extracted the essence of the shadow creature. How he smuggled the Opticus gun out of the UNIT Warehouse all those years ago was another matter. One likely to interest Pemberton.

'What is it?' Madeleine sounded breathless. 'It's a weapon. That much I can tell. Did Copeland plan to shoot everyone?'

'It's not that kind of firearm.' Bill reached in and lifted it from its concealment. 'I thought this must be what your father was on about when he said Copeland worked on a weapon for him. It's called the Opticus gun.'

Although he had no way to be sure, Bill *knew* this was the same weapon which fired on the shadow creature at that hospital in Scotland and, with luck, had secrets to reveal.

His first instinct said to take it back to Anne, but Bill hesitated. If he couldn't use brawn, he had to rely on intellect and...

The institute was full of intellectuals led by one old affable gent with more going on in his mind than the man pretended he did. Bill wanted to slap himself in the forehead for not thinking of it sooner. His gaze flicked to Madeleine who met his stare.

'Why are you staring at me?'

He didn't answer her right away, cursing his own hesitation. 'This is, for want of a better term, a light gun. Used in Scotland many years ago to eradicate a... shadow. We never knew what the creature was and I'm not sure it matters. It killed. We had to stop it. This did.' The story was more complicated than that, but he didn't have the time or the clearance to explain it all now. 'What I can tell you is Copeland helped develop this weapon.'

'Anne told me some of this.'

Though surprised, Bill was glad because it meant Madeleine was less likely to doubt him. 'I believe he utilised it somehow to collect something I'm not sure even Anne understands.'

'And it led him to become what he is?'

'Yes.'

'And I take it this is all confidential information and you're likely breaking many rules discussing this.'

'I wouldn't if I saw another option.' He gave Madeleine a moment to digest all of it.

'So, what do you need from me?'

He patted the gun. 'This used to run on a generator. A large one. Took several men to haul it around. There doesn't appear to be anything big enough here and I don't think running this weapon would interest Copeland. I think he got all he wanted from it.'

'So why keep it?'

Although her question was beside his point and slightly irritated him, Bill replied. 'I reckon he didn't want it to fall in other hands. His ego wouldn't allow it to be altered or discarded. For all I know he may have foreseen a time when he might use it again. I need a power source for this to work, and I'm thinking technology has moved on in the last eight years.'

'Maybe Anne...?' Madeleine fell silent as Bill continued to stare at her until she read his mind. 'No. She's overstrained, exhausted. We all are but not in the same way. What she's doing is important. What you're asking is something any lesser scientist could work on. Paul. Paul, with my help and maybe from one of the other men on staff, maybe my father. We can solve this.'

Bill grinned. 'I hoped you'd say that.'

*

172

'Anne, take a break.'

Easy for Bill to say after handing her extensive notes. She almost understood but... No. She slumped, trying to make sense of Copeland's experiments.

'Some of this is brilliant, but... I don't know. I don't know if Copeland left out something or I can't figure out something. I can't quite grasp how he did what he's done, let alone conceive of a method to reverse it.'

Bill lowered himself into a chair opposite, his expression one Anne didn't like.

'Anne, are you... certain, this is what you should do with your time?'

'What do you mean?'

'I'm suggesting perhaps your skills might be better suited trying to think of a way to stop this thing.'

'The thing being Copeland.' Anne tried not to bristle. She did her best to see things from Bill's point of view, but her hands clinched, fists screwing up the pages she studied. A violent reaction. She forced her hands to relax and let go of the papers, smoothing them out. 'Despite what he's done, he's still a man.'

The ensuing pause told her Bill would say something unpleasant.

'We don't know that. Fact is we don't know what he is any longer.'

She wanted to argue, unable to fault her husband's logic. 'Fine, but there's something of him in there. He may have killed Christophe, but he reacted to save the girl. I'm sure. If I can reverse this thing, I may save a man's life. I may save countless others.'

Bill opened his mouth, but clearly thought better of whatever he wanted to say because he closed it again.

'I know what you're thinking. It's Copeland, and he's a most unpleasant person, but he's not a terrible one. Fine, so maybe it depends on your definition of terrible.' Anne relented when Bill's eyebrows twitched. 'But he's also brilliant. And who are we to dictate who to save and who we shouldn't?'

'Anne, I don't disagree with you. I understand and your sense of morality and compassion are two of the many things I love and admire about you. I married you for the very qualities you are displaying. In time, if it's possible, I'm not saying we shouldn't try to save Copeland. But my military background demands I stop the immediate threat to the local population, which includes your friend. Then to extend the same protection to all citizens of the world. We don't know what Copeland is capable of, and I fear we may not be able to prevent him doing whatever he wants. Or from spreading more of a...' He hesitated, perhaps searching for the right word. 'From spreading a possible contagion. All that is more important than saving one man.'

The argument always came down to numbers. Sacrifice one to save many. Anne understood. Bill knew she did. Her husband also knew she never liked it. 'You know I must try.'

'Yes. But you know I must do what I can to stop Copeland, by any means. Are you going to hate me if I do?'

'Most certainly not!' How did he think that? Yet how could he not? They sat on two sides of a table, and of an argument, neither wrong nor right. She hadn't been happy to see the Opticus gun, though accepted it was the only likely weapon they had. Never had she been so relieved when Bill said she didn't have to work on it. 'No, Bill. I don't and won't hate you. I understand you have a level of care to the people of this world. It's a duty I share, though sometimes in different ways. I won't stop you in anything you must do. I'll help where I can if needs be. But I won't stop searching for a way to make Copeland human again.'

'I must ask you if there's anything in these papers to help us destroy him.'

Although she knew the question was overdue, she felt ill to have Bill ask it of her. She dipped her head, steadied her breathing, preparing herself for what was to come. How did one destroy something without substance?

'No gun or blade,' Anne said, thinking aloud.

'Gas?' Bill asked. 'Another chemical?'

The Shadowman came from some compound produced by Copeland, so maybe a similar thing was the best form of attack. Anne nodded, irritated with herself to be caught in solving the problem.

'But I'm not sure. I advise against it.'

'I hate to ask, but is it your professional opinion in the face of the enemy or are you still set on saving him?'

'Of course I'm still set on saving him!' Bill flinched as if her gaze scorched his skin. 'But I am not putting anyone at risk to do so. I'm saying if it doesn't work, there's no knowing how he'll react.'

'I realise, but we've no back-up. We don't have Pemberton issuing orders. Only a field of scientists and they are fumbling. I trust you. You know that. But, Anne, I have no jurisdiction here. If we don't stop him the local police will try to, and they will undoubtedly die in the attempt.'

Anne sighed. 'And we sit here picking each other apart. Bill, if a chemical can produce an effect, I'd rather use it to capture him. To contain him, until we reverse what he's done, but if it comes to leaving things to the local authorities...' Anne closed her eyes before finishing. 'Maybe we should do that.'

'What are you saying?'

Although she didn't wish to, Anne opened her eyes and met his stare. 'I can't explain it, but I have a bad feeling.'

'And I respect your instincts, but if it was the case, I'd have to tell them what we know. I'd have to stand by them.'

'Not for any logical reason.'

'It's the decent thing.'

'And if the decent thing gets you killed?'

There was a silence before Bill said, 'That's what you believe.'

'I don't... know.'

'But you know I couldn't let men die alone.'

How do you do it? How do you sit back and let your husband head off into danger yet keep so calm?

Paul's question haunted her.

'I want no one to die.' The words whispered out.

The next time Bill spoke, his voice was gentler. 'Anne, you're an intelligent woman. You understand. This is one of those things to plague all those in service. Whether to go to their deaths for a good cause, despite what it does to their loved ones. Goodness knows I must stand by knowing you put yourself in danger. A far from pleasant experience.'

Anne nodded. She clasped Bill's hand. 'You don't have to say the words.' It would be wrong of Bill to base his decisions

175

on his love for her. 'But, Bill, if you help them and fail, who will lead the survivors? Who will be there to help me contain the threat? We cannot know whether Copeland can breathe or absorb gas and if we try and it fails…'

'The threat could worsen.' Bill patted her hand and lowered his head, a ball of frustration.

'Now do you understand my desire to save Copeland isn't purely one of morality? I want to spare his life. I do, but if we're unable to stop him, it may be our only chance.'

'And the Opticus gun? You found no notes on how to get it working?'

'Nothing so far tells me anything definite, but I will keep reading.'

'We must hope your friends can work it out for themselves.'

Madeleine, Paul and Bonnaire, with a couple of others on site, collaborated on the problem, but Bill had asked Anne to keep a lookout for any notes to help.

Anne shook her head. 'I can't tell you what it may do to him. That it will be any more effective than any of our other ideas.'

'I know. But it's all we have. I best check their progress, but take a short break. If it's only for an hour. You've been reading most of the evening.'

'Please, Bill, don't suggest I nap. If I try to sleep I either won't be able to or I'll sleep too long and feel groggy when I wake.'

'Fair enough. But please stop long enough to get something to eat.'

Anne hesitated, but nodded. Bill was right. Exhaustion hadn't quite set in, but it would be good to stand, to stretch her back, walk about, and refuel. Bill stood by the door waiting for her, unwilling to trust her over even this small thing.

A group hovered outside the local pub tossing back beers. People laughed and joked. A few scary stories provoked more merriment than fear, but didn't fool Copeland. He needed only to peer into the eyes of the adults to fathom their anger. A boy had died, and they wanted to know why. A few police were out on the streets, one of them having wandered over, even accepting a drink, but they too knew trouble brewed. The atmosphere in town grew turbulent. Theodore Copeland waited, blending in with the deepening shadows and, sure enough, within an hour of him arriving the first fight began.

Copeland drifted back, observed from afar. This was his doing.

The boy deserved it.

The idea came as a certainty Copeland fought to shake off. The boy deserved… something, yes, but not what Copeland did to him. Not that.

He hadn't meant to kill him. Frighten him, sure, but… then he was inside, exploring, and testing his limits. The undeniable strength consumed him. Time expanded before it contracted and by the time he left the body, it no longer breathed.

The fight escalated, judging by the sound, but Copeland wanted no part. He could destroy them all, but it would gain him no peace.

'What have I started?' he asked of no one, unwittingly drawing the attention of someone standing nearby viewing the battle on the other side of the road. The man narrowed his gaze, staring at the shape that was Copeland, a stare so intent it was startling.

He sees me.

Destroy him.

Copeland battled the desire until the man blinked, a puzzled frown creasing his brow, the man relaxing, his attention drifting to the group of men the police had told to go home.

Laughter threatened to burst out of Copeland, so he floated away, fast. The man hadn't spotted him. He was no more than smoke, and every moment he remained in this form made it more difficult to recall how it felt to be human.

Although he hated to admit it, the voice inside him made him crazy. He needed help.

CHAPTER NINETEEN
No Going Back

AS ANNE had told Bill, Copeland was brilliant. In his field, he outshone her intellect. Copeland's interest in the living shadow though, read like an obsession lasting for years. She couldn't hope to dig through all the papers he collected, so aside from some skimming she concentrated on his most recent experiments. Some of his equations made her feel like a borderline imbecile. Yet if she showed them to some of her colleagues, they would be no more clued in.

He incorporated the work of others, she was certain. Perhaps people he worked with, but any attempt to locate who they were, to attribute each piece of labour to the right person, and to ask them to collaborate and discover what Copeland had done... They didn't have the time.

She stared at drawings of the Opticus gun, and the strange cartridge she worked out was a portion of the mechanism. From what she recalled from the original blueprints, they contained no such modification. The notes said the canister somehow collected part of what it distorted. Shooting out, but also drawing in. None of them had known of this aspect of the gun Pemberton had wielded in 1970.

If Copeland joined with the shadow creature, was he under its influence? She didn't know, but if so... Not entirely? At least not in the beginning, or he wouldn't continue to function as well as he did for so long. No. Copeland wasn't a host. Food? Possibly. Experience taught them the creature could consume a meal fast or slower. Much slower. Lie dormant, taking just enough to stay alive while hitching a ride, just like it had in Glencross and at Penrose Manor.

Copeland had done something to the creature, hoping to

use it, rather than allow it to use him. He'd succeeded, but Anne couldn't be sure to what degree.

She gazed around the room. She needed more than anything to talk with Copeland, but his appearance was the one thing she feared, positive he was the dark man of her dreams.

What possessed him? Was he truly possessed now? What little mention she found of a black inert liquid... Her mind skirted the edges of understanding. Copeland had to have created something like a vaccine, or rather the opposite of one. An infection, but not a disabling one. He switched back and forth between structures, changed form, manifested with an altered genetic makeup. The implications were stunning. Copeland collected part of the creature but changed its structure. Subjected it to several dilutions and outside stimulations: heat, cold, radiation, variations in UV levels and other light spectrums... Electricity. Although clear from Copeland's books that he took all relevant precautions with the base sample, Anne was positive none were necessary. The black liquid was harmless until jolted with electricity. Like something out of Mary Shelley's classic – Copeland's own melodramatic words – electricity appeared to be the final key. However, the reanimation, for want of a better word, was only partial.

Did Copeland have to die?

If captured, how would they contain him? Surely, he still required oxygen. So, if they could put him in a box of some sort, it would need to be a container into which they could pump air. Posed a problem. Any structure, unless completely sealed, the Shadowman might slip through. Any prison with access holes, even one to push air through, might present a possible escape route. No way to know through how small an aperture Copeland could slide.

Eyes burning, Anne lifted her head to stare at the wall, but what she hoped would ease the strain only made her vision double and blur. Good thing Bill was not around. He'd nag her into taking a break and that she couldn't do. Not that she understood the science behind Copeland's processes. When his extreme experiments failed, he reverted to ones more basic and returned to light refraction through lens and crystals, the point where her understanding fell short. Her failure was in part because Copeland, perhaps wisely, kept much to himself. His books referred to crystal X or lens Y. Some of the set-ups put down on paper were in some form of code. Anne would lay any bet the system for working out the cipher existed nowhere but in Copeland's head.

She swallowed, wincing. Not only did her eyes hurt. Her throat was scratchy. Bill or someone – she hated to admit she didn't know who – had brought her a glass of water at some point. How long ago? To her surprise, it now stood empty. She'd not eaten since Bill insisted earlier. Drank nothing other than the water, and she didn't think she'd taken a sip for the last two hours. Maybe some of the dizziness she experienced wasn't due to so much reading, or her headache. Now aware, she noticed several signs of dehydration.

'Bill would give me a talking to.'

So would Madeleine, and now she thought about them, where were they? No one had checked in on her for ages as far as she knew, but then they likely didn't want to risk her frayed temper.

Anne stood, hands braced against her lower back, prepared for the resulting ache. She took only a step when the view made her pause. Darkness pressed against the windows. She'd not closed the blinds and, at some point, she'd clicked on a lamp as the light outside edged into evening.

For how long had she sat in a room, highlighted to all who passed by in a halo of illumination?

She might as well paint a bull's eye on her forehead. Despite believing they should do everything possible to save Copeland, the sense of vulnerability and exposure was sudden and immense. She needed to find Bill, or Madeleine. Not that either could do much against the Shadowman, but she couldn't bear to be alone.

Anne opened the door, blinking in astonishment as she gazed into a dark corridor. Why had no one turned on a light?

No, not a dark corridor, for there would still be a way to distinguish the space, especially as light from the lamp should spear out into the hall. The lamp at her back should have sent her own shadow across the floor, maybe up the wall. Whatever she faced absorbed her shadow and pulsed, though she only noted this from the way it flexed at the outer edges, easing into the room. The darkness expanded and contracted as though a heartbeat, growing as if it pulled her shadow into itself and added to its volume.

A sense of losing herself, drawn into the mass molecule by molecule, made Anne's heart race. Although positive this was mere fancy, she half believed she dissolved, vanishing from the world. She started back with a small cry, but as she tensed, the darkness flowed at her... and attacked.

Copeland struck and Anne fell back, hit the ground, all the air in her lungs expelling in a bark of sound. The door slammed on the corridor, cutting them off, leaving them alone.

She didn't know what Copeland was comprised of, but it wasn't shadow. Her cheek stung. The blackness moved as vapour, and, if she stared hard enough, it swirled, but with form. Density. The mass billowed toward her and Anne instinctively held up a hand to protect herself, ready to push Copeland away. Her fingers failed to connect. The mist flowed over her hand, up her arm, scientific curiosity dulling her sense of self-preservation as she tried to understand. To *know*.

'Amazing, isn't it?'

The voice came neither from the centre of the fog, nor did it resonate in her mind. The sound came at her from no speaker or her thoughts but both. Could a part of Copeland already be inside her? Some particle sliding into her ear without her knowledge?

Anne shuddered, her reaction causing the cloud to make a noise she interpreted as disgust, while Copeland's real emotions remained as big a mystery as his notes.

'People fear what they do not understand.'

Anne mouthed the words though the thought wasn't hers. If Copeland were inside her, she could do nothing to change it, though maybe she heard him on a level the human brain struggled to comprehend. With what did a man made of shadow use to talk? Strange she'd not considered it until now.

'How are you speaking?'

'Will a mouth help?' From within the mist, a vague shape of lips appeared.

Anne sagged a little with some relief. Perhaps he wasn't

inside her at all. She wondered how much control he possessed over his form.

'Can you make yourself more solid?'

'You would like that. To have a target.'

'No. I would like to talk with you.'

'And your small mind would prefer to discuss things with a more human construct.'

'My small mind has seen things of which I'm unsure you've even dreamed. But I would share these with you and more if I could. What I would like is for you to show me you're the man I knew.'

'You never knew me. You didn't like me.'

'Said by someone who never attempted to make himself likeable.' Although speaking to him this way might goad him into a violent reaction, Anne was sure an act of pretence would be wrong. A lie or show of weakness would provoke him more. 'Copeland, please, we can help you.'

The shadow shifted. Hard to say how or why she knew, but its surface rippled and Anne knew without a doubt that Copeland gazed at her.

'Please, Professor Copeland, change back. Become a man again so we may speak.'

For seconds she felt he would refuse and billow away, but the temptation to talk to another scientist must have been too great. Anne's lips parted, shy of gaping as the centre of the shade paled, the edges drawing in, forming a rough outline of a man. Copeland's face emerged, his chest, shoulders, and upper arms. He hovered in front of her, half man, half shadow, sliding as if pushed by a breeze, but incomplete. There were patches through which she saw. Although glad not to view Copeland naked, his level of control was amazing, in part doubtful. The sight mesmerised the scientist, but horrified the woman.

'Copeland, let us... Let *me* help you.'

'Your intellect is beneath such a capability. Those who believed me a fool are no match for my intelligence.'

Although she wanted to argue, on this one occasion, at least at the current level of understanding, that much was true. 'I need a team, I admit. But the secret will remain.'

'Naturally, my dear. No one would wish to create

182

widespread panic. The stories abound in town, spread by a certain young teenager. The fights amuse me.'

He drifted a little closer as though implying a threat, but Anne stood her ground.

'Enough, Copeland. Enough banter. You know there's no time for this. You're more than wise enough to know someone will come for you. Let me help you. We can work together, or I'll be your assistant. Use the minds of others, those who've ridiculed you.'

A nasty grin spread over Copeland's mouth. 'For what purpose?'

'To understand what you've done. To reverse it.'

'Reverse it? My dear woman, why would I want to?'

'You're nothing. Nothing but a soldier in an army so unwanted no one sees it. Oh, don't take the comment to heart, my dear. Create a solution and what does it get you? Respect? Not a chance. Not a sniff. Not so much as a nod when passing a fellow professional in the hall. As far as I was concerned to Brigadier Spencer Pemberton, I, Professor Theodore Copeland might as well not have existed at all.'

'You're being terribly unfair.'

Her protest surprised him. Copeland laughed. 'Aren't you scared to talk back? No? Well, you've always been strong. Stronger than many know. And those who do know don't always like it. The age has not yet come where women are equal.'

'Says much about you that you've noticed.'

He chuckled. 'Oh, I noticed you. You're more intelligent than most and you may have a point. Fine, but when I and Pemberton concluded our business, recognition wouldn't have gone amiss.'

His thoughts winged back to the day he last saw Pemberton, staring at the man's back, glad to... well, see the back of him. Copeland chuckled again, easing off when he noticed the alarm on Anne's face. The confrontation of a laughing black cloud seemed to disturb her more than hearing him make threats.

He drew his shape together into a man and tried to wipe a hand down a non-existent trouser leg, attempting to remove the ghost of Pemberton's parting handshake, the action ungainly. Gestures of a drunken man. Maybe a little drunk on his own success. An accomplishment, which should never have progressed beyond speculation. Where was he? Ah yes. The handshake, a sensation to haunt him still, years later. The man's farewell words stung.

'Don't take this the wrong way, old boy, but I hope we never meet each other again,' Pemberton said. 'Let's hope the Opticus gun has done its work. For all our sakes.'

Theodore Copeland rather imagined he understood what Pemberton truly meant: the man was glad to see Copeland gone, and the feeling was mutual. Military men! Interfering where not needed. All the same. No clue as to the importance of science in the field. Damn fools thought to detonate all their troubles away, blow up every danger.

'For sure, the man had his reasons for not wanting me around, but the title of professor should accord civility. The surface politeness wasn't enough.' A professor of his standing deserved more. Took a mere few hours to realise he would not be accorded such courtesy at the UNIT Warehouse. Pity. He'd enjoyed his short time there.

Of course, he would have loved to get hold of some of the more classified technology, hear more about the unexplained cases that UNIT dealt with almost daily. He eavesdropped where possible, which hadn't afforded him much information, wetted the old appetite to learn more. He might have withstood Pemberton's regimented company if it provided him with the connections he longed for.

His irritation made him lose shape, so he drifted across the room, further from Anne, not wanting to terrify her.

Imagine. A learned man such as himself, instrumental in vanquishing a threat of national proportions, carted out soonest. If he had a head to shake, he would do so now.

Brigadier Pemberton had implied they should be glad to see no more of the strange phenomenon they called the shadow creature. The likes of Pemberton returned to work, celebrating that the light gun did what it should do and eradicated the danger.

Not Anne, though. She wanted to *save* everyone. Should he ridicule her for the trait or admire her for it? He struggled to pull himself together; the essence of his form twisting as though not part of him, wanted to break his control. He stopped at head and shoulders, too exhausted for more.

'Air Marshal Gilmore helped, but his indulgence only extended so far.' Was that something he'd already told her? Hard to be certain. Difficult to keep track of what he said aloud or only thought, being he spoke so little while in shadow form. 'Still, at least I gained enough access to examine both an injured combatant and the damaged capsule in which they tried to transport him. What I learned appeared to support my theories that the creature altered structures on the molecular level. I was most eager to collect samples from the wounded corporal, the only surviving man.' Copeland hesitated. Maybe he shouldn't go into detail on that score. Anne wouldn't approve.

What he'd wanted to do was to extract Corporal Weathers, set him up in a private lab, and run a few experiments on him. Gilmore wouldn't allow it, and as the air marshal had ultimate say on UNIT business, Copeland's days there became limited, fast. With no point to his remaining, he left as soon as possible. The pretence of needing to be on site awhile longer about drove him mad.

Hindsight, always hideous. He'd made such a fuss about examining the man, needed to tone things down, bide his time. Not good to cause trouble. Unwise to raise alarms. He had to appear to be the eccentric professor they all thought he was, but once he performed enough tests for it not to seem odd, he was leaving. Had left, of course. Happened years ago.

What was he saying? Oh, yes.

'Gilmore and Pemberton indulged me while it suited their purposes, although by then Pemberton was off to Glencross, not realising the shadow creature had hitched a ride. Even I hadn't known at the time. Gilmore believed what I didn't know caused no harm, and two can play the game. The crate I used to transport components to the Warehouse contained a secret compartment. With it I transferred a few samples, and the true reason I was there.' If he didn't require so much energy to form hands, Copeland would have rubbed them together in glee.

'And what did you go for?'

'Hmm?' He stared at Anne, his form wafting around. 'Don't you think it a shame, Anne? They never allowed me to examine the injured man the way I wanted?'

'Depends on the intended outcome of your actions.'

Her comment being an irritation, Copeland ignored it. 'They left me with almost non-existent options. Led me to this. Oh, don't be mistaken. I might have shared my intent, my ideas, if I ever found anyone with a mind open enough.'

The doctors at the Warehouse... oh, they took biopsies and tissue samples with such care, under anaesthesia and he didn't even get those.

'All I got was copies of the medical reports, or small specimens to examine under a microscope. So I edged my bets.' He let out a wild giggle, and noted Anne inched closer to the door.

'Don't you want to hear?'

She nodded, but she lied. She wouldn't want to know of his hinting at more invasive procedures, about him wishing to step over some line, which shouldn't exist in his field of work. Risks needed taking for the sake of learning. People must suffer. Where did people think all the advances materialised? He would gladly tell them it arose out of blood and pain in ages past where doctors set aside their squeamishness. Sadly, owing, in large, but not entirely to Pemberton's interference, Copeland quickly realised his arguments would do nothing but get him in strife. They'd not allowed him as much as a slice of a man's heart.

I wouldn't do. Not to a living man.

No, but the creature inside him would.

'I've been a fool.' The shame of the statement disabled him for some moments. If Anne had a weapon to use against him, he would have stood there and let her use it. 'They left me with one option. My greatest opportunity, the one I set in motion long before I went to the Warehouse. I hid it right under those fools' noses, too. Built it right into the design of the Opticus gun. You remember the Opticus gun?'

'Of course. Not that I know much about the way it operates.'

'Nor do you need to. Marvellous creature, don't you think?'

'Capable of random, mindless attacks.'

'Maybe not random.'

'If you meant it always sought the youngest of any…' She hesitated.

'The youngest available food source. You can say the words, my dear. We're not children. Not young enough to fear things under the bed.' He gave a little laugh, turning it into another cough because of Anne's lack of amusement.

The first field test of the gun took place in Kirkliston, in the home of a young boy, where the shadow creature crawled out from beneath the bed. Anne would remember. Not the last time someone used it. Not the time where Copeland altered it to do what he wanted. Ironically, the collection took place in a hospital where it ran to ground. Good thing it needed to, because the gun appeared to eradicate it, apart from a small trace… and the creature was never quite the same afterwards.

The creature. Oh, if only he and Pemberton could sit down and hold a conversation. What Copeland would like to tell the brigadier about the creature to which Pemberton had been an unwilling, unwitting host.

Copeland tried to spy his reflection in the nearby window but how did blackness reflect when the exterior lights shone more brightly than the lamp did in the room?

'Copeland, what did you do?'

He ignored Anne for another minute before swinging around. Did anything indicate he moved or was he all gloom and doom? Doom and gloom? He managed not to laugh.

'A good question, Anne. My opportunity came when they left me alone in the laboratory for a short spell. Alone with the gun under the pretence of improving the weapon. Sure, that part was true; I balanced the output so the power didn't burn out so fast, prolonging the life of the unit. They didn't know I'd already altered the gun's twin. Yes, a second gun. All I needed to do was make the swap. When I left, I took the gun Pemberton had used in the field. Complete with its secret.'

'A collection chamber.' Anne sounded stunned, maybe at his audacity.

Copeland smiled at her, though he couldn't tell whether she saw it at all. Praise where due.

'I always knew you were the smart one,' he told her.

'Copeland, please listen to reason,' Anne said. 'You're not

187

responsible for what you've done. I'll make sure they understand.'

'And they'll let me walk happily off into the sunset.'

'I'm not saying that. There may well be consequences for stealing a dangerous substance. For undertaking unauthorised experiments, and for the outcome of your actions, but I know you're no killer. Copeland, you're injured.' Anne wisely chose not to call him damaged. 'No one will blame you for those you hurt, but the killing must stop.'

For seconds it appeared as though he listened to her suggestions, head tilted, a small frown creasing his brow.

'Listen to yourself.' Copeland's quiet, sibilant voice disturbed her more than the strange sight of Copeland as this half being, not one thing or the other. 'Stealing. Unauthorised experiments. The outcome of my actions. Who are *you...*' Copeland roared and dived toward her, stopping only when Anne cried out and flinched back. '...to tell me I need authorisation? You're not as smart as I am, Anne Travers, but I applaud you for the intelligence you do have.'

Despite her fear, Anne bristled, but she held her silence. One wrong move and Copeland might well kill her. Although she didn't want to die, her thoughts were with Bill and Samantha more than herself.

'Think of the things you can accomplish if your hands were not tied,' Copeland said. 'Who has the right to say what is stolen? What rights do we have to test or not to test? Who should say lives cannot be forfeit if that is the cost of success?'

Did he believe all this, or did he say these things because he was not quite Copeland any longer?

'What about a moral compass?' Anne could not keep silent and, besides, Copeland awaited her answer.

'Morality comes with the too high a price of failure.'

Something stirred inside her. A woman's intuition? A mother's? She had searched through Copeland's records, though, and found nothing. No marriage. No children. Maybe... Someone not recorded? A lover? An illegitimate child? If so, the mother might not have registered him as the father. Such things happened. She might be way off base, but definitely something along those lines if not.

'Who did you lose, Copeland?' Her question came out as

188

barely a whisper, but the shadow swirled and what parts of Copeland appeared human faded.

'People die every day, my dear. You seek answers within the meagre boundaries of your limited mind.'

Maybe, but she didn't think so. Perhaps, unwise of her, but Anne pushed. 'You lost someone and yet you would blatantly take the lives of others and call that justified. How do you make those calculations?'

The query disturbed him, that much was easy to tell, but not enough.

'Why did you kill the boy in the woods?'

He took a few moments to consider this. 'Perhaps to see whether I could. To test the extent of that which I am capable.'

'Perhaps? Don't you know?'

'This conversation grows tiresome.'

'As does your attitude. I'm trying to help you.'

'If I didn't find you so amusing, I might kill you.'

'Will you murder everyone who dares to answer back? Who irritates you? Tell me, Copeland, if that's true, what kind of being are you now?'

His expression changed. Some of the human elements shifted to grey then black, fading into the mass. Although Anne wanted to call out, to tell Copeland not to fade away, she kept silent. As much as she wanted him to remain at least partly human, she didn't want to interrupt.

'No. No, I would not destroy you because you are an annoyance. I would only do that to a threat.'

Anne suppressed her own irritation, seen as non-threatening. 'Then why kill the boy?'

Christophe had been the least danger to Copeland, so she circled back to that, hoping to prod Copeland's conscience. If he possessed one, surely that incident would provoke the greatest response. When he remained silent, he left her no choice but to fill in the blank.

'I spoke with the girl. She wants me to thank you for saving her. Pity you killed to do it.'

'That was... unfortunate. But the boy was not so innocent. He wanted more from the girl than she was prepared to give. More than was right.'

'So, you avenged her?' Although not right, his actions

revealed a level of humanity in him even then. 'Couldn't you have chased him off? Copeland, you cannot be an avenging angel.'

'I was... not trying to be. I meant to frighten him. I...' Copeland frowned and more of him faded to black. 'Once I flowed inside him, the things I saw, what I could do...'

Inside him? Anne froze, fighting the sick feeling that rose within. Although she suspected as much, to hear how Copeland suffocated the boy made her feel ill.

'It's not too late to repent.'

Copeland's gaze lifted to meet her. 'I don't. The boy deserved his fate, a good way to test my limitations, or rather lack. You see me as somehow diminished, but I see evolution. In this form, I'm not prone to disease or injury. I may have lengthened my lifespan. And I can escape from anyone. I'm mist. I'm smoke. I'm shadow.' Copeland laughed. 'Try to catch me.'

'You're not shadow permanently. You're partly human now.'

'When I wish to be. Sometimes.' He appeared to notice more of his body was now black, and drew together again.

The change seemed to require effort and concentration.

'How long have you been smoke this time?'

Copeland regarded her, his gaze one of suspicion. 'Why?'

'Let me guess. You began this thing. Moved from one form of existence to the other, and back again. You required your formulation to become shadow.' She wasn't sure what to call it, but formulation was as good as using any other word. 'And then you needed less.'

Copeland's gaze narrowed. 'How do you know this?'

'An educated guess.' That and reading extensively through his notes. 'If not the case, you would have used up your supply ages ago. So, like Jekyll, you first controlled the change and then it controlled you.'

'That's not... true.' Although Copeland protested, he didn't sound certain. 'I alter at will.'

'But how long have you been shadow this time? How long before? Are you spending longer as shadow than man?' He must have been or they would have found him before now.

'Are you suggesting I'm now Hyde? How gothic.'

190

'Then prove you're not.'

'How? By becoming a man so you can try to kill me?'

'Copeland, if you know me at all, you know that is the last thing I want to do. I'm maybe the only one who doesn't want you to die. I want you cured.'

'And if I don't want to be?' Copeland shouted. 'Look at me! Do you really see nothing but something monstrous? Anne, you are better than that. You above all others. Think of what this means.'

'I do! I'm thinking what it means if man could transform, become vapour, move where he wanted to go. The implications of space travel alone may be ground-breaking. It can be used to rescue people, in the medical field, in operations, curing people from within, but, as you've proven, someone can also use it for... ill.' She almost said evil and stopped in time. 'They can use it for espionage. To kill.'

'I... Well, yes, there are those in the world who would... But...' He shook his head; black streaks materialising in his skin, making it appear as if his flesh were disintegrating. Despite his claim to change at will, Copeland seemed unwell as he struggled to remain part man, part shadow. The blackness crept up on him and, as he winced, and more of him disappeared, Anne became certain Copeland knew he fought a battle already lost. 'There must be precautions, but this is too miraculous to ignore.'

The scientist in her wanted to agree, but that same clinical mind believed they were better off without this ability. Some breakthroughs best lay buried. She didn't want to bury Copeland along with them.

'No. No one can cure me. This keeps me from harm. If I agreed to change back, even you cannot promise to keep me safe.'

'There are those who will do everything they can to help you. I promise you there'll be a whole team working on this and with your help we'll save you.'

'You... don't understand. You don't know what you're asking me to give up.'

No, but she could imagine. 'And what about your work, Copeland? If you disappear, where will you go? How will you live as smoke, as you call it? Because if you do, those in authority will eradicate all you've done. They'll call your work smoke and mirrors. They must. You'll be an enemy because they'll fear what you can do, and fear will control their decisions. But if you come in, under my guidance, then we'll work to—'

She stopped talking because of the way Copeland stared at her. 'You're too clever for your own good, Anne.' His expression grew sad. 'You can see as well as I can feel, the shadow is winning and I struggle to keep this form. I had made peace with it.'

'Had?'

'You're overlooking one thing.' Black spots appeared in Copeland's skin, spreading darkness overtaking his body, though he clearly fought to hold his face together. 'You are assuming I've not already tried to reverse the process.'

CHAPTER TWENTY
The End

MUCH TO her surprise, Copeland allowed Anne to stand, and to move back to the table and his notes.

Something bothered her, but she dismissed it as too implausible. Copeland *was* brilliant, but was he too brilliant for his own good?

'You're not sure how it worked. The collection method. Therefore, you don't know what you gathered.' She shifted through papers. 'I thought we had missing entries, but it's plain from what I read, all the early tests, those where you tried to work out what you collected, failed. It's liquid more than it is anything else, but it's not conforming to any known substance. It's why you referred to it as essence in your notes, because you don't know what it is. There's no way you could.'

'Clever sssspeculation.' Copeland's voice emerged from the darkness, having reverted to shadow. The occasional word sounded slurred. Not a good sign.

'But I'm right. Therefore, your experiments weren't... haphazard, not random.' He had followed a thought-process though she was unsure what, but there *was* a pattern. 'Yet you must have reverted to some speculative work yourself.'

Luck. Damn, but she didn't want to believe it. The thing Copeland had become was part creative genius and part accident. Not something Copeland would want to hear voiced. Her warning instinct kicked in, proved a second later as the darkness moved closer.

'Be careful, Anne.'

'I intend no insult. Much in science is by mishap as intent. It's nothing to be ashamed of.'

'I am not a man who knows shame.'

'Remorse then? Killing someone to test whether you can is not a good enough reason. There are other ways to explore your capabilities. You're no killer, Copeland.'

'You have no clue what I would do for a scientific breakthrough.'

'I think I do. You ran a few animal tests. And yes, I think you're not above causing others pain, but when it came to the big experiment, you put your own life at risk and tested it on yourself.'

'And I wouldn't have, if not for you!'

Copeland shoved a chair at the wall. The sudden clatter made Anne jump, but no one came running. Her gaze shifted toward the door, uncertain whether she wished someone to show. They could do nothing against Copeland. The discovery might scare Copeland away, but she didn't like the odds. Any would-be rescuer would likely be killed. Anne didn't know if Copeland intended to kill her, but either he would or he wouldn't; she didn't want someone else to die by her side. While she lived, a chance existed to talk him down. Get him to hand himself over. Although she grew sick with fear, her bravado kept her alive so far. Patronising Copeland, wheedling, speaking down to him; she remained convinced it would end her faster.

'Not going to assssk me to…to esplain?' Copeland's words came out muddled again.

'I was. I am.'

'Your ar… arrival. Didn't na-know if you knew I waszzz here.' Copeland struggled but pulled his speech together. 'Didn't… ma-matter. Couldn't chance…'

'I'm sorry.' How should she handle this? She hadn't known of his presence and if her appearance forced his hand, he might consider her accountable for both his change and the boy's death. Responsibilities Anne was unwilling to accept. Each person was responsible for his or her own actions. Occasionally, sometimes people could be coerced but something like this… No, she refused to be answerable. If her being here caused him to panic, she didn't force him to murder. Still, he might turn his hatred on her, seeing her as the source of everything wrong.

'I can kill you. Choke you. Suffocate you. I can sssslide

194

inside you.'

The thing to scare her most. Anne fought her terror. Copeland might not end a fellow scientist, but he would destroy a sobbing woman. A sobbing anyone. Copeland hated weakness... because he feared it in himself. The insight might have been accurate, but it was one she didn't dare voice.

To have Copeland inside her though... The dread proved difficult to control. Crawling through her veins and ventricles, blocking the flow of blood, the entry of oxygen. Invading like a parasite. A disease.

The shadow advanced. All blackness. All shade. She searched for a trace of something human and failed to discover it. What to do? To say? What good would it do to beg? Showing weakness would not help her. Copeland admired strength. A twisted lack of compassionate strength was preferable to him than cowering.

The urge to step back remained strong, but Anne stood her ground. She lifted her chin a little and stared into the black void – easy to think of the darkness as an abyss – where Copeland's eyes should have been.

The cloud slowed. Now if only she could think of the right words.

'Anne, get back!' Bill's voice called out from the other side of the black mass.

A whirling rush took place, suggestive of movement. Did Copeland now stare at Bill? She no longer saw anything of the man. Her mind raced ahead, divining the many scenarios of what might happen next. She didn't expect Copeland to laugh.

'So, you found the gun,' Copeland said as his chuckles peeled off.

No! She had told Bill it might not work. She stepped to the left, wanting to edge around Copeland, to put herself between Bill and the blackness, though it would do no good. If Copeland attacked either of them, the other would rush into help and maybe die too.

Samantha. Mother. The thought of her daughter and mother froze her in place. How would Samantha fair without a father? How would she continue without a father or mother? And Margaret Travers; she'd lost her husband only nine years ago, how would she cope with the death of her daughter too?

Anne fought to drag herself back to the events in the room, aware Copeland spoke.

'I'm invulnerable.'

'Maybe,' Bill said. 'Maybe not. I don't want to use this on you. I don't want to use any weapon against you. All I ask is for you to move away from Anne.'

Bill's gentle words may have worked if not for the weapon in his hands. Hard to tell how she knew, but she was sure. Not that she blamed Bill. Using weapons was part of his training, and Copeland posed a threat. If Bill stood here in her place, she couldn't say she wouldn't reach for a weapon too, though she would do her best not to use it.

Copeland's voice contained a sneer now. 'Such small-minded individuals. Determine a potential danger; obliterate it. Didn't you ever want to know where a creature like that came from? Didn't Pemberton?'

'Yes, I did. Old Spence? Maybe not, he's never been an officer blessed with an enquiring mind. Why do you ask?' Bill edged to the left as Copeland moved to the right so at last Anne and Bill spotted each other.

'Because it's not your priority.'

'My priority is King and Country, and protecting civilians.'

Anne knew her husband well enough to know it would irritate him to defend his position; he wouldn't consider the need. No, he spoke mostly to keep Copeland occupied and talking. Every scrap of information might make all the difference.

Copeland snorted. 'It's what sets men like me above men like you. We will always put scientific interest over the safety of others, including King Edward. And sometimes our own.' The cloud drew in, gathering, taking on the rough outline of a man, but nothing human showed through. 'I sought such a creature for so long I almost gave up hope.'

'Sought?' Despite Bill's plain dislike of the professor, Anne's husband sounded curious.

'Oh, not this one, but... something. I chased so many tales, folk legends, mysteries, hoaxes, and... this. This was meant to be. The moment I learned the creature existed for real I knew I needed to capture a part of it.'

'We know all about that.' Irritation crept into Bill's voice. His gaze darted to Anne, and she didn't need him to tell her to edge closer to the door.

'The biggest joke. Took it from under your noses. All those tissue samples I wanted from Corporal Weathers... No, I never forgot his name. I would have liked those, but all the fuss I made when what I truly wanted was a sample of the creature itself. And it was right there in Pemberton's hands. All I required was the opportunity to swap the gun.'

'We know all this,' Anne broke in, earning a frown from her husband. 'What about the creature? What can you tell us?'

'Ah... the creature. Impossible to identify or explain in terms the pitiful human mind can understand. Our language is inadequate, too. I can tell you it's primordial. It found itself borne in primeval ooze in some part of a far-off galaxy.' Copeland hesitated. 'Or dimension. Sometimes it's hard for one with my intellect to interpret the images it reveals. It thinks in terms of age and distance in a way we don't. So expansive it threatens the mind. All I know is it found itself here, one of a whole, of an ancient being. Dying, starving, unable to feed on anything until it stumbled across us. Humans. Then it learned fear and anger, and hostility and hate, malice and malevolence, levels of violence, and it *feasted*. Us!' Copeland postulated. 'Our most basic, base emotions a veritable banquet. So, it slipped and slid and lived among us until it found the thrill of the kill.'

Copeland faltered. 'Not condoning its actions. No, not pardoning its behaviour, but now I understand. I'm in a unique position. The best. It's why it learned to go for the children. It discovered them easier to terrify, and an excellent meal.' He paused but went on. 'Oh, it didn't refuse a tougher repast, and the psychology of adults varies greatly. Some provided it with more nourishment than several young, but children... They more than anyone believed in the monster under the bed. They believe in Santa Claus. They're easier to manipulate.'

'Abominable,' Anne whispered.

'Abominable?' Copeland sounded dreamy. 'Yes, one might call it that.'

'And now you've given it another host.' She had to know.

Did anything of Copeland still survive?

Copeland burst out laughing. 'Host? Well, yes, but no. Do you think me so foolish? You think I'd be a willing shell for a parasite. One that would drain me dry. Oh no. I had no intention of dying.'

Bill adjusted the gun as the Shadowman moved closer to him.

'So how does this work? You took it into you and… What comes next?'

'Took it in? Took it in! I guess the small mind would think such a thing. But you think I'd allow this creature, as magnificent as it is, to live as a symbiont? No. I always wanted it to serve.'

Bill shot a worried confused glance at Anne. 'Bonnaire said you were here to work on a private project.'

'That fool.' Now the cloud swirled, giving Anne the impression he looked at her and not Bill. 'You think I would ever work on such an idiotic idea?'

'Idea?'

'To come up with some kind of contentment drug.'

'Don't such things already exist?'

'Not in the form Bonnaire wanted.'

'No. And that wasn't your plan at all. Your plan…' Anne stared into the black cloud. 'To cure disease. It's what you wanted all along.'

'That and so much more. Think of the uses of this technology. Changing one's DNA may enable men to go where they've never been before. We might travel to the depths of the ocean, to the far reaches of outer space.'

'You can't make the human race into something it was never meant to be.' Anne spoke without thinking.

The Shadowman set its gaze on her. 'I can do anything I want.'

They received a mere second of warning and the Shadowman moved fast, so fast Anne understood no one ever stood a chance. The weapon tumbled away, out of the room into the corridor, Bill engulfed by the dark.

Please no. Anne sent up a silent plea for many things. Most of all for Bill not to be hurt, for nothing to force her to pick up a firearm again, not even one that fired a spectrum of light.

The black mass stood between her and the doorway, blocking the exit. Unable to get to the gun, Anne tried to grab at the blackness, only for her hands to pass through. Anne searched the depths of the swirling fog. Should she dive in? Two things made her hesitate. Thoughts of Samantha, and instinct told her the moment she did Copeland would turn on her, too.

Which meant Bill might be suffocating, dying, cut off from her, alone.

'Professor Copeland, please! Stop this! Don't hurt him!' What to say to reach the man? What to say they'd not said already? 'Copeland!'

Never had she felt so helpless, and the most terrifying aspect of the attack was the silence, the... stillness. The fog hung in the air. Bill uttered no sound, and after the first few seconds where she heard his body flailing on the ground, the man she loved grew still.

'Cope—' Anne took a step closer, pausing at the edge of the cloud. She blinked the tears from her eyes. 'Theodore. Ted. Please. I think you know what it's like to lose someone. Please don't take Bill from me. Nine years ago I lost my father to an alien entity... Please, don't let me lose Bill too. I'm not your enemy and you know it. I will still help you if I can, and I know you didn't start all this to change who or what you are. You said it yourself. The clues are there throughout your notes. You wanted to cure people, not destroy them. Somewhere something changed. I know it. I know you were interested long before you encountered the shadow creature, but the last few years... The truth is you can't tell whether it influenced you.'

Did she imagine it or detect a subtle difference in the way the cloud lingered? Did it withdraw a little? Her confidence grew along with the strength of her voice.

'You blamed me, my presence here, for making you rush ahead, but I think you know it's not true. You worked with this stuff for years. There's no knowing what it did to you over time. It always required a host. What if it *wanted* you to introduce it into your system? What if, though changed, there's something of the original creature left?'

'I wanted its genetic code.' Copeland sounded puzzled.

'But there's no knowing what influence it has. If it isn't the same, if even a part of the original exists, even on a genetic level, maybe the instinct to survive in any form remains. Maybe it made you experiment on yourself way before you were ready.'

'No, you're trying to trick me.' He didn't sound certain and she wondered why, but the minutes ticked by and Bill was out of time.

'If you don't believe me, if you blame me, if you don't think I want to help you, kill me instead. Let Bill live and I'll leave with you, if there's no time for you to kill me here. Just let me save Bill first.'

'You would...?'

Copeland's uncertainty became her only hope, but Anne ran out of words. Every time she blinked, a tear fell; she couldn't think.

'Theo, please.'

'Theo.' Copeland repeated the shortening of his own name with something like laughter in his voice as he floated off. 'Someone else called me Theo once...'

Anne let out a cry. Too late. She had found the right words but too late.

Bill lay sprawled on the floor... dead.

CHAPTER TWENTY-ONE
Resolutions

ANNE HAD heard people scream. Heard people shriek when told their loved ones were dead. The same cry came out of her now. She flung herself forward sliding to Bill's side. No pulse. He wasn't breathing. What to do? What to do? She knew. CPR. Anne ripped open his shirt, pressed her hands to his chest, and began compressions. Breathed into his mouth, watched his chest rise and fall, pushed again. Breathing. Compressions. Breathing...

'Come on. Come on!' she said on a shout. 'Breathe, damn you! Breathe!' She went through the same ritual. It wasn't working. Nothing did. She gazed around the room, cursing they were not in a lab. She had nothing to hand to get his heart started. If she didn't get him breathing soon...

Anne laid her forehead on Bill's chest and sobbed.

He's dead. He's gone.

She couldn't bear the thought, but it intruded. No. This wasn't right. She was unprepared for this. This was not her Bill losing his life in the line of duty. Not her Bill forsaking his life to save countless others. This was Bill lying on a cold hard floor, while Copeland hovered like a dark winged harbinger.

She turned her stricken face to the Shadowman, doing nothing to conceal her anguish. 'You did this.' The words carried the depth of her hate.

Damn you, Copeland. Damn your arrogance. She didn't believe he was all-bad. His actions may have been borne from good intentions, and some of what happened might be from an alien influence, but Copeland's arrogance set him on the wrong path.

'You wanted to save lives, start with this one.' She didn't know where the demand came from, but it shocked her.

The cloud hung there for a suspended moment before it

flowed toward Bill, tendrils snaking out, sliding into his mouth, threading into his nose. No. What was she thinking? She couldn't allow this. Not that Copeland would stop even if she told him to, and he'd already been inside Bill. That was why he'd died. She looked away, unable to withstand seeing this, forced herself to watch. If Bill was dead, what difference did it make what Copeland did to him now.

All the difference; Bill would hate this even if it saved his life, but would he feel the same way if their positions were reversed? If Copeland tried to save her?

Copeland flowed away.

'What? No!' Anne panicked. Felt Bill's pulse. Nothing changed. Had Copeland failed? Not tried? Should she start compressions again?

She opened her mouth to shout at Copeland, to convince him to do more, when the room filled with light.

Copeland screamed and reared back, the beam pressing him. Anne jerked her gaze to the source. Bonnaire stood in the doorway, a clumsy grip on the Opticus gun, swinging the beam, making Anne duck. If it hit her or Bill... well, she didn't know what it might do. They used it once many years ago, and it saved a man's life, but she didn't know whether Madeleine and Paul had repaired it well enough.

Copeland screamed again, and he roared. Tables and chairs, all his notes, went flying, caught up in a whirlwind the Shadowman carried across the room. The darkness tried to fall on Bonnaire, but the old man raised the gun again and at such close quarters couldn't miss.

'Bonnaire, wait!' Anne staggered to her feet. Copeland was worth trying to save, if only so he could save Bill. 'Stop! I need him!'

The light swung across the room. At first, she thought it cut a path following Copeland as the Shadowman tried to escape but, through the glare, Paul Larousse appeared, battling Bonnaire for the gun. The beam zigzagged as they wrestled, making Anne duck out of its path until it at last winked out. The weapon spun from Bonnaire's hands, flying against the far wall of the corridor and to the ground with a crack. Bonnaire and Larousse still tussled.

Madeleine came running, shouting at her father to stop, until the two men fell still, and pushed apart, Bonnaire gasping, reaching into a pocket, taking out a pot of pills and fumbling one into his mouth.

Anne crouched over Bill... Her husband's body. For a moment it felt like her own heart had stopped. What would she tell their daughter?

When she finally glanced over to Madeleine to say they needed help, she stopped, unable to utter a sound at the expression on her friend's face.

Anne spun around searching for what captured Madeleine's stare, gaze falling on the sorry sight of what remained of Theodore Copeland.

Madeleine Bonnaire stared at the telephone on her desk, having replaced the receiver several minutes ago but unable to move. Would another eight years pass before they saw each other again? It might well be more. As much as she loved Anne, she was in no hurry to remake her acquaintance. Unfair on Anne, not fair on Madeleine, but she couldn't help how she felt.

Although she'd expected Anne's call, and in no way blamed her friend, speaking to her was another reminder of how much changed. Not owing to her friend's visit. Worse things might have occurred without Anne's presence and if not for her previous affiliation with Copeland. Although not worse for Anne. Madeleine could think of nothing worse than losing the man you loved.

The institute was now wholly hers; Madeleine made certain. She ejected the scientists working there under assumed names or with dubious backgrounds. She put a stop to all animal experimentation that did not pass her consent and her approval was hard to gain. Victor Bonnaire only oversaw paperwork she took to him on her weekly visit. Those... encounters were strained. Sometimes the conversation flowed, and they could forget for a short while. More often not.

'Any good news?' Anne tried to make the question sound casual, but the raw pain of her loss edged her voice with... something Madeleine did not wish to contemplate.

'I'm still seeing Paul,' she said, hoping that bit of news would lighten Anne's heart a little.

If not for Paul, they might not have got the Opticus gun

running again. Though Anne didn't like what Victor Bonnaire had done with it, and Paul blamed himself for the result, Madeleine feared what might have happened if Paul hadn't made the repair. They may have lost more than just Bill.

Anne walked down the corridor, exchanging nods and smiles with members of staff who came to recognise her on sight. Bill's body was in the morgue, awaiting transport to the UK for the funeral. She had rang her mother, who had agreed to ring around to friends and family. Anne wasn't looking forward to returning to England, to her life... without Bill.

She stopped and took a deep breath. Time for that later, right now there was something she had to do.

Room 36 B wing. Anne paused as she always did, readying herself for any alterations.

Not this time. No change, not since Copeland's skin took on the patchy colour of bruising.

'Hel—' He got no more out, a rough coughing overtaking him.

Anne walked fast but without dashing to his side. She poured a small cup of water and held it to his cracked lips. Copeland sipped, a little of the liquid dribbling out the side of his mouth and running over his chin. Anne snatched a tissue and dabbed at the wetness as Copeland fell back against the pillow lacking strength. To her dismay, her hands shook a little, though showing kindness even to Copeland, the man responsible for her heartache, was an inherent part of her nature.

'Hello, Anne.' Copeland gave her a feeble smile. 'I'm sorry about...'

Anne held up a hand. Copeland had apologised so much about Bill, about what the Shadowman had done, and how he wished he could have prevented it. Anne couldn't hear that again. Not now. She managed to blink the threatening tears away, though her throat closed forcing her to swallow.

'So.' Copeland shifted position as much as his stamina allowed. 'Are the... bruises what I feared?' He glanced at her. 'They're a little worse.'

'No, they're not.'

'They look worse to me.'

'They're not, and they're just bruises.'

'Not…?' Puzzlement flickered over his face. He didn't trust her.

'You're not slipping back.' That was what he feared when the first bruise – the first dark shadow – appeared on his skin. 'Theo, I don't even understand how your organs rearranged themselves but as we both know…'

He nodded. 'Yes, yes. They're damaged.'

Anne bit her lower lip, amusement toying with her regardless of her sorrow. Despite the situation, he sounded so impatient with her.

'So, the bruises to the skin are like the damage to my organs?'

'Essentially. They will take more time to heal than normal bruising and in the meantime…' She glanced at the plethora of drugs on his chart.

'I'm a walking medicine cabinet.'

'Well, there's much to fix.'

'Yes. Anne, if I could fix…'

'Please. Don't. I can't…' Anne looked away, sniffed, then turned back to Copeland. 'But it's looking good. I told you, it's like your body needs to relearn how it works.'

'I'm an old man.' Disgust encrusted his voice. 'I'll never be the same.'

'No, but with us working together you'll live. And your life can have purpose.'

Anne had given it some thought, and decided she could harness the power of the light gun differently, treating Copeland with a kind of out of this world chemo. She also took it upon herself to make sure his brilliant mind didn't go to waste, though he'd never walk freely again, would never be allowed. He'd told her that she got through to him when she talked about possible influences. He'd told her of his early uncharacteristic thoughts and clumsiness before he ever took the formula. Unable to determine how much was an alien influence and how much the man, where able, yes, she would work with him.

'And I have Pemberton to thank?'

'Yes.' Anne spoke the truth, though she remained guarded. Despite everything, Copeland struggled with his feelings over Brigadier Pemberton. 'No voices in your head?'

'None. And you? Any dreams of dark men?'

Strange when she considered why, but she had told him about

the dream, though Bill wouldn't have approved. 'No. We may be safe.'

'Safety is an illusion.' He sounded almost wistful.

'What makes you say so?'

He became lost in his own thoughts, giving her time to study his scared face, dry skin, and the dark bruising. No doubt about it, he'd aged. Might have shortened his life span, though by how much only time, or a time traveller, might tell.

Copeland at last swung his gaze her way. 'Forgive me. I'm maudlin. Now tell me, Anne, what's to be our first project together, and did you bring me some grapes?'

Anne stood outside the lift. She wanted to visit Bill, spend some time with him. Talk to him, but the thought of looking on his face. If it wasn't for the lack of colour, she would believe him asleep, but...

'Anne Travers?'

A woman's voice. Anne turned and was surprised to find a short woman standing behind her. Dark hair, an intelligent glint in her eyes, and dressed in the uniform of the World War II Woman's Auxiliary Air Force.

'Oh. You look like your mother,' the woman said.

'I beg your pardon?' Anne blinked, and something clicked in place. 'I've seen you before. Days ago.'

'Yes. Actualising hasn't been easy, dear. Now, I have something important to...'

'What's your name?'

The woman smiled and held out a hand. 'Section Officer Le Croissette.'

Anne shook the section officer's hand. 'I assume you've come from the past?'

The woman didn't answer. They released hands and Anne looked down at the item Le Croissette had left there. A coin of some sort.

'What is this?'

But when she looked up, Section Officer Le Croissette had vanished. Moments later, though, that didn't seem to matter, as the entire hospital blinked out of existence around Anne, too...